Four Summers

by

Nyrae Dawn

Other Books by Nyrae Dawn:

CHARADE

WHAT A BOY WANTS

WHAT A BOY NEEDS

MEASURING UP

FREEING CARTER

$\mathcal{T}$able of Contents

Dedication

To Kelley York.
You're the type of friend who always comes through.
So glad we met all those years ago.
Thanks for having my back,
and taking this wild writing journey with me.

Summer One

I'll never forget the first time I saw Nathaniel Chase. I was fifteen-years-old and leaving cabin 3B with my best friend Alec, who up until that moment, I'd always figured was the boy for me. It wasn't that Alec and I were in love with each other, but we still knew that was our future. Without ever talking about it, we accepted it. Everything changed when Nathaniel pulled up to our lake cabins for the summer. Now, I had another boy in my life. Another best friend, but this one only part-time. This one, I loved.

Charlie Rae
Chapter One

My legs hang over the dock, feet dancing in the water as they do every summer. It's early June, but already sticky hot. Any time I can, I sneak away from Dad before he finds more work for me to do. The water is the only way to stay cool on days like this.

I make circles with my toes, watching tiny waves ripple out until they disappear and I wonder how long I'll be able to avoid Dad. He seems to be immune to the heat. He's spent all day every summer working outside at our lake cabins since he was a kid and Mom's parents gave him a job. My grandparents are long gone now and the place belongs to him and Mom. I get the joy of working alongside him.

"Hey, Charlie Rae. I've been looking for you." Glancing up, I shield the sun from my eyes to see my best friend Alec standing next to me in a pair of cut-off denim shorts and a red, sleeveless shirt showcasing the firm muscles that haven't always been there, running the length of his arms. He smiles, showing me the little chip in his tooth he got when he fell off the tire swing when we were eight. Alec pushes a hand through his sun-bleached hair.

"Let me guess, my dad's looking for me?" I groan.

"How do you know it's not me who wanted to find you, huh?" He winks.

I shake my head. Alec is such a flirt. He playfully does it with all the girls, but he's the only one who does it to me. Which, embarrassingly, makes my cheeks warm up a little bit. I know it doesn't mean anything. Alec is just nice like that, but when he's the only boy who's nice to *me* like that, it makes it hard not to get girly. Even though he's only my best friend and I know that's all he'll ever emotionally be.

When I go to stand, he holds out his hand, and I let him pull me up.

"So...your dad's looking for you," he says, making me roll my eyes.

"See! I told you, Captain Liar. Where is he?" Crossing my arms, I try not to pout. I'm not sure why I feel like it. Maybe because of his stupid teasing. Maybe because I'm annoyed that Mom and my sister, Sadie Ann, are sitting in our air-conditioned store right now and I'm the one who has to work outside with Dad. Not that I wouldn't rather be with him than them. Dad and I have more in common, but it's still not fair.

"Captain Liar?" Alec laughs. "You're such a dork. I mean, a cool dork, but a dork all the same." My face feels hot again, but for a different reason this time. Shoving past Alec I try to walk away, but he runs after me. "I'm kidding, Charlie. Wait up! Hey, what's the problem?"

4

Actually, I don't know what my problem is. Or maybe I do. I'm tired of being the "dork". Tired of being teased and just plain old Charlie Rae. Never Charlotte. Charlie. "Just grumpy. And hot. Where's Dad?" I pull my hair tie out before putting my long, dark hair into another ponytail. According to Sadie Ann, ponytails are "so out" but it works for me.

"He's busy getting some boat rentals ready. He wanted me to tell you he needs you to make sure cabin 3B is ready. Got a family coming in. They'll be here the whole summer."

I don't try to stifle my groan. Why would people choose to come here for a whole summer? They think it's such a great place to spend time, when really it's just because they don't live here. I do. I know how much it sucks. Luckily, the people who come the rest of the year never stay very long. "What do we know about them?"

"Some rich family. Parents and two sons. They're probably too afraid of getting dirty to end up in our way much, though." We've seen it enough to know. Usually, we don't pay much attention to the people our age who come here, and they're the same to us.

"I hope so," I say. "Okay, thanks for telling me. I'm going to go grab the key and get the cabin ready." I wave at Alec, but he keeps going.

"I guess they're going to be here earlier than your dad thought, so we gotta hurry. I'll help you."

I smile. What a sweetheart. These are the things Alec does that make him my best friend. He's the only boy in Lakeland Village, Virginia that I can stand.

Really, there isn't much to do in the cabin anyway. It's already been cleaned, but we like to freshen the cabins up before people get here so they aren't so musty from being closed up.

Our store's a little white building with blue trim. It matches our house, which is off to the side and behind it. When people say, "one-stop shopping" this is what they mean. The building houses the limited products for purchase, the rentals, and the office.

Taking the back door, I run inside the office to grab the customer key so I don't have to run into Mom or Sadie Ann out front. My blue baseball hat is sitting on the counter so I grab it to help keep the sun out of my eyes while I'm working today. After putting it on and pulling my ponytail through the hole, Alec and I are on our way to cabin 3B.

The cabins? They're much cuter than our house or the office, each one decorated in a theme or color. They're actual cozy log cabins. I can see why people would want to come here. It's the living here year 'round I'm still a little lost on. But what can I say? I know this place is going to be my future.

The area of land isn't huge. There's a small pond off to one side. We have ten cabins, some on the lake and some a little farther out. 3B is one of the nicest.

"You don't have to help, Alec. I'm sure you want to go home and enjoy your summer or whatever."

Just because I have to be stuck here doesn't mean he should have to be, but because he's a nice guy, Alec says, "Nope.

Plus, I need the money. Your dad's letting me help out this year."

Alec is a year-rounder like us, though he doesn't live at The Village, which is the name of our "dream getaway". He lives up the street. Our parents are best friends, too.

He doesn't realize how lucky he is not to *have* to work here, but I don't say that. "Thanks."

We do a quick sweep of the place. I freshen the potpourri, make sure the rooms are spider-web free, and all sorts of stupid things. Just as we're walking out and I'm locking up, car doors slam behind me.

Great. I had hoped to make it out and put the keys back before they got here so Mom or Sadie Ann would have to be the ones to talk to them. They're much better with people than I am.

As soon as I turn around, everything changes. My heart speeds up. I feel hotter, almost like I can't breathe. I swear I'm not one of those annoying girls who pine for their stupid dream boy at fifteen-years-old. I've never even had a boyfriend. Or wanted a boyfriend. I've looked at tons of boys though: Alec, boys at my school who used to call me "flatty-Rae" instead of Charlie Rae because God obviously decided he could only give boobs to one Gates sister and chose Sadie Ann.

I've seen how boys look at my sister, but when I've looked at them, I've never felt...well almost like I have the flu, to be honest, but I've never looked at a boy and felt *this*.

I can't see his eye color from this far. His hair is bark-brown, with streaks of gold when the sun hits it. One look at him says he's so different than me. I shouldn't be staring, but my eyes won't move away.

I believe everyone has certain key moments in their lives they'll never forget. Moments marking the beginning or end of something. Moments that will always own a little piece of you. You can track decisions you make or paths your life follows and they always lead back to one of these defining moments.

This is one of them.

I'm not stupid enough to think I understand it. I don't believe in love at first sight or anything like that. I don't even know this boy, much less feel anything, but he... *This* is one of my moments. I know it like my body knows it has to breathe to survive.

Mom, Dad, Sadie Ann, or probably anyone else would think I'm crazy, and maybe I am crazy because I'm sitting here thinking tons of thoughts that have no business in my head. Thoughts I'd laugh at if anyone else had them. I know who boys like him are. They're stuck up, rude, think they're better than us, and everyone here knows they always, always leave, but still...this summer boy just gave me my first *moment*. A piece of my life I will never forget.

"Hello? Earth to Charlie." Alec grabs my shoulder. Immediately I feel the blush crawl over my whole body.

"Um... Sorry. I'm not feeling too well."

The family is walking toward us. The dad is in crisp, new jeans, but with a button up shirt that looks like it goes with a suit. The mom is wearing a bright red summer dress, heels and a big red hat. The other boy looks exactly like my summer boy, but somehow...different. His hair is a little darker. He's maybe an inch taller. They're dressed like only summer boys are in expensive tennis shoes and ironed shorts. But still, I can't stop looking. There's an ease about him I don't usually see in summer boys. A laid back expression that doesn't completely fit what I'm used to.

"Hello! We stopped by the office, finished filling out the paperwork, and they said you'd have the keys?" The dad walks up to us, a perfect smile on his perfect face.

"Umm...yeah. Here. They're right here." I try to hand them to him, but they slip through my fingers and fall to the ground. My moment boy has reached us, and he bends to pick them up at the same time Alec and I do. All three hands zoom toward one destination. Mine touches his. It's not one of those "electric" sensations books and movies always talk about. Maybe I wish it is or maybe I just feel silly touching him, but I jerk my hand back. In my rush not to look like I'm trying to hold hands with him, I lose my balance a little. The more I try to catch myself, the more I stumble until I'm on my butt. On the porch. And I'm dying.

"Charlie? Are you okay?" Alec abandons his quest for the keys and reaches for me instead.

"Charlie?" moment boy asks. Yes, I want to tell him. Yes, I have a stupid boy's name! And no boobs, and I just fell in front of you! But of course, I don't.

"I'm fine. I think I'm getting sick, or something. I need to go home and lie down." And die!

"Okay...okay. I'll help you." Alec pulls me to my feet, putting his arm around me. Then to the summer family, he says, "Sorry about this. Everything you guys need should be in there. If not, call the office. I better get her home."

"Definitely. I'm so sorry you're not feeling well, dear," the mom says.

"Thanks." I can't even look at her, so I talk to my feet instead. I let Alec lead me back home where I fake being sick again, lock myself in my bedroom and die of embarrassment.

"Charlie?" Alec's voice sounds through my door before he knocks. I try to ignore it. Want to, but I know Alec. He'll come right in. Hell, my parents have let him sleep over before. They don't care if Alec has free reign in my house or my bedroom, which actually makes me feel like crap. Sadie Ann could never have a boy stay over. But me? I'm just Charlie. It's not like any of the boys are going to want me anyway.

"Come in." I sit up in my twin bed and lean against the wall. As soon as I do I remember my reaction to the summer boy and how big of an idiot I must have looked like. No wonder they probably wouldn't care if Alec moved into my bedroom. It's not like I'm real smooth with guys.

"Are you feeling better? Your dad asked me to come and check on you."

Ah, so there must be outside work that needs to be done. Charlie work. Not work for Mom or Sadie Ann. "The only time you come looking for me anymore is when my dad sends you. Are you sure you don't want to just be his best friend instead of mine? You love The Village as much as he does." I cross my arms and turn away from him. I'm acting like a brat, but I don't care.

"Shut up. Stop acting like such a girl." He playfully pushes my arm before sitting next to me.

"I am a girl, you jerk."

He laughs, but when I don't join him, he quiets. Alec's good at stuff like that. I get annoyed with him, but I know he cares about me. "Hey." He scoots closer. "Believe me, I know you're a girl, Charlie."

I turn my head, feet on the bed, knees pulled up to my chest. My head rests on my arms that lie on my knees. "Yeah?"

"Of course. Your arms are puny." He squeezes my bicep. "And your voice is high pitched. Oh, and you pout a lot—ouch!" He winces when I make a fist and hit him with all the strength in my "puny" arm.

"You're a jerk!" I try to push off my bed, but Alec grabs my arm and pulls me back down.

"I'm kidding. You know that. What's wrong?"

Everything and nothing at the same time. I feel both stuck and at home and comfortable and uncomfortable and I suddenly want to be free even though I don't know what that means. "I told you, I don't feel well." I let him keep his arm around me and then rest my head on his shoulder.

"You're a shitty liar."

"I thought you would be too big a gentleman to call me on it."

Alec sighs. "You know you can talk to me, right? What's wrong? Is it Sadie Ann? Your mom?"

Alec's the only person in the whole wide world who knows how I feel about my mom and my sister. Mom will never love me like she does Sadie and I know I'll never be as good, or as pretty as my sister. Well, I'm sure people know that, but I don't know if they know that I know all those things. Alec does, and even though he drives me just as crazy as they do sometimes, and he would be happy on this land every day like Dad, and wants me to be right here with him, I couldn't imagine my life without him.

"I don't know what it is, Alec. I just feel...lost. Like I want more."

"More of what?" he asks and I know he doesn't get it. I don't even get it, so I answer the only way I know how.

"More life."

Chapter Two

I don't see the family from 3B for the rest of the day. I spend it out in the sun, working with Dad and Alec on boats. One of them is having some trouble and Dad considers himself a boat mechanic even though half of the time he makes things worse than he does better. We waste hours on something that we'll have to call a mechanic about later, who will have to fix the original problem, plus whatever Dad messed up.

I get it. I know money is tight, and Dad has to hold onto every penny he can. I'm not dumb, but when it ends up costing more than it originally would have? That doesn't seem like good money management to me.

We're up early the next day. There's a lot to do to get ready for The Village Bash. It's the big night in the beginning of the summer. It's basically the kick off to the summer season where the people in town come out and all the out-of-towners staying at The Village come and we pretend to know how to party and have a good time. We pretend we're this fun place where everyone wants to hang out. I guess people seem to enjoy themselves. I used to. I'm not sure why that changed last year, or why this year I'm really not looking forward to it.

"What time is the band supposed to be here?" Dad asks. There's a huge open area in front of the lake, not far from our store. The trees crowd in behind the area and behind our house where the bash takes place. The party area goes partway down the little strip of "beach" that leads around the lake. People don't travel too far from the main area for the bash. This is where everything "happens."

"Same as every year, Dad. Bash starts at four, they'll be here at two to start setting up."

"Shit." He runs a hand through his slightly graying hair. He's not old. I'm not sure why he's going gray suddenly. "We need to set up the stage."

I wait for it. Know it will come so I stand up, and as soon as I'm on my feet he says, "Charlie Rae? You think you and Alec could set up the stage?" It's not hard. I mean, we can handle it. It's not a big deal to just have Alec and I do it. Or...

"What about Mom and Sadie? I thought you wanted me to fix the fire pits?"

He shakes his head. "You know your mom or Sadie Ann can't do the stage. I'll finish the fire pits. Come on, Charlie. You're the only one I can count on."

He means Mom and Sadie won't, not can't. I'm pretty sure they're not helpless. They probably wouldn't even break a nail. But when he says that, reminding me how much he needs me and gives me that kind smile, it's hard to stay mad at him. "Let me go grab Alec."

Dad pulls me to him and kisses my forehead. "Thanks, kid. I love you."

"Love you too, Dad." Then I'm off to find Alec to put up a stage and then end up finishing the pits and to do whatever else to have a huge bash that I want no part of. One I wish I could disappear from all together.

The Bash is in full swing. I manage to hide out through the first couple hours, making excuses for reasons to go in the house or to the store. There's live music, dancing, games, and food. People are laughing and talking and singing. Even Mom and Sadie Ann like The Bash. It's their day to dress up and give people a reason to envy them. It's the only time they seem to like having The Village.

I see Sadie dancing on the small dance floor in the sand and watch people circle it, clapping for her. Her dress twirls around her hips and long legs, and I look down at my cut-off shorts and take a minute to thank God that I realize comfort is more important than showing off the assets I don't have.

Alec peeks his head through the door. "What are you doing in here, Charlie? Get'cha ass outside and dance with me!"

"I don't wanna." I know protesting won't work. Alec comes in and grabs my hand and he's dragging me outside. God, he loves this. Not the showing off and stuff like Sadie, but he loves The Village. A part of me wishes I could love it again, like I used to. It would be so much easier that way.

He smiles and it's almost impossible for me not to do the same thing. I see his parents standing with Dad who has actually taken a small break to enjoy himself. Out here in the middle of it, I see how much busier it is than usual. I should be enjoying this. Why aren't I enjoying this?

There's a family of redheads who are staying in one of the cabins a little farther from the lake. They have a two-year-old who's running around, making everyone around them dance. An older couple that Dad says is on a celebration of life. I guess the husband has cancer and they want to spend a month together on the lake. It's both sad and romantic and I find it hard to look at them as they hold hands.

I know the other people filling our cabins are around too, so I try to focus on them.

They're all having a good time.

"You're going to dance," Alec says.

"I'm not," I tell him. "Plus Sadie is drawing everyone's attention. I'm not going up there to dance by her." Her black hair is shinier than mine. Longer than mine, just like her legs are.

"Then we'll dance in the sand." He's still pulling and I'm still digging in my heels, but I soon give up because I know Alec won't. He finds us a spot and we start to dance. I'm a tangle of arms and legs, but I don't care and Alec doesn't either. That's part of the best friend code. Thou shall dance stupidly with friends.

I see some of the girls watching us, and they must be wondering what Alec sees in me. He's gorgeous and way more social than I am. I know he doesn't really *see* anything in me. He's a flirt, but he never dates any of the girls. He plays sports and has his sporty guy friends, but when he's not with them, he's always with me at The Village.

The fast song changes to a slow one and Alec pulls me to him. I'm just as sweaty as he is, but I know he won't say anything. I know he won't care.

"See? Having fun isn't so bad."

"You really think this is fun?" I ask in his ear. I think maybe there's something wrong with me. Something I don't get or somehow lost in the past year. I always say Sadie thinks she's too good, but can that be me, too? Do I think I'm too good for The Village, only in a different way than Mom or Sadie Ann?

"Sure." Alec shrugs. "It's always been fun. What's not to like?"

I don't know. I wish I did.

We dance a couple more songs and then hang out with some friends from school. Dad calls me away to help once in a while or to grab something or fix something or whatever other "Charlie" job brings itself to his attention.

After my errand to go get more ice, I come back outside. They've lit the tiki torches and the little twinkling lights that hang all around are lit as the sun starts to go down. It's getting dark, my favorite time of the day. I love it at night. Love the darkness with those little specks of light decorating the sky. I like to pretend I can visit the stars. That I'll ride one far away from here one day. It's a kid's dream. I know that, but I like it so I plan to keep on dreaming it.

Alec is surrounded by a group of people from school. Girls are all around him and a couple of the guys from his football team. I know I'll hear it later if I leave, but I have to get away. Dad might need me or Alec will come looking for me, but I want to chance the stars by myself. Heading back into the house, I go out the back door, which leads to the woods. I don't go deep, but stay hidden enough that I can walk around the Bash and toward the far area of the lake without anyone seeing me.

Once I clear the party, I head back toward the beach, staying close to the trees as I make my way down. I can't go all the way to my favorite spot tonight. There isn't time and I can't stay long, but I just need a few minutes to...*be*. It has a good view here anyway.

I find a place to sit down by the water. The sky is painted midnight now and I watch the little lights I love start to dot the sky. They're like candles, and every time a new one is lit, I smile.

"I'm pretty sure girls who sneak away to go exploring in the woods can be nothing but trouble."

I jerk my head to the right to find the face that matches the voice from beside me. But I know. Without looking, I know it's the summer boy.

"You're not going to try to kill me or something, are you? You look like you want to kill me. Not that I would be scared. I just wouldn't want to have to fight a girl." He looks amused and I'm not sure how to feel about it.

Don't be an idiot, don't be an idiot, don't be an idiot. "What? Because I'm a girl I'm nothing to be afraid of? That's a little sexist, don't ya think?" I'm not super proud to admit this, but I kind of like it. Not that I don't want to be a strong girl, because I do. But I like that he notices I am one. It lessens the chance he's going to ask me to put together a stage or lift something heavy.

"I bet you even followed me in case I needed help," I say. "Who knows, a girl alone at night? Something scary might happen to her."

I can't see him real well, but I think he's smiling.

"Nope. Didn't want to protect you. You look pretty badass. Just wanted to see what you were sneaking away from—or *to.*" He sits down next to me. I feel a little jolt of excitement zip through me when his arm brushes mine before he pulls away.

"I'm not running from anyone."

"Then why did you sneak around through the woods? You went back in the house, out the back door and through the trees to get here."

"Holy stalker." I scoot over a couple inches. "FYI, I *am* bad ass and I'm not afraid to use those bad ass skills if I need to."

My summer boy laughs. "I don't doubt that. And I'm not a stalker. Just...curious."

Those words do something to me. Turn me inside out. They're so simple, but there's never been anyone in my life that's been curious about me. Probably because everyone knows everything about me. I'm Charlie Rae Gates. My family has lived in Lakeland Village since it's creation. Mom's family opened The Village right after they got married. Dad was Mom's high school boyfriend. He worked here. They got married and took over the place. One day it will be mine. Not Sadie Ann's, but Charlie's.

It's my destiny. I was born to take care of The Village.

"I know. It sucks here. I don't get why people come. You must be pretty bored if the only thing to do is be curious about me."

"Ouch," Summer Boy says. "Is that your way of telling me to get lost?"

"What?" I look at him and he's looking at me and I wonder if this could be another one of my moments. No, I tell myself. That's ridiculous. I don't know this boy. I'll probably never see him again after this summer. "I didn't mean it like that. I just meant..." I shake my head. "Never mind." It's not like I'm going to tell him I don't understand how someone could be curious about me. I may be lame, but I'm not real stoked on making that public knowledge.

"How ya feeling?" he asks.

"Huh?" Then I remember yesterday. I ignore the urge to puke, not out of sickness, but embarrassment, and say, "Oh. Much better."

"You live here?"

"Yep."

"Like, all the time?"

"Yep."

"Cool."

"I guess." Gah! What's wrong with me? I sound like an idiot. "Where do you live?"

"Upstate New York."

I look up at the sky and pretend the stars are lights in New York. I wonder if they'd compare to the stars here. If you can see the stars in the city. "I bet this place sucks compared to there."

I feel him shrug. "It's a whole hell of a lot smaller, I can tell you that."

I laugh and wonder if maybe he won't be so bad after all.

"So...is your boyfriend going to realize you're gone, coming looking for you and then freak out when he sees us sitting here? My dad might freak out. He gets mad when I get caught fighting."

It takes me a minute to realize what he means by boyfriend. I know, I know. It should be obvious, but everyone knows Alec isn't my boyfriend. They all know I've never had one. "Oh, God. He's totally not my boyfriend."

"Looked like it to me." I think there's a laugh in his voice. I wonder if he's laughing at me.

"Well, he's not, okay? He's my best friend."

Summer boy stands. I do the same. Neither of us moves, we just stand there side by side.

"I'm pretty sure that's code for he wants you. He just hasn't made a move yet."

I don't reply because it's so not Alec's style and this summer boy just doesn't get it.

"Well, now that I've figured out the mystery to where you were sneaking off to, I had better go. I don't want my parents to freak out. No, that's a lie. I know they won't freak out, but I'll pretend they might. My brother might be bored and wonder where I am though."

"Oh...okay." I'm bummed he's leaving. I'm curious about him and liked the idea of him being curious about me. Waiting for him to go, I look out into the forever night at the stars I love.

"You like stars?" he asks.

"I love them. I sneak out a lot at night just to come look at them." I don't know why I said that last part, but I figure if I try to make up a reason, I'll screw it up.

"Cool," he says. "Sneaking out is fun. Maybe I'll see you sometime."

That quickly, summer boy turns and starts to walk off. He stops about ten feet away. "Do you want me to walk you back? I feel kind of wrong leaving you out here like this. Not trying to be sexist. Just...what's that word? Oh, yeah, nice."

I giggle. I'm not sure if I've ever giggled in my whole life. He's funny. I like that. "Thank you for asking, but I'll be okay."

"Okay. Cat'cha later. Oh, what's your name?" he asks.

I stall a few seconds and he probably wonders what's wrong with me. He only asked my name. Shouldn't be that hard of a question.

"Oh, yeah. It's Charlie, right?"

I shake my head and look at him. "Charlotte. My name is Charlotte."

"I'm Nathaniel. Cat'cha later, Charlotte."

This time when Nathaniel walks away from me, he doesn't stop.

Long after all the guests have gone back to their cabins, and everyone from town has gone home, Dad, Alec, Alec's parents—Maggie and Randy—Sadie Ann and I are cleaning up the mess. It has to be ready for tomorrow, where we'll be up bright and early for another day. That's probably the only reason Dad made Sadie help.

"It sucks he makes us do this. It's not *our* job," she whines for the millionth time, as she walks by me. Like all the other times, I ignore her.

I'm thinking about Nathaniel. Still wondering what made him decide I was a mystery. Yeah, I know it was probably just because I went off from the group and hid out in the woods, but he had to have been watching me to know that, right? So why? What made him watch me?

Suddenly looking less annoyed than before, Sadie whispers, "Oh my God. Did you see the boys in 3B? They're freaking gorgeous!"

No! No, no, no, no. I don't want her to think that. Don't want her to have anything to do with 3B and Nathaniel because he's intrigued by *me.* He talked to *me.* She gets a part of everything, and I want this for myself. "No. I didn't notice them."

"I swear, Charlie. When are you going to grow up? You wouldn't notice a cute boy if he kissed you. That tomboy stuff might be okay when you're younger, but you need to get out of it."

"I'm not a tomboy." Kind of a lie. We both know I am, but who cares? Can't I be both? Not like to wear dresses *and* notice cute boys?

"Whatever. I think the younger one is your age. Not that you aren't practically married to Alec already, but still. The other one is my age. I can tell. I think I heard them say his name is Brandon."

"Cool." I try to ignore her as I pull down keep filling the bag with trash.

"He's going to be the perfect way to spend the summer, Charlie. I'm finally excited about something. I can't wait to have him."

She dances away. Sadness wraps its ugly, lonely hand around me. Brandon has nothing to do with Nathaniel, but I don't want her to want him. Being around Brandon means being around Nathaniel and no one notices me when Sadie Ann is there. No one but Alec, who I know to the marrow of my bones doesn't see me as more than his best friend. The one who doesn't understand when I say I want more than the life I have right now. I think Alec looks at me and sees The Village he loves so much.

Chapter Three

The next day, Sadie Ann doesn't stay in the store. She's outside with the rest of us, working in the sun. And when there isn't work to do, she's still out here, which I guess isn't as unusual as her breaking a sweat for The Village. She suntans by the water, and again, that isn't anything new. She does it every summer, but it feels different right now because I know she's hoping to see Brandon. It shouldn't bother me, but no matter how hard I try I can't stop the anger from glaring daggers every time I look at my sister.

"What'd Sadie do? You've been giving her the evil eye all morning." Alec says. Leave it to him to notice.

"Nothing." I walk over to the dock, which isn't too far from Sadie, and sit down. Alec sits beside me.

"What do you wanna do today?" he asks.

We spend a lot of time working, but it's not like that's all we do. Lots of the guests are pretty much on their own and don't need us often. There are boat rentals and sometimes people want us to take them on a tour, but usually they're good to go by themselves. It isn't like I don't have any free time here, even though it never really feels free. I'm still always inside the cage of this town. Of my life. "I don't know. What do you want to do?"

Alec shrugs, pushing his blond hair out of his eyes. As he does, I see something in his expression change. He's looking over my shoulder. While I turn to see what it is, he says, "Looks like Sadie found a way to keep herself busy this summer."

My stomach sinks as I see her smiling up at Brandon. He's standing beside her and she's holding her hand over her eyes to block the sun, a huge smile on her face. Her red bikini looks perfect against her golden skin. Especially when you count the boobs she has holding them up. The bumps under my tank top aren't even a quarter of hers and she's only a year older than me. I dust off my shorts like it matters.

A movement behind Brandon catches my eye and I notice Nathaniel standing there. He has a Yankees hat on, that I watch him turn around and wear backward, with cargo shorts and a white t-shirt. He gives me that nod that boys do, slightly lifting his head and sends a partial smile in my direction.

"You know him?" Alec's voice has a strange sound to it.

"No," I shake my head, but I'm still looking at Nathaniel. "I ran into him, but I don't know him." Which I guess is really what Alec is asking. Nathaniel hasn't been here long. It's not like I can really know him.

Brandon sits down next to Sadie and Nathaniel nods his head again, this time calling me over. Well, me and Alec over, I mean.

My heart darts through my chest like a shooting star. He steps closer to his brother and Sadie before sitting down, too. His feet are flat on the ground, his knees up with his arms resting on them. He looks so relaxed. So comfortable. I find it hard to breathe.

Which makes no sense. I don't know this boy. But he's different. I see it and feel it and that calls to something deep inside me that I don't understand. But I want to. Being here at The Village, I know everything. I always have. Nothing is ever new, no matter who comes and goes. Alec and I will probably always be best friends. We'll probably grow up and get married like Mom and Dad because they were best friends.

Sadie will leave. Mom will wish she could. Dad will grow old and Alec and I will take over. It's written in the stars. Probably our destiny and I suddenly want to cry.

I stumble forward at the nudge to my back.

"Oh crap. I'm sorry, Charlie. I didn't realize you weren't paying attention." My eyes find Alec to see he's not looking straight at me. He's glancing back and forth between the group of three sitting down and me.

"It's fine." I fight the embarrassed heat I feel pushing to the surface. Alec grabs hold of my arm, as though he's trying to steady me, despite the fact that I'm not falling. I wait for him to let go, but he doesn't.

It's awkward having Alec hold me like this in front of the others. It's not like he's never touched me before, but part of me wants to slip out of his grasp. Then I feel like a horrible person for it, so I don't.

We walk over to the group and Sadie looks up at me. "Hey, Charlie! Hey, Alec." The fake sweetness in her voice makes me want to throw up.

"Hey." When I sit down, Alec's hand comes off my arm. I nod to Sadie Ann, then Alec, Brandon, and Nathaniel.

"What do you guys usually do for fun around here?" Brandon asks. His voice is totally different from Nathaniel's. Not deeper, but maybe a little rougher. He almost sounds like my grandma who smoked sixty-five years of her eighty. Okay, maybe it's not that bad. Maybe I just want to find something bad about him so Sadie won't want to get close to Brandon or Nathaniel.

"What do you do?" Alec replies with a strange kind of tightness in his voice.

Brandon shrugs. "Whatever."

Alec's eyes dart down. I try to keep looking at him. Or to look at Sadie, or even Brandon, but I can't stop from peeking over at Nathaniel. He smiles and shakes his head as though he thinks they're all being ridiculous. It's impossible not to smile back at him.

Sadie speaks up. "You should let me show you around Lakeland Village. There's not a lot to do, but it would get us away from here for a little while." The way she looks at Brandon, it's as though the rest of us aren't sitting there. She looks confident and beautiful and a mixture of jealousy and pride blends inside me. I never thought I would look at Sadie and feel pride like that, but I do. I wish I could look at a boy I liked and feel that confident.

"Sure. That would be cool. You guys wanna take off?" Brandon looks at Alec and I, then at Nathaniel. "I know you do."

Sadie's confidence looks a little dinged. "Charlie and Alec hardly leave The Village if they don't have to. I'm sure they don't want go."

"I'll go," shoots out of my mouth, unplanned. "I mean..."

"You should go." Nathaniel replies. "We'll all go. But my douchebag brother failed his driver's test, so hopefully one of you can drive."

"Screw you. At least I'm old enough to take it." At that both Brandon and Nathaniel push to their feet. They play around with each other; pushing and fake punching and I can't help but watch them. Maybe boys are the same everywhere. Right now I don't see anything different in the way they act and Alec. Except when it's Alec, it's me he's goofing around with.

I fidget in the backseat, sandwiched between Alec and Nathaniel. Sadie Ann is driving and of course, Brandon is sitting in the front with her.

Dad about had a fit when we told him we were leaving. All it took was Sadie pouting out her bottom lip and he was a goner, though. He was happy the two of us are hanging out, apparently. I didn't tell him Sadie would rather I stay home.

I shift again, uncomfortable in the too-tight shirt Sadie made me wear. I don't know why she cares what I have on anyway.

"You okay over there?" Nathaniel asks. "You're squirming around like you're about to jump out of your skin. You're not about to go all Incredible Hulk on me or anything, are you?"

His comment stings. "No!" leaps out of my mouth, with a harsh edge to it.

"She doesn't usually dress like that. She's uncomfortable," Alec grits out. I want to thank him for sticking up for me and bury myself in a hole at the same time. Nice of him to out me like that.

"I was kidding, man." Nathaniel leans closer to me. "You know I'm kidding right, Charlotte?"

The car goes deathly quiet at the name. No one calls me Charlotte. Sadie laughs while Alec gives me a strange look, but Nathaniel doesn't seem to notice or care.

"Yeah. It's cool," I tell him. We pull into a parking lot in town. I'm thankful that we're here so I can get out of the car. Alec gets out first and I stumble out behind him. It's a bright, sunny day like it always is in the summer. Sadie is smiling as she slips on her sunglasses.

Alec cocks his head at me. I can see the wheels turning in his head as he tries to figure out what's going on with me. The truth of the matter is, I don't know. I wouldn't even know what to tell him. It's not just about the summer boy...it's everything.

"There's not a ton to do, but we can show you guys a few places," Sadie tells Brandon.

"Sure. Sounds cool," he replies.

"Charlie, if you guys wanna take off by yourselves and meet up with us later, that's cool. I know you're more comfortable around just Alec anyway."

Dude. I'm going to kill her.

"If you wanted to get Brandon alone, you just had to ask," I shoot right back at her. I'm used to taking crap from a lot of people, but most of the time, I don't take it from my sister.

For the first time in forever, she blushes. Alec laughs and I hear Nathaniel mumble a "well played."

"I have to keep this twerp with me anyway. My folks made me promise." Brandon tries to flip Nathaniel's hat off, but he dodges him.

"I was just being nice. I don't mind if we all hang out." Sadie's smile is forced and I feel a little guilty for embarrassing her.

Brandon and Sadie walk in front of Nathaniel, Alec and I. One of the boys flanks either side of me and it's impossible not to accidentally bump against them. Alec here, Nathaniel there. A brush of an arm, the touch of a hand.

We show them a few of the shops. There's this ridiculous Lakeland Village Museum, which is really nothing more than an old, white house stuffed with Lakeland Village history. The boys walk through like they care and Alec and I pretend we haven't seen it all a million times before. It was our first field trip in Kindergarten, then again in third grade.

We go to the ice cream shop where Brandon buys Sadie ice cream. Nathaniel turns to me and says, "What do you guys want?" And as stupid as it is, it makes me swoon a little. A boy has never offered to buy me ice cream before.

"It's cool. You don't have buy it," Alec replies just as I opened my mouth to answer. "You want your usual, Charlie?"

Nathaniel shrugs like it isn't a big deal and steps forward to order his ice cream. I try not to let it bother me, and nod at Alec.

We sit at the little tables with ice creams painted on them. One of the girls in Sadie's grade did it. She's planning on leaving Lakeland Village as soon as she graduates to pursue art school, and I envy her that.

Soon, we're all piled in the car again and heading back home. I'm stuck between the two boys again and I'm kind of bummed I can't make myself enjoy it. They're both cute, super cute, but Alec is my best friend and Nathaniel's only here for the summer.

"Anyone around here play ball?" Brandon looks toward the backseat. I actually feel Alec's body go haywire.

"Football?" Alec asks, excitement in his voice. And I know, as much as he didn't want to like these two boys, he's just found a new best friend.

"Is there any other kind?" Brandon asks.

"Baseball. Anyone can tackle someone else," Nathaniel says from beside me.

Brandon and Alec start rambling about teams and the next season and blah blah. It's not that I don't like to play around. We get together and have tons of games. It's fun. Alec always picks me for his team and most of the other girls sit around watching, but I don't care. I like being involved. But it's different liking to play sometimes and being in love with it.

Alec is in love.

I wish he would try to leave this town one day to play somewhere.

"You want to get a game together when we get back?" Alec asks.

Brandon's eyes glow with excitement. "Really?"

"Yeah. I'll call a few people."

Sadie Ann has a cell phone, but I don't. "You're only fifteen, Charlie Rae. You don't need one," Mom told me when Sadie got hers. I don't really care. It's not that I would call anyone but Alec anyway.

Alec pulls his out and starts texting a few people. Since he gets paid for helping out at The Village, he actually has money sometimes.

"You going to watch us play?" Brandon asks Sadie.

"Sure. I guess." Even thought her words sound nonchalant, I can tell she's happy he asked her.

"You're down to play, right, Charlie?" This from Alec. He would never ask me to watch. He knows better than that.

"Yeah. Sounds cool."

"You play?" Nathaniel asks, but it doesn't sound like he's making fun, just curious.

"Yeah, sometimes."

"All the time is more like it," Sadie says. "She likes playing with the boys."

I hate it when she says things like that. It makes my gut twitch, but part of me doesn't blame her. It's true and I don't think she's always trying to be mean. She just doesn't get me, and she likes to make sure everyone knows that.

"Cool," Nathaniel replies.

"Her and I are awesome together. We kick ass out there," Alec says.

No one replies to that. We pull up back at home and turn off the car. Everyone piles out. My insides don't know if they're excited to play, to hang out with Alec and the people we know. To do something comfortable, or if I'm freaked out because being around Nathaniel seems to make me that way.

"You ready?" Alec asks, but he's not looking at me. He's looking at Brandon.

"You know it." Brandon grins.

"Charlie Rae! Thank God you're back. I'm going to need your help a little bit, kiddo!" Dad calls from his perch by one of the boats.

I deflate. It doesn't matter if I was excited before. Doesn't matter if I wasn't sure how I felt because now there isn't a choice.

"We were going to play football," I say, knowing it won't change anything.

Dad looks bummed. "It won't take long. I'll make it real quick and then you can get back to your friends."

I turn back to the group. This is where Alec would usually say he'd stay and help me. We'd get done quickly and go play, but the look on his face—the guilt blending with the desire to play is as plain as day

"Go with them. I'll be over when I'm done."

"Thanks, Charlie. That's why I love you." He gives me a hug and then bounces on the balls of his feet. All energy, like he always gets when he plays football.

"Want me to stay?" Nathaniel asks. "I can help."

That causes Alec to pause. It makes my heart stutter, too.

"No," I shake my head. "That's okay."

"Are you sure?"

"Charlie! Hurry up, please!" Dad shouts.

"I have to go," I say, and turn around to walk away.

Chapter Four

It's dark outside when I slowly slide open my window and sneak out. I'm not sure my parents would really care. I'm sure they wouldn't. It's not like I'd be sneaking out to meet a boy or do anything dangerous, but I still never let them know. They wouldn't understand my fascination with the night. With the stars and how they amaze me and make me wonder what else there is in the world.

Sure they know I like them, but they don't know how the stars carry my dreams. That I wish I could drift away on one and see and explore everywhere.

That's a fact I like to keep just for me.

Tonight, I need a little piece of that thing that's just mine. By the time I finished helping Dad this afternoon, the football game was over. Sadie was angry because Brandon disappeared with Alec to do some stupid boy stuff and, according to her, she didn't know or care where Nathaniel was. I'd used the home phone twice to call Alec, but he didn't pick up or call back. That's never happened before and I know I shouldn't let it bother me, but it does.

It's not like I should want to hang out with them anyway. Alec can be best friends with that stupid summer boy if he wants to.

When I walk by one of the cabins, a noise startles me. Looking over I see the older couple in chairs on their porch. The light shows me they're holding hands. Pausing, I watch them for a second, my heart going pitter-patter as I think about how much they much love each other and how hard it must be to know, they'll soon be separated. Shaking my head, I start walking again.

It doesn't take me long to walk to my spot. There are other places I like to go at The Village, places that are more private and harder to get to, but tonight I don't go to them. Tonight I want to be here, in this same little place I snuck off to the other night with the cool view, down the beach.

I have my telescope in the bag over my shoulder. My eyes are following the light from my flashlight as it dances across the ground. I'm not even wearing any shoes, because it doesn't matter out here. For a minute I think of my toenails and how plain they are without all the colors that Sadie Ann and Mom like to use. Maybe I should paint mine too.

I shake my head. I have no idea why I'm thinking about my toenails right now. I've never cared how they looked before, so I'm not about to start now. I'm so lost in thought, that I don't see anyone in front of me, just hear the voice in the darkness say, "Boo."

I don't jump, but my heart does. Not because I'm scared. It jumps in excitement. Maybe even wants to do a little dance in my chest.

"I'm not very scary, huh?" Nathaniel says.

I look over and see him sitting close to where we met last night. He has his legs out in front of him, a pair of Nikes on his feet, and I suddenly wish I was wearing shoes. Or that I would at least be the kind of girl who painted her toenails. "What are you doing out here?" My voice sounds a little sharper than I meant for it to. *Don't be a dork, don't be a dork.*

"Waitin' on you."

"Why?" I don't mean for the question to come out, but no one really waits for me, except Alec, but I feel like he kind of has to. We bathed together as kids. We learned to walk together and our parents threw us in the pool to learn to swim on the same day. Alec grabbed my hand under the blue water and we found our way to the surface together. I'm not sure he has a choice but to wait for me, but Nathaniel doesn't.

"I felt bad you got ditched today."

Oh. That's not really the same thing as wanting to be here. "I didn't get ditched."

"So you didn't want to go with us?" he asks. It takes me a minute to make sense of him. Boys are so strange. He seems to say whatever is on his mind and he's so literal. Alec is like that with me, but not quite as much. Alec wouldn't tell me I got ditched. He would say he was sorry my dad made me stay, which, yeah might be the same thing, but they sound a whole lot different. Choice of words is important.

"Whatever," I say, and go to turn around, but he speaks again.

"I'm just asking. I'm not trying to be a jerk."

I pause, wanting to walk away, but knowing there's a bigger part of me who wants to stay with the summer boy who came out because he felt bad I got abandoned while everyone else got to have fun. And when I put it that way, it doesn't sound like such a bad thing.

"What's in the bag?"

I turn to face him again, shining the flashlight in his direction, but not right in his face. The moon is bright enough to give some light, but it gives me something to do. "My telescope."

"Can I see it?"

I shrug. "It's not that nice."

"So?" He sounds confused by my words and I have to bite my cheeks not to smile. My face is hot and there's a game of tackle football going on inside my belly.

I walk over to him and sit down. My fingers are all shaky and I cover my plain toes with my pack as I pull out the old, black telescope. I hand it to Nathaniel and our fingers brush. It makes me feel like little fairy wings are brushing my skin. I turn so he doesn't see my smile as I pull the stand out of my bag. My back is still toward him as I set it up. I turn to grab the telescope from him and Nathaniel is looking at me. His eyes are this dark blue that somehow reminds me of the moon.

Once it's all set up I scoot over and nod my head toward it. "Look."

Nathaniel gets up on his knees; so super close to me that I swear I feel the heat from him. It's like I'm sitting by the woodstove. Like I'm freezing and he's giving me the warmth to keep me alive even though it's a billion degrees out here and I know my thoughts make me sound like an idiot.

He looks through the scope and I watch, excitement burning in my insides because he's going to get it. I know he is. He's going to understand me in a way no one from The Village can. I hold my breath, wanting, needing, waiting, flying.

"Look like stars to me," he says, leaning back, and I crash to the ground. My eyes prick with tears. I'm stupid. So stupid. Why did I think he would get it? Why do I want him to?

"Oh," I say, those fairy wings replaced by little pins poking my skin.

The look on his face changes thing. His eyes crinkle and he removes his backward hat. "Show me what you see up there, Star Girl."

My pulse stutters and then tries to catch up. "Really?"

Nathaniel shrugs. "Sure. Whatever."

I'm not sure if it's something he really wants, but he asked me and so I do. I start off easy and show him the big dipper. I move to Orion and Pegasus and on and on. I don't know how interested he is, but he at least pretends to be. He asks questions and looks at each one and listens to me talk.

"So is it the scientific aspect you like?"

I almost say no, but change it to, "Both. It's fascinating, but I also love the legends and stories. I like that it's so...well, space and stars could be anything."

"That's cool," Nathaniel replies.

When he first showed up, I thought that was one of my moments, but it has nothing on right now. How it feels to just sit back and talk about something I like without feeling guilty for it or like I'm some stupid kid. Dad doesn't understand loving anything but The Village, Sadie only loves herself, and Mom just doesn't get me. Alec would listen, but it's different.

Soon we've abandoned the telescope, and we're just talking about stars, and then The Village, and it feels different to talk to someone on the outside of everything. I don't tell him how it feels like it's suffocating me, but I wonder if he knows.

An hour and then two passes by. There's a pause in the conversation and I realize I've been blabbing forever. That's not me; especially not with someone I don't really know. "Sorry. I talked a lot. You probably didn't expect me to say so much."

"I asked. Duh." But he leans to the side and nudges me with his shoulder. "I'm kidding."

"I better go," I reply, even though I don't really want to.

"Yeah. Me too."

He helps me pack up the telescope and then stands. I move to get up and realize he was holding his hand out to help me, but I missed it. I'm glad it's dark so he can't see me blushing. "Sorry."

Instead of replying, he says, "I'll walk back with you."

We're quiet as we walk back to the cabins. The whole time my heart is beating like crazy and I'm way more exited than I should be, just from walking next to a boy.

When we're close both of us stop. "Thanks for hanging out," I whisper.

"No problem. I'm kind of a night owl."

"Oh," I say. We're just standing there and it shouldn't be a big deal, but it is. I wish I was older. And more like Sadie Ann so that I could lean forward and like kiss him or something, just because I want to. If I were Sadie Ann, maybe I could totally know if he wanted to kiss me, too. I am completely lost. I'm sure she'd kissed lots of boys by the time she was fifteen.

"See you later," I say.

I make it ten steps away, yes, I counted, when his voice stops me. "Wanna do it again tomorrow night?"

My smile is so huge I know I'll look like the biggest loser in the world if I turn around, so I don't. "Yeah," I say. "Yeah, I do."

That was how it began, our summers of sneaking out and watching the stars. Where we shared our secrets with each other and the night. We'd meet in secret and sometimes sit in my favorite spot. Other times, we'd head down the lakeside and I would pretend we could walk forever. I think I was really the one pretending and Nathaniel just listened. I wanted those summer walks with that summer boy to be my way out of The Village forever. But, really, I knew that couldn't happen. Nathaniel would leave and I would be the one who stayed.

Chapter Five
July

"Thanks for helping me wash the boats," I tell Alec as we work on the second to last one.

"Don't I always help? Plus, it's my job," he replies. At that I give him a small laugh.

"Most of the time you help, but you've been super busy this summer. I think Brandon has replaced me as your best friend."

"Shut up. You know you'll always be my best friend, Charlie. Brandon just likes ball as much as I do. He's cool." Alec looks away and starts scrubbing the boat again, his blond hair hanging in his face. He's still been working at The Village and if I'm being honest, I guess it's not that he hangs out with Brandon *all the time*, but it's different. Alec has never ditched me for a guest before, though I guess he's right. They are both obsessed with football and we don't get a lot of people close to our age that would want to hang out and play as much as Brandon does.

Still, that doesn't mean I'm not going to tease him. "*He's cool*. You sound like you're in awe of him!" Which in a way makes sense considering Brandon is supposed to be really good. Nathaniel says there's no doubt he'll play college ball.

As soon as the words leave my mouth, I regret them. Alec grabs the hose and turns it my way.

"No! Alec you better not!" I'm wearing a plain tank top and cut off shorts like I always am, and a pair of flip-flops. None of these articles will hold up well against a hose assault.

Alec steps closer.

"I said no, Alec Andrews!"

It really gets him when I add in his last name like that. Alec pulls the trigger to douse me in water. I scream and stick my hand in the bucket, ridiculously trying to fling water at him with a soppy sponge. Alec laughs when I give up and try to take cover. I turn to run and don't make it very far before I'm crashing into someone. I bounce off of whoever it is, assuming it's Dad who is going to freak out because Alec and I are playing around instead of working, but as soon as a pair of hands come out to catch me, I know it's not Dad.

It's Nathaniel.

Alec stops spraying and I stand there with Nathaniel's hands on my arms. I shiver and hope he thinks it's from being wet when really it's because he could totally be letting me go by now and he's not.

"What are you guys doing?" Nathaniel asks. I'm a total sucker for the backward way he wears his hat.

"Workin'," I say, which is sort of silly because it's obvious we're not. My eyes take him in and I realize his t-shirt is all wet. "You're all wet. Crap. I'm sorry."

At that, he laughs. "I'm pretty sure you're the one who's all wet."

His eyes trace down my body and I can't help but look down, too. Oh my God! My white tank top is sticking to my embarrassingly small boobs. You can see my bra through it. I pull away from him and bump into Alec, who I totally forgot was there.

"Chill, Charlie," Alec says.

Pulling away from him, I cross my arms over my chest.

Nathaniel looks at me, then Alec, and back to me again. I can't help but wonder what he's thinking, wishing his eyes or his face would tell me something.

"I came to see if you guys want to do something," Nathaniel says.

"Yes," I say at the same time Alec says, "We're working."

"Didn't look like it to me." Nathaniel raises his eyebrows. There isn't a chance to reply because Brandon and Sadie Ann walk up. They've been hanging out a lot over the past month. She brags about it all the time. It's so hard for me not to tell her about my nights spent with Nathaniel, but I don't.

And it's obvious she doesn't like how much time he spends doing guy stuff with Alec.

Brandon is the one who speaks. "Sadie said there's a spot everyone goes to watch the movies at the drive-in? Maybe we can get a big group together to go."

"I'll call some people," Alec says, right as Sadie replies, "I didn't know we were inviting other people, too." She crosses her arms in the way she does when she's trying to get what she wants. It usually works.

"Aw, come on, beautiful. It'll be fun." Brandon pulls her to him and wraps his arms around her. He nuzzles her neck and I'm pretty sure, for the first time, someone other than Sadie is going to get his or her way.

I'm shocked when Alec steps closer to me and wraps an arm around my shoulders. It's something we've done before, but it feels different this time. My heart races and not in the way you want it to when a boy touches you. Oh, God. What if he tries to get all close to me like Brandon's doing with Sadie? I've never kissed a boy, and I'm not like scared to or anything, but I don't want to kiss Alec.

I look over at Nathaniel, hoping to see something from him that says he cares, but he's screwing around with his iPod. *Stupid, stupid, stupid.*

Why would Nathaniel care? I should feel lucky if Alec wants me. I'm not exactly a real hot commodity around The Village like Sadie Ann.

"I'm going to get ready if we're all going out tonight." Sadie pulls away and when she does, there's a huge smile on her face. Behind Brandon's back she gives me a thumbs up as though it was ever any question that she would get Brandon.

"Cool." Brandon glances at Alec and grins, looking an awful lot like Nathaniel. "You calling people up, Andrews?"

When did Brandon start calling Alec by his last name? It's this strange guy thing that I'll never really understand.

"Yeah. Sure," Alec replies. "I forgot my phone though."

"You can use mine." Alec and Brandon walk away as though Alec wasn't just helping me wash the boats. Sadie is already halfway back to the house by now and I know there's no way I'm getting her out here to help me.

"Looks like your boyfriend left, Gates," Nathaniel says. Since when did he start calling *me* by *my* last name?

"I told you he's not my boyfriend," I snap.

"He wants to be."

"You don't get it. You don't understand us."

His blue eyes see right through me. He has a little dimple in his cheek when he smiles, which he does a lot. There's a kind of rope necklace around his neck that he always wears. It's tucked away under his shirt, and I don't know what's on it.

"Then why don't you explain it to me while we clean the boat?"

I look at the very light, few freckles on his face. The smile curling his lips. The necklace that keeps me up at night. I don't know what it is about this boy. Why he makes my heart dance and my stomach flip. Why he makes me wish I painted my toenails, but also makes me nervous to try.

He cocks his head and stares at me. I want to turn away, should turn away, but I can't make myself.

Then, Nathaniel says, "Sometimes when you look at me like that...I don't know...I wonder what you're seeing."

My cheeks burn with an embarrassed heat. My eyes dart away from him as my mind starts going at Mach speed. I am so stupid! Why do I stare at him? He knows.

I take a step away, and then another. My feet move faster each time. It's so ridiculous, but I feel like I'm going to cry. He's probably going to want to stop sneaking out with me and stop talking to me because he knows I like him.

"Hey. Where are you going?" Nathaniel asks.

I keep going until I'm on the other side of the last boat where no one can see me.

He follows. "What are you doing, Charlotte?"

"Washing the boat."

"Why are you pissed at me?"

"Why are you following me?" I try to walk away again. It's stupid that I'm mad. It's not his fault I can't hide the fact that I like him, but it is his fault for basically calling me out on it. Doesn't he see I want to be alone?

Nathaniel grabs my arm. Not hard, but enough to make me stop. We're still hidden around the back of the last boat. My chest is heaving up and down I'm breathing so hard and I try to forget about my wet shirt and tiny boobs and unpainted toenails.

"Why are you running from me?"

I let out a deep breath and close my eyes. His hand is still on my arm, and I'm shaking. I don't look at him yet. Can't, but I'm also not a runner. Dad taught me to be strong, not just physically but mentally too. There's no reason to run because it's not going to change anything, so even though I kind of feel like I'm going to puke right now, I open my eyes.

"You know why I'm running and why I'm embarrassed." *Because I like you. I like you and I know you don't like me the same way. Because even if you did, you'd be leaving at the end of the summer and it wouldn't matter.*

I want Nathaniel to let go of me. To walk away or laugh or something like that, but instead he just looks at me the way I looked at him. Not that I think he likes me, too, but I think maybe he sees something there no one else does. Or at least that he's searching for it.

His right hand still has my arm, as his left moves toward me. I can't help but think, this is it! I'm going to get my first kiss and it's going to be perfect because it's with this summer boy who gets lost in the night with me.

But instead he touches my hair. Lets it fall through his finger tips and I know it's not silky and pretty like Sadie's but it looks beautiful when my brown strands wrap around his fingers. You can see the highlights from the sun.

"I've never met anyone like you," he finally says.

I don't know what that means, so I say, "I'm just Charlie." It's a stupid thing to say.

"Charlotte. You told me to call you Charlotte."

It's the perfect thing he can say. I'm not Charlie Rae, the girl who plays football with the boys or the one who has no future but to stay here and take over The Village. With him I'm Charlotte and that feels entirely different.

"You going to let me help you clean the boats?" he asks. A nod is all I can manage.

Nathaniel lets go of me and we walk over to the hose and buckets. Right before he gets started his voice stops me.

"Charlotte?"

I turn to look at him. "Yeah?"

"I'm glad we came this summer. I'm glad we're friends."

I chew my bottom lip, not sure how to reply. His words pump my heart up, because I want that. To be his friend, but then it gets so big it shatters, too, because I know that's his way of telling me that's all we'll ever be.

Chapter Six

I get halfway to my room when I hear Mom. "Charlie Rae! You're tracking water all over the house!"

"Crap," I groan as I grab the kitchen towel off the counter. "I'll clean it up."

I'm sopping up the water—which is ridiculous, I might add, since I'm still wet and just making more of a mess—when she walks in.

"What were you doing out there?" She leans against the counter in her pretty summer dress.

"Washin' the boats."

"Your sister's going out with those Chase boys tonight. She and the older one, Brandon, seem to be getting along well." Mom smiles. She would love Sadie to end up with a boy like Brandon who would take her away from here. I know she wishes she had a man more like their dad rather than mine. That makes me sad, because he loves her so much. Because no matter what, he's the best man I know. I'm sure she loves him too, but maybe not *in* love with him. I think her hatred of being here changed her feelings for him.

"They're leaving at the end of the summer," I remind her.

Mom sighs. "I know. They always leave us behind, don't they?" She looks sad. Part of me wants to tell her they don't have to leave us behind. We could go. All of us. For once I want her to know I want to leave, too. It's one of the only things we have in common, but I can't do it. It would feel like stabbing Dad in the back.

I don't think she would get it anyway. Not my wanting to leave. It's something she shares with Sadie because their reasons are different from mine.

"I'm going with them tonight, too," I say.

Mom smiles and I can tell she's not trying to be mean when she says, "That's nice of them to let you tag along."

It doesn't stop the words from hurting though.

I don't want to be the one who's tagging along.

There's a spot way off to the far right side of the drive-in movies where we like to hang out. Not many other people come here because the view isn't the best. But I guess when most of us come, it's more to hang out and not watch the movies anyway.

Alec was able to borrow his parents' truck, which Sadie wanted him to bring so we'd have the back. Of course she still brought her car, I'm assuming so she could have more time with Brandon, which means it's Nathaniel and I riding with Alec. Talk about awkward. They both talk to me, but neither of them talks to each other. Alec keeps calling me Charlie and Nathaniel, Charlotte, which always gets a snort from Alec. It totally sucks.

Alec jaw is tight and he keeps squeezing the steering wheel. I'm not sure why he doesn't like Nathaniel. Maybe because no boys are interested in me and we spend so much time together, he just sort of considers me his. He's never had to share me, even with another friend. But he's friends with someone who stayed at The Village for the first time too.

I'm not anyone's. Not Alec's, and I'm definitely not Nathaniel's.

Nathaniel leans forward from the small cab in the truck. "Do we even know what's playing?"

"No one watches the movies anyway," Alec replies.

"So I'm not allowed to watch the movie? Shit. You guys should have told me." There's laughter in Nathaniel's voice and I can't help but smile.

Alec shakes his head from the driver's seat, but then as we pull in, he says, "Your brother and Sadie are getting awful close."

Nathaniel just shrugs like he doesn't care and leans back again. My head whips toward Alec. "Why do you care? Don't tell me you're worried about Sadie Ann."

It's selfish of me, I know, but Alec is the only thing I've ever had that Sadie could never take away from me, even if she wanted to. Everyone else loves her more and I've been okay with that because I had Alec. His statement hurts me more than it should.

"You know that's not how it is, Charlie." Then he reaches over and puts his hand on my knee. It's a comforting move because he knows I'm insecure when it comes to my sister. He's been around long enough to know that and I both want to squeeze his hand back as a thank you, and also feel strange about it being there, too.

Nathaniel clears his throat. Without looking back, I know he's smiling. His eyes are dancing with laughter and saying, I told you so, because he sees more between Alec and me than there really is. I ignore him.

We drive to our private spot under the trees. Sadie's car is already there as well as a bunch of other people we know. All in all there's about six vehicles parked. As soon as Alec kills the engine, we all three climb out.

Everyone gets busy making beds in the backs of the trucks and setting up camp chairs. My chair is stuck. As I fight to get it open, I see a few girls from school looking over at Nathaniel and smiling. My stomach sinks. The stupid chair becomes even more annoying as I struggle with it.

"You're going to pulverize that thing. Let me do it." Nathaniel grabs the chair from me and pulls, trying to open it.

I can tell he thought it would open easy so I laugh when he fights with the thing as hard as I did.

"You're trying to put a dent in my masculinity, aren't you?" He grunts like he's struggling even more than he is.

"I don't think I have to. The chair is doing a good enough job," I laugh. Nathaniel looks up. He's bent over messing with the chair, but his eyes are on me. There's a teasing playfulness to them and then half his mouth lifts in a smile. His dimple shows and I don't know how I'm able to read that look, but I turn and run.

I hear Nathaniel drop the chair behind me and know he's right on my tail. I don't get far before his arms wrap around my waist. My back is lined up with the front of his body, his mouth right next to my ear.

"Think you're tough, do you, Star Girl," he whispers. Shivers flow in wave after wave down my body. It's only the second time he's called me that, but I like it.

"Maybe not tougher than that chair." I try to keep my voice calm, but then a laugh jumps out of my mouth when Nathaniel starts to tickle me. His hands play at my sides and I can't stop the giggles that fall out of my mouth.

I feel the eyes of everyone else on us. They're probably all wondering what the heck is going on. I don't play around with boys like this. Sadie does. Other girls do, but not Flatty Rae.

I'm laughing and trying to get out of Nathaniel's arms, but he doesn't loosen his grip. He's strong. I wish I could melt into his hold and that he would never let go. Still I pretend to try and break free as he keeps tickling. Then my foot gets caught in something and I start to go down. I don't know how he does it, but Nathaniel turns us before we fall to the ground so it's him that hits the dirt first. I land on top of him, gasping as I realize how I'm laying on him.

I pause, stare.

Nathaniel pauses, then smiles.

And we both bust up laughing again. I don't think I've ever laughed as hard as I do at this moment. He doesn't push me off and I don't move just yet. We just lay there in the dirt, my body resting on top of Nathaniel's, his hands on my hips as we laugh.

All too soon, we're quieting and Alec is walking over, holding out his hand to help me up. I let him and then Nathaniel gets up behind me and he's dirty and I know I'm dirty and my cheeks hurt from smiling so much.

Nathaniel dusts himself off, but then looks over at me from under his lashes. He's facing to the side of me and not head on so it's just this side look and this half smile and I can't stop from returning it. It feels like there are secrets in this look. Like there's knowledge and fact, and I wonder if it was written in the stars.

I know then, I will never, ever forget this moment. I hope he won't either.

They always play two movies at the drive in. When the first one is over, all the girls decide that we need to take a group trip to the bathroom. Makes no sense to me, but I go anyway. I don't want to be that girl who stays behind with the guys because that's the easy way of them seeing you as one of the boys.

There are eight of us in the dirty bathroom where no one really pees, but fixes their hair and touches up their make up and does girl talk.

"Brandon is so hot," Cissy tells Sadie.

"I know, right?" my sister replies. "And seriously, such a good kisser!" Everyone laughs. I'm probably the only one who hasn't kissed a boy so I keep my mouth shut.

"His brother is hot, too!" Danielle adds and they all agree. I grab a paper towel from the dispenser and pretend to wipe my hands. The last thing I want is to listen to them talk about how hot he is.

"Eh, he's okay," Sadie replies. "A little young for me."

Yeah, because a year is so much younger than she is.

As awkward as it was sitting between Nathaniel and Alec for the first movie, it was better than being a part of this boy-talk cluster in the bathroom.

"If I didn't know better, I would think Charlie had two boys fighting over her!" Sadie laughs, which everyone follows and starts to do the same. My gut clenches, but I try not to show my discomfort. Try to laugh it off, but really, I'm wishing it wasn't so hard to believe. Not that I want boys fighting over me, because I don't, but...why does it have to sound so impossible?

"For sure," Bridgett says. "Everyone knows Charlie and Alec are going to be one of those couples who just end up together and then they'll get married and that will be that."

"Alec isn't my boyfriend," I grit out.

Bridget replies, "I know. You guys make that painfully obvious, but we know you will be one day. Which is a shame because Alec is hot, too. Since he's not yours yet, you should tell him it's okay to spread the love around a little."

Everyone laughs again. I want to throw up. I toss the paper towel in the trash, planning to walk out, but Sadie's voice stops me. "They might not admit it, but her and Alec have been together since they were born. It's ridiculous. Plus, it's not like she could have Nathaniel. Brandon told me he has a girlfriend back home."

It feels like she just punched me in the stomach. I try to ignore the pain. "I'm not interested in him, anyway." But I am. I know it and Nathaniel knows it and I think even Alec knows it. Why didn't he tell me he had a girlfriend?

He didn't have to tell me. It's not my business.

"We need to hurry. I want to get back to Brandon!" My sister winks at the girls. They're all giddy and giggling and my chest hurts so bad I feel like I can't breathe. They've just reached into my chest and wrapped a fist around my lungs, my heart, and they're squeezing the life out of me.

My brain keeps trying to tell me nothing has changed. I always knew Nathaniel would never be mine. He'll leave in a few weeks and then probably be out of my life forever. My heart doesn't get it, though.

Just a couple of hours ago, I knew I would remember this night forever. Now I know I'll remember it for all the wrong reasons.

I'm quiet through the second movie. Quiet still as we pack up. Quiet the whole drive home. When we get back to The Village, Nathaniel whispers in my ear, "What time do you want to meet tonight?"

I know right here what I have to do. I want nothing more than to keep having my nights with him, but I know I can't. If I don't look out for myself, no one else will. To protect my heart, I look at him. Study his eyes, his dimple, wish I could pull his necklace out from under his shirt to see what it is. I don't do any of that. Instead I tell him, "I can't come out tonight. I can't meet you anymore."

He doesn't stop me when I walk away.

The next day Dad tells me to clean the cabin the old couple was in—that they left. I remember them sitting on the porch together that night, and all the other times I've seen them just enjoying each other for the past month. Loving each other.

I don't know why, but I cry the whole time I clean their cabin.

Chapter Seven
August

I miss the night. Miss the stars. Miss talking to Nathaniel.

For the past couple weeks I've done a good job ignoring him. I help Dad as much as I can, even when he doesn't ask me to. Alec is off with Brandon when Sadie isn't and he doesn't try to get me to come. I'm surprised he hasn't pushed me, asked what's going on, but he's too busy playing ball and trying to impress the summer boys to care about much else.

It hurts more than I'm willing to admit.

Nathaniel's tries to talk to me a few times and I always reply. I'm nice and professional just like Dad expects us to be to our guests, but that's as far as it goes. I wonder if he misses me the way I miss him, but then I try to push those thoughts away. They won't do me any good.

A week left. That's all I have until they're gone and I can work on forgetting I ever knew them. Sadie will forget Brandon and date someone from our school and Alec will be my best friend again and things will be as though the Chase boys never happened.

I'm sitting on one of the docks with my feet in the water. It's dusk. I love this time of day because it's the bridge from day to night. Day where I work at The Village and know that's all my life will ever be and night where I think I can be anywhere else in the world.

Footsteps sound from behind me and I flinch, wondering who it's going to be.

"Night games tonight." Alec sits next to me, a huge smile on his face. "Last man standing. Everyone's coming down. It's going to be awesome."

We've always played a lot of night games in the summer, but haven't done it much this year. It's normally one of my favorite things. We have the area marked off from part of an empty field, not too far from The Village and going into a certain area in the woods. There are forts out there from when we were younger, along with an old house with tons of places to get lost in.

I love Last Man Standing.

Alec and I always own it. There are two main groups, but we usually break up in two man teams on each group. We're always on the same team and we almost always win. We play with paint ball guns, in full gear.

The moon is pretty bright out here, but each group is still allowed a flashlight. Dad has portable lights they we set up in a few spots, too. It doesn't give us too much light, but enough. It's a cutthroat game. Someone almost always gets hurt.

For the first time since the drive-in, excitement burns through me. I want to play. I want to win.

"Sadie and a few of the other girls aren't playing. They're setting up the flag. You got your paint gear? Some of the others are lending theirs to Brandon and Nathaniel."

All the happiness deflates from my muscles. How could I have forgotten Nathaniel would be here? Of course he would want to play. "I don't feel like playing."

"What? You never skip out on Last Man Standing, Gates. What's up with that?"

"Umm... You never call me 'Gates.' What's up with *that*?"

Alec grabs my hand when I try to stand up, but I pull it away. He gets up right behind me. "I've been a jerk, Charlie. I'm sorry. It's just...he's cool. You know he'll probably play college ball?"

"So?" I shout. "You could play, too. I know it. Don't stick around here and you'll be out there doing the same thing!"

Alec moves in front of me, blocking my way. "It's not that easy and you know it. Our lives are here. Plus, I don't want to leave. I wasn't saying that. It's just..."

He doesn't continue so I ask, "What?"

"Never mind. You wouldn't get it. Just play with us, Charlie. It won't be the same without you out there. You know it. Hell, I don't think I've ever played it without you."

Alec gives me the sweet smile that's impossible to say no to. He has this innocent, little boy look to him that the girls love. But the thing about Alec is, most of the time, he's not working it. He doesn't do it on purpose. He's just sweet and it's part of who he is.

No matter what, I love him and I do want to play this game of Last Man Standing with my best friend. I can do this. *I'm not a runner*, I remind myself. I can deal with a night around Nathaniel. Looking at Alec, I say, "Okay. I'm in."

He pulls me into a hug and we set off to get ready for the game.

Once we get everyone all set up, the big group of about twenty meet in the middle of the field. We're all decked out in camo clothes and paint gun gear. It's not completely dark yet and the lights definitely help.

Nathaniel hasn't tried to talk to me the whole time and I haven't tried either. It makes me sad, but it's for the best. I know it. I just have to keep reminding myself of it.

Everyone's arguing about team captains, but I don't pay much attention. It's not until I hear them announce that the two captains are Alec and Nathaniel that I perk up. I'm suddenly disappointed I won't get to be on Nathaniel's team.

Alec wins the coin flip, meaning he gets to choose first. The rest of us stand in a group with him and Nathaniel in front of us. I try not to look at him, but my eyes keep darting his way.

"Come on, Andrews! Choose!" someone yells at Alec.

I'm about to step forward to walk to his side when I hear Alec say, "Brandon."

My heart stops. Everyone suddenly gets quiet like they can't believe what happened. Alec has never, ever not picked me first for something. My cheeks get hot, but I try to stamp down the embarrassment.

Brandon walks over to Alec and they do this stupid boy, shake-hand, high-five thing and I'm about to leave. Screw Last Man Standing. Screw Alec and Brandon and even Nathaniel, too. Alec knew I didn't want to come here tonight; the least he could do is not throw me for a loop by embarrassing me.

"Charlotte."

My eyes shoot over to Nathaniel and he's staring at me, hard. My heart is running a race in my chest and I hear Alec in the background saying, "What? Charlie's always on my team!"

"Then you should have picked her," Nathaniel tosses back, still looking at me.

"Everyone knew I would!"

But he didn't. He always does, but this time Alec didn't pick me.

"Then I guess you should have picked her *first*." Nathaniel nods his head, like he's calling me over, and I walk right over and stand next to him. My feelings are hurt that Alec didn't pick me first and my heart is soaring that Nathaniel did, but I'm also trying to ground the freaking flight because I am not supposed to be feeling this way about him.

"Charlie?" Alec says and there's a little bit of shock and regret in his voice, but I feel the same thing. It's just a game and he didn't pick me.

"It's cool. We got this," Brandon tells him. I glance at Alec and he looks at me, something strange in his eyes that I don't understand. There's never been a time I couldn't understand Alec, but right now I don't.

And then, we break eye contact. He looks at the group of people and picks someone else. Nathaniel asks me who he should pick and I tell him who the best is. Back and forth we trade picks until everyone is in a group, and we have our two man teams decided. The goal is for one team to work together to try and take out the other, then it goes all Lord of the Flies and we go after each other.

Once there are only two, two-man teams left, we go for the conch with the flag. Whichever group gets it, wins.

Nathaniel looks at me, competitiveness that matches my own glimmering in his eyes. We're going to win. There's no question about it.

All hell has broken loose. This is unlike any game of Last Man Standing we've ever played. People are brutal and it's getting darker and darker but we still don't have a winner. There's one group left on the other team, Alec and Brandon, and then me and Nathaniel on ours.

The flag is in the middle of the field, waiting for us, as Nathaniel and I hide behind one of the forts on one side of the field. We have no idea where Brandon and Alec are.

"How good a shot is your brother?" I ask. Everything else is put behind us out here. It's like life or death and even though I can tell he wants to ask me why I've been ignoring him and I have the urge to either run and hide or just grab him and steal my very first kiss, he doesn't ask and I try to ignore my instincts.

Out here, the only instinct I can let grab me is the one telling me to win.

"He's all right. Not horrible but not great."

"You better than him?"

"Absolutely. What about Alec?"

I shake my head. "Not better or worse, either. We're pretty evenly matched, but he's good. Really good."

"So that's your way of saying you're good?" Nathaniel smiles.

I shrug. "I guess." We pause for a few minutes and then I ask, "What's the plan?"

Just then, Nathaniel grabs my arm. My first thought is they snuck up on us, but he points to the sky and I see the tail end of a shooting star. I love shooting stars.

I can't help but smile. He saw one and knew I would like it.

"I think that's our sign. I say we go for it. They're probably sitting somewhere waiting to snipe us, but let's let them be the passive ones who sit back and wait. We'll run out there, get it, and win."

"It's a risk."

"Not if you run fast," he laughs.

He's right. We can sit here forever waiting for them to find us or we can go out there and take our win. I'm determined to grab it with both hands and own it. But we can't let them shoot us either. If we do, it doesn't matter if we get the flag or not.

"Let's do it."

Nathaniel grabs my hand. "Run like hell. Don't look back. Leave your gun—"

"What? I can't leave my gun. How will I shoot them?"

"You won't need to. I'll have your back. I'll be right there and I'll take out anyone who gets you in their sights. You get the flag and we got this, Charlotte."

This is not usually how Alec and I do it, but I will be able to run faster without my gun. And...maybe it's not something I should be thinking, but it feels good to think of him having my back.

"Let's do it."

He squeezes my hand tighter. I forgot he even had it. "If we win, you have to meet me tonight."

My brain tells me to say no, but my heart is beating to say yes. The word is pumping through every part of me. There's no other option. "Okay."

Nathaniel smiles and I think it might be the best smile in the whole wide world. I bet his girlfriend loves that smile, too.

"Ready?" he asks. "On the count of three."

I set my paintball gun down.

"One," he says. Pauses. "You can do this. Run fast. I'll be right behind you."

I nod again. Who knows if he can see me but once we step into that field, everyone will be able to. The lights are that bright.

"Two."

Another pause.

"Three."

As soon as the word leaves his mouth, I run. Run with everything I have. My chest hurts. My legs hurt. Nathaniel is right behind me.

"Keep going. Shooting on your right," he yells. I hear the *pop, pop, pop* of his paintball gun. I keep running. Brandon curses. Alec and Nathaniel are shooting at each other. I don't pay attention. Just keep moving. As soon as I get there, I grab the flag and Nathaniel grabs me and jerks me into his arms. He lifts me up and we laugh, not a drop of paint on either of us.

Chapter Eight

I sit in the dark, waiting for it to be time to meet Nathaniel. It's like there's electricity inside me. A live wire that's flipping all around because I'm anxious to have another of our nights together and because it seemed so important to him that I meet him. I know it makes me sound bratty, but when he didn't push for it sooner, it made me feel like it didn't matter. I think maybe I wanted him to...maybe not *fight* for me to meet, but to pull for it. To show me he wanted it and he did and that means more to me than the knowledge that this will make it hurt more when he leaves. He's here now and I don't have anything else I look forward to.

I'm taking this.

Quietly, I push my widow open and crawl out. The "pillow me" is under the blankets. Not like anyone will check on me, anyway. As soon as my feet hit the ground, I hear Mom's voice surfing on the wind as it drifts from her and Dad's partially open window.

"I'm so tired of this place! I tried to make it work, but I don't want this life, Richard!"

"We've been okay," Dad replies. "Things have been better. We'll close for a week or so and take a trip this fall. Get out of here for a while. This is our life, Tabitha."

"A life only you want! You and Charlie Rae love it here. This place fits you. I just...I want to take Sadie and go. You can go, too. We can sell and—"

"No! I'm not selling. This is our past and our future. How can you just want to throw it away? And what about Charlie? You're going to leave her?"

"She can go if she wants."

I grab my chest. Fight to breathe. Tears fill my eyes and I turn to run. I stumble and fall, but get right back up again. They're leaving? She wants to take Sadie and leave? Leave *me?* I stop when hope fizzles in my veins. I could get out of here. How could I want to leave Dad? I don't. I love him. And it's not that she really cares if I go or not.

Her words hit me again and I dry heave. I fall to the ground again and cry. They're going to leave and I'll be stuck here. Then the guilt mixes in, making me nauseous. Is here really that bad? I don't like it, but I would never just bail.

"Charlotte?" Nathaniel's voice comes from behind me. "What's wrong?"

I scramble to my feet, embarrassed that I'm on the ground crying. All I can think about is the fact that they'll get out of The Village to find a new life, and then I hate myself for wishing for the same thing.

Nathaniel steps toward me. I try to turn my head away, but he ducks and follows, tilting my chin toward him. "What's wrong, Star Girl?"

I watch him in the moonlight. His eyes look like they belong in the sky and I want to talk to him. I want to tell him things because I need to get the words out. Nathaniel has the key that can set them free before they eat me alive.

I can't talk to Dad, Mom, Sadie, or even Alec. Not about this, but more than anything I want to tell him. "I hate my life." If there was a way to snatch back those words, I would. They sound so end of the world and I'm not like that. I'm a realist. I know how things work and I usually don't run so high on emotions, but...I think he might get what I mean. I hope he will.

"Wow...that's pretty brutal." There's a laugh in his voice and it's just what I need. It makes me smile when two seconds ago it felt like I'd never smile again. In this second, I'll do anything to forget what I just heard. The thoughts are still there. They can't disappear that easily, but they aren't what I want to focus on right now.

"I want to show you something," I tell him.

Nathaniel nods and I head down path that will lead us where I want to go. When I get there, I disappear into the trees. Nathaniel steps up beside me and grabs my hand. It's not the way Alec and I have held hands before. Our fingers are weaved together and I like how his hand is a little bit bigger than mine.

We don't talk as we follow the trail into the night, each of us carrying a flashlight in our free hand. It doesn't take long to get to the fort my dad made us when we were kids. It's a decent size. Alec and I used to have secret meetings out here with our friends so it's big enough for a small group of kids to stand inside.

The little plastic table we used to keep out here is long gone, and the place is empty, but I like to come out here now and again. Alec and I used to play in the creek running behind the fort.

"What is this place?" Nathaniel asks.

"It used to be my hideout." I shine the light inside. There's no door or anything like that. "It's not much, but when I was younger I used to think it was the most amazing thing in the whole world. I helped my dad build it." That was back when I thought The Village would always be the place for me.

"That's cool. None of my friends back home have stuff like this. And my dad was always too busy to help us make one."

I nod at him. "Let's go out back."

If I'm being honest, I'll admit it's a little scary out here at night, but I grew up stomping through this place. Kids party on the mountains in Lakeland Village. It's just a part of our lives.

When we get behind the fort, Nathaniel asks, "Why were you crying?"

I sit down and he follows right behind me. "I thought you were so different that first day. I thought you would be scared to get dirty or something."

Nathaniel laughs. "Wow. Thanks. And you're stalling."

I pull my knees to my chest and wrap my arms around them. I let my light dance around the trees and look up to see the stars. "Why do I feel like I can talk to you?"

"Because you don't know me."

Maybe that's true, but I also want to tell him I do. I do know him. Maybe not everything that matters, but I know him.

"When I was little, I thought The Village was magical. We were so lucky, right? People paid us to stay here. We cleaned boats and took people on tours and I could swim all I wanted or explore out here. Dad and I would make things and Sadie and Mom would mostly stay inside, but they'd tease us and we laughed and everything felt okay. I never thought I wanted to leave.

"And then as I got older, I realized that Mom hated it more and more every year and Sadie never really liked it and I started to watch the stars. It feels like nothing matters when I look up there, ya know? I used to dream about getting to study them one day, but I never really got the fact that I would have to leave to do it. When that occurred to me, I thought I would just be happy watching them. It was then that the stars became my magic instead of The Village."

For a second, I think maybe I should be embarrassed saying all of these things to him, but I'm not.

"You don't want to leave one day?" he asks.

"No. I do. That's the problem. It's like, I'm suffocating here now. I love it, but I don't."

"You only have a few more years till you're off to college."

I shake my head. "Who would help Dad if I left?"

"Can you just come home for the summer to help him?"

"We're open all year. It's not nearly as busy, but there's ice-skating on the pond in the winter. There's an apple orchard close that people like to visit in the fall. Wagon rides take them back and forth from here to the orchard. We don't get people who stay months at a time, except in the summer, but people do come."

He still doesn't look convinced, so I add, "You don't get it. It's always been Dad and I versus Mom and Sadie Ann. He depends on me and he loves this place so much. He thinks I love it too and I do, but—"

Nathaniel brushes the hair back from my face. "You want to follow the stars."

"I do... And planets. They all fascinate me."

"What happened tonight?"

Automatically, I open my mouth to tell him. "I don't think my mom loves my dad anymore. She said she wants to leave...to take Sadie Ann and go." The words make it all too real again. My chest aches.

"Shit," Nathaniel mumbles and puts an arm around me. I drop my head to his shoulder and let a few silent tears trickle down my face. He doesn't talk and that's perfect. He just lets me be and holds me because nothing he could say would fix this. I'm grateful he seems to know that.

We sit like that for a long time. He smells fresh like after the rain, but with a hint of something else. I hear him breathe and wonder if he hears me, too. Finally, after who knows how long, I can't stop myself from asking the question that's filled my head since Sadie told me.

"Do you have a girlfriend?"

Nathaniel stiffens beside me. It's all the answer I need, but he offers one anyway. "Um... Kind of."

I chuckle and pull away from him. It hurts my chest, but it's not something I didn't know. "You can't kind of have a girlfriend."

"I'm serious. We were together. We've been together since December, but when summer came, and we knew I would be leaving, we decided to take a break."

I sigh. "But you'll get back together when you go home."

He looks like he doesn't want to answer. "Probably."

I nod, not willing to let myself cry again. There's no point. What will the tears do? It's not his fault I like him. That I...what? Became infatuated with him the second I saw him? It's so stupid. It serves me right that he 'kind of' has a girlfriend.

"You're so freaking cool, Charlotte. I wanted nothing to do with this place when my parents told me we were coming. Both Brandon and I were pissed, but we've had a kick ass time. You're fun to talk to and I've never met another girl like you. You're like...hell, you're almost like my best friend."

Talk about ironic. Of course I would end up with another boy for a best friend. One who's always been there for me, and the other who makes me breathe faster and my heart bounce. Who makes me feel like a girl when no one else does and who looks at me like he sees something that only he can see.

One that if I gave into my heart, I would love.

"You're my best friend, too."

He shakes his head. "That's Alec."

"He is. He'll always be my best friend, but...I don't talk to him the way I do you. We don't talk about the sky and I never could have told him what I told you tonight."

Nathaniel's quiet for a few minutes before he turns to look at me again. "Things would be different for us if we lived close, huh?"

It's not what I want. I want things to be different for us *now*, but I feel lucky to hear that. Because I believe it. I don't know what it is, but I know he's right. Things would be different for us if we lived closer. I wouldn't be afraid to follow my heart.

"Yeah...I think they would."

Nathaniel puts his arm around me again, and together we watch the night.

Chapter Nine

It's Thursday, August 8th, and Nathaniel leaves tomorrow. He and his family have been gone all day. It's their last day here and we won't even get to see them. Sadie Ann is mad. She's locked herself in her room and even though I'm sad, I don't let it get me down. What's the point? It won't change anything.

I work with Dad around The Village. No one has said anything about what I heard the other night so I haven't either. Part of me wants to, but I'm scared to hear the answer. Or of how I'll respond, so I just try to forget it.

Even though I don't want to, I keep watching Nathaniel's cabin, waiting for them to come back. Soon it's dusk and Dad goes back to the house. I follow him and he kisses Mom on the cheek and I take that to mean she's not leaving.

She has this sort of resigned look on her face that breaks my heart.

After changing clothes I go back outside, hoping to see their car, but it's still not there. Nervously, I pop my knuckles, before kicking my shoes off to walk along the edge of the water. Joy bursts inside me when I hear footsteps behind me. *Please be him, please be him, please be him.*

"Charlie. Wait up!" Alec calls and I let myself smile. I refuse to be disappointed. He's still my best friend. He always will be.

Alec catches up to me. "What are you doing?"

"Taking a walk."

"Mind if I come along?"

"Sure."

We wander and talk about school starting next month. He's excited about football and we're going to be sophomores, and I know I should be excited about it all too, but I'm just not.

"I've kind of been a jerk this summer," he says after a while.

I shake my head at him. "No, you haven't." And he hasn't. Not really. There's no rule that says he has to pick me first for games or that he can't meet new friends. No matter what, I always know Alec will be here for me and he knows the same about me.

"I don't know what got into me. I...It's not important, but you know I love you, Charlie. You're my best friend and I didn't work with you as much as I usually do and I didn't pick you first—"

"It doesn't matter," I tell him. "And I love you too." We've been telling each other that since we were three years old and both of us know what it does and doesn't mean.

We meander down the lakeside for another few minutes before we turn to head back. The Chase family still hasn't returned.

Alec gives me a hug before heading home. I eat dinner with my family and then go to bed. Just past eleven PM, a knock on my window wakes me up.

Nathaniel.

I hold up a finger for him to wait. He nods and disappears from my view. I slip on another shirt and some shoes before grabbing my flashlight and crawling outside.

"Wanna go where we went the other night?" he asks. I grin when I see his dimple and his backward hat.

"Sure." I'm not sure how to feel right now, so I try not to feel anything.

We head out to the fort, mostly quiet. Nathaniel tells me his parents dragged him and Brandon around all day even though he wanted to be here hanging out with me. His words make me smile as we slip into the night. Our night. I think I might always think of it that way. I'm not sure I'll ever see another moon and not think of Nathaniel.

A moaning sound comes from the darkness and I reach out and grab Nathaniel's arm. There's a little light ahead of us and he puts his finger to his lips as we sneak forward. We hide behind a tree and look toward the clearing where there's a small fire and...holy crap! Brandon and Sadie are on the ground, under a blanket. Brandon is on top of her and I might be naïve and never kissed a boy, but it's pretty obvious they're having sex. *Sex!* I have no idea if it's Sadie's first time or not, but I don't care. I turn away, my cheeks hotter than they've ever been. I can't believe I just found my sister getting it on with a boy. I start walking away.

Nathaniel's jogging to catch up with me. It doesn't take me long to find my fort and I'm scared I'm going to die right here of embarrassment.

Four Summers

"My brother has game! Who knew," he laughs and I swat his arm.

"Oh my God. I can't believe we just saw them having..."

He cocks a brow. "Sex?" he supplies for me.

"Yes!"

At that, Nathaniel laughs harder "You couldn't even say it. Damn, your face is bright red, Star Girl. I know it was awkward, but why are you embarrassed?"

I shake my head, knowing I'm getting redder by the second.

"It's not like they saw us. Why are you so shy?"

"Do you really have to ask that?" I bury my face in my hands. He's so quiet I have to peek out, afraid he walked away.

"Have you ever..." he starts.

I drop my hands. "What? No! Of course not." I can't help but ask him the same thing. "Have you ever?"

"No."

He doesn't add the of course not.

"Me and Roxi...we've messed around and stuff, but not that far."

"Okay, that's enough for me!" I turn my back to him. It's not like I want to talk about the girl he's going home to. And of course she'd have some cool name. Roxi versus *Charlie Rae.*

"What about you?" He steps up beside me. "Messed around, I mean."

Ugh. Why is he doing this? I think about lying, but know I can't. "Nope."

"Nothing?" He says it like he's shocked.

"Thanks! Make it sound like I'm a freak or something."

81

"No, no. That's not what I meant." He steps in front of me so I'm looking at him. "I just figured you and Alec..."

Oh. "No." I shake my head. "We haven't. I've never even..." There's no reason to continue because I already told him I haven't done anything. Why embarrass myself more by repeating the fact that I've never even kissed a boy? But then, this is Nathaniel and I like talking to him and can't seem to stop myself from continuing. "No guys have ever really been interested in me. They all assume Alec and me are together, or will be together. Who knows if that's really why. Maybe that's just an excuse because—"

"—Charlotte," he cuts off my rambling. And he's looking at me funny, all serious. Like he was by the boats that day and suddenly my heart starts a stampede and my stomach feels wobbly, maybe the way someone looks if you're looking at them through a pool of water. Little waves making everything feel off.

"What?" I finally reply.

Nathaniel steps closer to me, his voice low. "I wanna be your first kiss."

I can't believe he said that. This is really happening and I'm licking my lips and nodding my head. Before I thought I wasn't frightened of my first kiss, but I am. I'm so scared I could burst out of my skin, or set on fire, but I've never wanted to burn so much in my whole life.

He leans forward. I close my eyes and it's not a second later that I feel his lips on mine. His hand pushes through my hair and rests at on the back of my neck. His lips tease mine with little kisses. I return them thinking nothing has ever felt this good.

Against my mouth he asks, "Can I kiss you more?"

Another nod from me and I feel his tongue trace my lips. I open my mouth and now I really know I've never felt something like this. Nathaniel's tongue touches mine. Dances with it. I try to mimic what he does, slipping mine in his mouth and he lets me. It's a trade off, and we learn to move together.

He pulls me closer, his whole body lined against mine, and kisses me deeper. I wrap my arms around his neck and his heart is against mine and I can't stop it...can't block it anymore. My heart opens and I know he'll forever have a home there. It's stupid and I'm young, but I don't care. I love him and for the rest of my life, this moment will be engraved into my heart.

He pulls his mouth away, but doesn't move his hand. I don't let go of him either and all I can think is our breaths are mixing the way our tongues just did.

Wow...

"I saw something when we were out today." He pulls away and I wish he hadn't, but then he's reaching into his pocket and pulls whatever it is out.

It's a necklace. Thin, black leather cord with a silver star hanging from the middle. My eyes water as I reach for it. "I love it," I whisper.

"Turn around. I'll put it on you." I twist and lift my hair as he ties the necklace on me. When I face him again, he says, "Is it stupid that I got myself one, too?"

The tears spill out of my eyes and I shake my head. "No. It's perfect."

I look at his neck and the rope is gone. In its place is the black leather, just like mine.

There are so many times I've been with Nathaniel that I've thought, *this is my moment.* I'll never forget this. I realize as I stand here with him, they're all true. I'll remember every moment I spent with him this summer.

He pulls me to him and hugs me as I cry. When my tears finally stop he grasps my hand and we walk back to my house together. He takes me all the way to my window this time and I wish the walk would have never ended.

"I'm going to miss you," I tell him.

"You too," he replies. We exchange emails and promise to write. He hugs me one more time before turning to walk away. I wish we could kiss again. I wish we could kiss all night. He gets a couple steps away before he stops, turns, and says. "Follow your stars if you want, Star Girl. Don't let anyone tell you that you can't."

Crying, I watch him walk away, knowing I may never see him again.

When I wake up in the morning, Nathaniel Chase is already gone.

We email back and forth every day. He's back with Roxi. I pretend to be happy for him, like a friend should. He asks about

Alec and Sadie and I answer all the questions. He told Roxi about me. Not about our kiss, I don't think, but about his "best friend." I get the feeling he thought it would make me feel good, but it doesn't.

I imagine his dimples when he writes LOL and his backward hat.

Even being busy with school, we still write. I tell him that Alec invited me to Homecoming and he says he hopes I have a good time.

I do, but I still wish it was him.

After that, our emails become less frequent.

In December the emails from him stop. I write a few times, but he doesn't reply and I know this must be the end. He's moved on. It was destined to happen anyway.

Summer Two

He's changed since last year. He's sadder. I guess I've changed, too. I'm more wary of him, scared to get too close. I've had my first boyfriend since he was here last. I've taken to helping Dad more often. He seems to struggle sometimes and I don't know why. Nathaniel looks at me differently when he doesn't know I'm watching, and even though I can tell he's in pain, we still have our nights. And they're even more magical than they were before. ~Charlotte

- Nathaniel Chase -
Chapter One

I sit in the backseat with my headphones in. My iPod hasn't been turned off once since we got in the car for Lakeland Village. Not that I keep it off much these days anyway. Makes it harder for people to talk to you when you don't feel like talking.

It's crazy because I don't know how I feel coming back here. When we came last year, I wanted nothing to do with it. It was supposed to be a one-time thing because Dad is always busy. But then we went and I met *her*, and she made it okay. No, she made it fun and I started to really fucking like her.

Charlotte is cool. Different. She would talk to me half the night, and as lame as it sounds it was almost like I was the only person she ever talked to. Like she would burst open and everything would spill if she didn't get those words out and that made me feel good. I wanted to be that person for her and I liked listening to her talk. But, hell, what could we have had besides a summer friendship? One that meant more to me than I really thought it would because I missed her when I left and I looked forward to her emails, but we also live a thousand miles away from each other.

It hurt more than I thought when I wasn't sure if I would ever seen her again.

But then everything in my life crashed in on me. I screwed it all up; people got hurt because of me and I stopped talking to everyone—even her.

Right as the song switches, Dad says, "Almost there!" from the front seat. It's the pseudo-happy voice he uses with me all the time now.

I click the power off on my iPod to hear Mom add, "This is just what we need. Another family summer like last year so we can spend quality time together."

Brandon huffs from beside me and I nod at him. Yeah, like we spent that much time together last summer. He was always with Alec or Sadie and I spent my time with Charlotte.

Mom and Dad get lost in their own little world together and I look at my brother. "I'm sure you're stoked to see Sadie again." I want the words to sound teasing, but they're rough and serious like everything I say nowadays.

"Eh. Not really. She was too prissy. I'm hoping she's got someone else so I don't have to deal with her."

That surprises me. Though it's not like the past six months haven't been hard on Brandon, too. We had to deal with half the town being against us, and then we had the trial too. Brandon had to leave our school with an awesome football team, to one with only an okay team. He was pissed. Once we moved, he met friends because that's Brandon; he's always talking to someone about something but he hadn't screwed around with any girls. Hell, I don't even remember him messing with anyone since last year. I teased him about getting his heart broken by Sadie, but I never really thought that was true.

In a low voice, so our parents don't hear, he says, "What about you and the sister? Don't tell me you didn't touch her last year."

A little flash of our kiss from that last night climbs into my head. I haven't thought about that in a long time and it makes me want to smile. She was so nervous. How she'd never even kissed someone, I don't know, but she'd been good. I liked it way too much. Was glad I was the one who got to do it. I shake those thoughts from my head.

Without realizing it, Brandon helps with that when he says, "Nah, it don't matter anyway. She's probably hooked up with Alec by now."

I groan internally, a strange sort of ache taking root in my chest. I should be used to feeling like shit by now, but I'm not. Not when it comes to Charlotte. She deserves way better than Alec. She deserves her stars.

Without answering, I turn the iPod back on and hit play, and turn to face the window. When my brother shuffles next to me, I glance over to see he's doing the same thing.

We're getting the same cabin as we had last summer even though we booked last minute. It doesn't surprise me. Dad has a way of getting what he wants, which I guess is why it pissed him off so bad when everyone turned their back on us after everything went down this year.

Mom leans back and pats my leg. "We're here!" she says with cheeriness. A weight lands in my stomach. I want to see Charlotte, but don't. I'm scared as hell she'll be different. After all the other changes, I need her to be the same. Maybe that's not what I should be worried about at all, though. It's not like I don't know *I've* changed. What if that makes things different with us? I didn't realize it until we pulled in how important it is to me that things be the same, though after the way I treated her, I'm not sure how they can be.

How am I going to explain to her why I disappeared? She sent three emails that went unanswered. I like that about her. That she's caring and was worried, but also that she's strong enough that she didn't dick around when I treated her in a way she didn't deserve.

We pull up in front of our cabin and Dad kills the engine.

"Looks just how I remembered," he says and I want to tell him no shit. It's not like they were doing a big remodel or something.

We get out of the car and head for the trunk to grab our things. "Nate, why don't you go to the office and grab the keys?" Mom asks. Nate. That's a new thing too.

I'm caught between telling her yes and trying to get out of it. If I go to the office, I'll probably run into Charlotte and, it might make me a wuss, but I'm not sure I should see her yet.

"I have your keys for you already, Mr. and Mrs. Chase."

I look over to see Alec standing on the porch. My eyes immediately scan for Charlotte. He's always where she is.

"Thank you!" Dad calls to him. Alec takes the stairs to help us with our stuff. I'm still looking around for Charlotte, but she doesn't come out of the cabin and I don't see her anywhere.

When Alec gets to us he gives my brother a quick nod and he returns it, before Alec's eyes cut to me. And damned if I don't see the anger there. It's not like we were ever buddies anyway, but he's pissed and I can pretty much guarantee I know why.

"You guys are welcome to go inside. I can help Nathaniel with the bags," he says.

"I didn't realize I'd offered my help," I toss back at him.

"Nate!" Mom screeches.

Alec doesn't take his eyes off me and I stare him down, too. I get it. I really do, but whatever went down is between Charlotte and me. I'm not going to let him push his way in the middle of it.

"I was kidding, Mom. We got this."

"Why don't you help, too, Brandon?"

My brother nods, but as soon as my parents start to walk away, he grabs the smallest, closest bag he can find and goes inside with them.

"I knew it. One look at you last year and I fucking knew you'd hurt her." He steps closer to me, but I don't back down. He's gotten bigger since last year, but so have I.

It really sucks that I don't know exactly what he's talking about. Does he know I kissed her? Did that hurt her? That was the last thing I'd wanted, but she'd been standing so close and her lips looked so good and I couldn't let myself leave without having kissed her. Maybe it was a mistake, but I can't regret it because...hell, I don't know why. She's Charlotte, my friend, and she's cute and funny and maybe I'm a prick for being the one to want her first kiss. But I did and I'm glad.

"Whatever went down between Charlotte and me isn't your business." After I say it, I realize it might really be his business. What if Brandon was right? They might be together now.

"Charlie's my best friend. If she's hurt, it's my business."

"She's my best friend, too, and in case you didn't notice, she's strong enough to take care of herself. Plus, I'm pretty sure I'm not the only one who's ever hurt her." But it still feels like a knife to the gut. Out of everyone in my life, she's the last one I would ever want to cause pain.

He balls his hand in a fist and even though my parents will freak, I'm not about to let him hit me. I've been in enough fights this year to promise I can come out on top.

"Alec!"

We both freeze at the sound of her voice. I turn toward the office and she's standing on the porch. For a second I feel like someone has knocked the breath out of me. Her hair is longer. It's kind of whipping around her head in the breeze. She looks a little curvier. Not big or anything, but last year she looked even younger than she was. Now? Not so much.

The first thing I wonder is if she's still wearing the necklace. If she has the star that matches the one in my pocket. It got ripped off in a fight this year and it took me forever to get a new clasp on it, but it's there now and even though I don't wear it, I keep it.

The second thing is she dresses the same and it's almost like some of the weight slides off my chest. She's still in cut-off shorts. Still wearing a tank top and it reminds me of our nights last year when everything was easier.

"Alec!" she calls again, but doesn't look at me. She crosses her arms and I smirk. Damn, I missed her.

"Go ahead. I got this," I tell Alec, but my eyes don't leave Charlotte. Alec doesn't need to be told twice. He jogs off toward Charlotte who waits for him. I watch them, tightness taking hold of my chest. All the shit that I've been through this year, I didn't realize it, but somehow I thought things would get better when I got here.

Look at me. I feel like such a pussy for silently begging her to turn back, but I need someone to see *me* and not the one whose family had to uproot their lives for, or the guy who would have gotten himself in that kind of situation in the first place, the nark who ratted out his friends when they were just having a good time.

Alec gets to her on the porch and wraps an arm around her shoulder. The tightness in me spreads and I tell myself it's just because she's my friend and I think he'll hold her back.

Alec turns her so her back is to me and they start to walk away. It's not until they get to the far side of the building, just about to go around the corner, that she glances over her shoulder and her eyes find mine.

Somehow, just that one look, makes it so I can breathe again.

Chapter Two

Brandon and I unpack all our stuff in our room. Mom and Dad went to town, but they said they want us to all go to the Bash tonight. I forgot about that from last year, though we must have come a day later this year since it's tonight. It was the night I saw Charlotte sneak off and I followed her. I'm surprised she didn't think I was a creeper. Hell, maybe I was. It's not like I make it a habit to follow girls at night, but I'd noticed her that day. How she kind of always looked like she was on the outside looking in. Not really that people treated her that way, but she felt it. The way she would step out of the circle or how many times her eyes darted toward the sky.

It was like she'd been in on a secret that no one else could begin to fathom. She looked lonely, carrying that secret on her shoulders, and I wanted to be the one to discover what it was.

I look over at my brother lying on his bed. He's tossing his football up and down in the air and I wonder what it would be like to love something the way he loves football. Yeah, I like baseball, but *like* is the key word. I don't love it. Brandon deals with school because he has to in order to play ball. I actually don't mind school and work to be good at it.

"You find out about Alec and your girl?" he asks.

I shake my head. "She's not my girl. But, no, I didn't find out." He said she was his best friend, so maybe that means they aren't together. I roll over so my back is to him, hoping it will make him shut up. I don't feel like talking about Charlotte, Alec, or anything else.

It does the job and Brandon doesn't say anything else. Pretty soon our parents are home and they're telling us it's time to get ready to go. It's not like it takes that long so Brandon and I are ready in about five minutes. My brother looks nervous, making me wonder why the hell he's so sketched out to see Sadie. She can't be that bad.

Grabbing my iPod off the bed, I stick the buds in my ears before dropping the iPod into my pocket.

"Nate, you don't have to bring that thing, do you?" Mom asks.

Yeah. Yeah, I really do. "It's not on," I tell her, but that doesn't mean it won't be really soon.

It's almost dark when we go outside and everything is decorated just like it was last year with a small dance floor right in the middle of the sand surrounding the lake. There are tiki torches, white Christmas lights, only this year a DJ is playing instead of a band.

"You guys hungry?" Dad asks.

The barbeque smells good, but I'm not really in the mood to eat. "I'm good."

Mom and Dad shrug, and then wander off in search of food from the row of grills. The cabins line a circular driveway, with the office-slash-store directly across from 3B. To our left are the boats and lake, and behinds us, nothing but trees.

I sit on the stairs of the porch and my brother does the same. Crap, what is this? Usually we're doing our own thing.

"I really wish we didn't come back here," he says. Brandon's seventeen. Our parents thought about letting him stay home, but didn't. They probably would have come home to the house burned down if they had.

Since I don't really know what to say, I don't say anything. Part of me wishes the same thing, but it feels good to be here, too. Mixed emotions.

"You're trippin' out."

"Fuck off," he replies.

We sit there while the party goes on around us. So far Charlotte and Alec are both missing. Sadie comes out not long after and I see her eyes shoot right to my brother. Shoot is the perfect word because she looks as though she wants to murder him.

It's not until I see her that I remember what Charlotte told me last year. That her mom wanted to leave and take Sadie with her, leaving Charlotte behind with her dad. I'm glad they didn't go, but it pisses me off that she could even think to do something like that when Charlotte wants out too.

Brandon shifts and watches still hot as ever Sadie as she heads over to the group of people about our age. This tall guy grabs her hand. Sadie looks over her shoulder and the smile on her face is nothing but smug. Yeah, she definitely has something to prove.

"What went down with you guys?" I ask. When we'd come home I just assumed he was still talking to her the way I continued to speak to Charlotte. It wasn't like they would stay together. We hadn't planned to come back. Plus they were sixteen and nine months apart is a whole hell of a long time, but I figured they were still cool.

Brandon shrugs. "I kind of didn't call her or anything."

My brother is a fucking idiot. Not that I didn't end up doing the same thing to Charlotte, but it was different. I hadn't been having sex with her. Plus, I was talking to her until everything went down.

"Did she call you?"

"Didn't answer."

"Are you shitting me?"

He just shakes his head. It's going to be a long summer.

I don't leave the porch when Charlotte comes out, Alec right by her side. They aren't holding hands or anything, but I can't help but wonder if they usually are. If she wants to be. Maybe she's changed and this is what she wants, and she and Alec will end up together, running The Village one day like everyone expects they will.

I shake my head. No, not her. Not that there's anything wrong with it, but it's not her dream.

Last year I would have just walked up to her. Found my way to the middle of their group or by her side and cracked a joke or whispered something in her ear. Anything just to be a part of the group because it was easy for me.

This year, I don't do that.

All their friends laugh and talk. They dance some of the time and Charlotte dances with Alec. Her dad steals her away to help him every once in a while and she leaves her friends to do whatever he needs, like always.

He never asks Sadie.

My hands tighten into fists. It's shitty that it's like that for her.

I turn my music on and Brandon throws his football to himself.

Yet again, I feel this crazy, unexplainable pull to her. Questions swim around in my brain and I wonder if she still likes stars or if her feelings for Alec have changed or if she's still scared of her mom and Sadie leaving her behind.

Even though I know I shouldn't do it, I can't stop myself from pushing to my feet. Then, turn off my music.

"Where you going?" Brandon asks, but I don't answer.

I feel my brother step up behind me and I'm pretty sure he thinks I'm about to do something stupid so he's here to have my back. Maybe it isn't the smartest decision, but I'm still going and don't stop until I walk right up to their friends.

"Hey! What's up?" a guy with a shaved head asks. We all played night games and some football with him last year, but I don't remember his name.

I pull the hear buds out of my ear and shove them into my pocket.

Everyone's saying hi. Sadie is giving Brandon the evil eye and he isn't so much as looking at her. Alec's jaw is tight and I see him step closer to Charlotte. Is it just me or did she move away?

I want to ask her to leave with me. To go to our spot so I can talk to her, but I know Alec won't let her go and that just pisses me off more.

"Can I talk to you?" I ask her. She still has those few freckles on her cheeks and her skin blotches red. I wonder why she's embarrassed.

"We're busy, man," Alec says.

"She knows how to answer for herself."

I feel a little guilty but he's been an asshole to me since the first time we met. I'm not stupid. I know he's never liked me.

Alec takes a step toward me, but Charlotte grabs his arm. I study her holding him for a second, before I pry my eyes away to look into hers. What am I doing? I don't know. I want to talk to her. It doesn't feel right to be here if I can't talk to her.

"I just want to talk, Charlotte. Dance with me."

Her eyes go wide and she gasps quietly. I wonder if it's because I called her Charlotte or because we've never danced. Or maybe it's none of those reasons at all. Maybe she hates me.

I hold out my hand and try to plead with my eyes. *I just need to talk. I'm sorry.* A girl giggles, but I ignore it. Sadie huffs, but that doesn't matter either. She looks at me as though she expects me to turn away. Like she's not worth holding my hand out to her and I wonder why no one pays her more attention. When I don't turn away, she places her hand in mine. Her fingers quake gently and it reminds me of how her lips trembled when I kissed her.

Alec curses and we walk away. I don't go to the dance floor, but not too far away either. Off to the side of the party, close to the same stretch of beach she walked down that first night we really talked.

They're playing a slow song and I pull her to me. My arms wrap around her waist and hers around my neck. People are all around us, some I recognize from last year and others are probably new guests. We're silent as we move together. This is the quietest my thoughts have been in months.

I want to tell her what happened. That I'm sorry. That I'm a jerk and she really is my best friend and I shouldn't have turned my back on her.

I want to know how things have been here for here. Like if she's told her parents she wants to leave one day, Or if she's learned anything new about the stars she can teach me.

What comes out first is, "Are you and Alec...?"

"No." She answers quickly, honesty in her features.

My muscles relax. I would have felt like a jackass if I asked some other guy's girlfriend to dance.

I feel her hand knot in the back of my shirt. I don't understand it, but I'm glad if I'm giving her some kind of support. Someone to lean on.

"I'm a jerk," I tell her.

"Yeah."

It feels good to laugh.

We keep moving in a circle. I let my hand move up and down her back and she buries her face in my shirt.

"I missed you, Star Girl."

She stiffens and I wonder if I went too far. Maybe I shouldn't have assumed or shouldn't have pushed, but it's the truth and I want her to know it. I need her to, so I keep going.

"A lot happened and I was in a bad place, but I shouldn't have stopped talking to you."

She pulls away to look at me. "What happened? Are you okay?"

I think maybe I might be. I mean, I had to have been, even from the beginning, but right now I actually feel it. "Yeah...I'm okay. It's just..." How do I say it? How do I tell her what I let happen?

"Charlie Rae! Come here for a few minutes! I need your help."

Something in her dad's voice tells me he's calling her for more reasons than needing her.

"I gotta go." She pulls away.

An urgent need takes me over and I blurt out, "Do you still sneak out?"

She nods.

"Meet me tonight and we'll talk. Shit...I never said sorry. I wanted to tell you sorry first."

"Charlie Rae!" her dad calls again.

Charlotte backs up a few steps, turns, and takes a few more. All I can think is she never told me if she would meet me or not. She never said if it was okay.

As though she could read my mind, she stops and glances back. "I...I missed you."

And then she runs, kicking up sand behind her.

She doesn't hear me say, "I missed you, too."

Chapter Three

"You're sneaking out with her already? I thought she hated you." Brandon sits up in his bed and turns on the bedside light.

"Shh. You'll wake up the house, and that's not how it is. I just need to talk to her. It's not like what we saw you doing last summer."

Brandon's face pales. I swear to God he's about to get sick. His mouth drops open and then he lunges off the bed at me.

"What the hell!" I hiss as he grabs my arms.

"Did you tell? What did you see?"

I rip away from him. "You're tripping the hell out. Like I'm going to tell Mom and Dad you screwed Charlotte's sister. I'm pretty sure we wouldn't be here right now if I had."

He lets out a heavy breath and falls back onto the bed. "I just..." he trails off. "It kind of got out of control. She started talking all serious about her moving with me when she turned eighteen and all this stuff. And it's just...she's not... It's not like I want to hurt her, but it was just so easy with Sadie, ya know? I wanted it to work out. Maybe."

I look at my brother, not sure where all this opening up is coming from. "You're seventeen. You don't have to be serious about anyone. It's not like—"

"—You don't get it. You know what? Never mind. I'm tired. I don't know what the hell I'm talking about." He turns off the light and gets back into bed like we weren't just talking about, whatever we were talking about.

"Want me to stay?"

"Shut up. Go get laid," he replies.

"I'm not sleeping with her, you prick. She's my friend."

"Whatever. No one spends as much time together as you two if you're not going at it, but whatever."

Ignoring my brother, I open the window and climb out to go meet Charlotte.

I wait off to the side of her house because we weren't able to decide where to meet. After about twenty minutes, I start to wonder if she either ditched me, or if she went to one of our spots to wait.

Finally I see her sneaking around the building. A smile tugs at my lips. She's wearing a baseball hat with her hair sticking out the hole. I love how she's comfortable like that. It makes me miss wearing mine. I don't know why I don't anymore.

"Hey," I whisper.

"Hey," she replies.

"Where do you want to go?"

She shrugs. "I don't know... The creek?" The way she looks down, I wonder if she's blushing, but I don't want to shine the flashlight in her face to check.

I lead the way; surprised it comes back to me so easily. We twist and turn through the woods until I see the little wooden fort she made with her dad when she was a kid. Those are my favorite things about her. That she does all these cool things. She works harder than any guy I know and she's just as rough and competitive, but she's also all girl. Especially in the way she melted against me when I kissed her.

It's not like Charlotte was my first kiss. I've done more than that with Roxi, but I still remember how it felt when my lips touched hers.

I've definitely thought about doing it again.

We get to the fort and she leads me around back. The moon is so bright out here that it's easy to see, especially with our flashlights.

I stop when I see there are two wooden chairs behind the building with a little table between them. I know she said she used to come out here a lot when she was a kid, but I didn't realize she still did.

"Where'd these come from?"

Charlotte sits in one of the chairs. "It was a project for my dad and I this year. He says he needs to keep busy because he's getting old and doesn't want to lose his touch. Which I think is ridiculous. Guest are always coming and going all year around. No one keeps as busy as my dad and—"

"—Charlotte?"

She looks up at me, face awash in moonlight. "Yeah?"

"You're rambling." Before I probably would have laughed. Maybe said more to make *her* laugh, but I don't. Instead I only sit in the chair next to hers. She pulls her knees up so her feet are flat on the chair, and wraps her arms around her legs. She does that when she's nervous, like when we sat out here and she told me about her parents and how she wanted to leave.

I guess it's my time to man up and talk to her, too.

"It wasn't you." As soon as the words leave my mouth I know it's a stupid thing to say.

Charlotte laughs. "Is it one of those *it's not you, it's me* speeches? I didn't realize those went with friendships, too. Unless you think it's because we kissed, but it had been months so that doesn't make sense."

She rambles more this year than she did last. It's cute. "It's not because we kissed. It's not you that I wanted to stay away from. I was just...having a hard time."

"And I would have made that harder through emailing? If you didn't want to talk anymore, that's fine. I get it. But I deserved at least a kiss off email—"

"—A girl got hurt because of me, all right? She got attacked and could have died and I'm the one who set up the fucking meeting!"

Charlotte goes quiet. The only sound around us is the water in the creek and the rustle of the trees mixed with crickets. Those words were so hard for me to get out. I know it's stupid. They're just words, and if I could live through what happened, I could say them, right?

"Nathaniel..."

"Chrissy was Roxi's best friend. She was my best friend, Adam's girlfriend. He'd been acting kind of different, and not in a good way, but I didn't realize how *much* different. I guess part of it was playing Varsity as a freshman and then sophomore. I don't know, but he started turning into a prick, but he was my friend and I didn't want to just bail on him.

"Anyway. They'd been fighting a lot. Adam cheated on her and she broke up with him. Adam kept trying to get Chrissy back, but she wouldn't talk to him. He talked me into getting her to meet me. He wanted me to tell her I wanted to talk to her. And because she trusted me...she agreed."

I stop talking, feeling more like an idiot as I go along. Why did I listen to him, anyway? It wasn't my business to get in the middle.

"What happened next?" Charlotte asks.

"It was at a party, which again, stupid, but I wasn't thinking. We'd all been drinking so she comes and we meet in this room, and then Adam comes out with flowers and stuff for her. She was upset at first, but then he gave her the flowers and said he was sorry and started to beg her to talk. I left them in there and I went outside. It wasn't long that I was gone, but...damn, I don't know. I guess I just had a bad feeling so I went back in and the door was locked. I knocked, but nobody answered and I started freaking out.

"I'd been in there a million times though and knew they kept keys on top of the doorway so I unlocked it and he had his hands around her throat, Charlotte. He was choking her and her shirt was ripped."

My heart is thundering like it did that night.

"I pulled him off of her, and she was crying, and he kept saying he was sorry and he had too much to drink. Over and over he kept saying he didn't mean to hurt her. She ran out of the room and I went after her. She didn't want to tell anyone, but I kept seeing the look in his eyes. The hold he had on her. I could hardly get him off, so I kept pushing her to tell. We stayed out all night and I drove her to the police station to file a report. Things were a mess after that. Half the town was pissed at her— she went in the room, she'd been drinking too, it was an accident and shit like that. They all kept saying how Adam was a good kid and a good ball player. It was like that stuff you see on TV, only real.

"So yeah, I testified against him. People lied and said it was because I liked her and all sorts of other things that don't matter. We ended up moving and I just...I couldn't talk to anyone. Not even you. I just felt like—"

"It wasn't your fault, Nathaniel."

I want to smile at the way she seems to read my mind, but I can't make myself do it.

"Feels like it is."

She shuffles beside me and I wonder if she's going to get up and leave, but she doesn't. Charlotte reaches over and grabs my hand. I thread my fingers through hers, hold her tightly, and think maybe...just maybe everything would have been a whole lot easier to deal with this whole time, if I'd had her hand in mine.

Chapter Four

When I get up the next morning, my brother isn't here. Our parents decided to go get massages in the city, which is all kinds of screwed up if you ask me. We just got here yesterday. I'm not sure why they need a massage already, but if it keeps them from getting on my case, I'm not going to complain.

I wonder what Charlotte is doing. I'll feel like crap if she has to work with her dad today after how late we were out last night. We didn't go in until after three—just sat out and talked. She's good for that. Telling me about life in The Village and her stars. She never expects me to do more than listen unless I want to and it's not the same as it is with everyone else.

Mom and Dad might not try to get me to talk because they're not really good at that kind of thing, but I know they're always trying to figure me out. Trying to decide how to be the kind of parents who sit down and open up to their kids when we both know they're not. Whatever. It's cool. It doesn't bother me.

But with Charlotte, I can just chill.

Brandon's sitting outside with his stupid fucking football when I go out, and I wonder if he's had the thing surgically attached without me knowing. I don't know what it is about him and that ball, but I know it was important for him to bring it and he's been screwing with it since we got here.

"What's up?" I ask him. "Sadie come and bust your balls yet?"

"Fuck you. And what's up with you? Why are you all chatty all of a sudden? You've been walking around like a kicked puppy for six months and all of a sudden you're cracking jokes. " He's palming the ball tightly between his hands.

I look at my brother, who's usually one of the most laid-back people I know, and frown. It's not like him to lose his temper. All he usually cares about is football and having a good time. Did I miss something these past few months? No. Not with Brandon. He's never been able to keep anything to himself.

"What's your problem, man? You're being a douche."

Brandon drops the ball to the ground and pushes me. Caught off guard, I stumble before lunging at him and pushing him back. My brother hits the ground and I know it's more from shock than the fact that I'm stronger than him. We screwed around and got in fights when we were kids, but not in a long time.

Brandon gets to his feet. "My problem is we're here because of you. We had to move because of you. You fucked everything up!" Just like that, he's gone. I sink down to the porch stairs, knowing everything he just said is right, but it's the first time he's actually said it to me.

I feel like hitting something. Slamming my fist into something as hard as the guilt pummels me. I screwed up getting Chrissy to meet Adam. I pushed her to tell when she didn't want to and then I screwed up my family's life, too.

"Hey." Charlotte steps around the side of the house.

I'm looking at the ground, trying to calm down. "Hey."

"So...your brother just totally lost it."

I almost laugh and I'm pretty sure that's what she wants me to do.

Charlotte stands in front of me for what feels like forever before she asks, "Wanna go for a hike?"

I risk looking up at her. She has this soft sort of smile on her face like she's unsure of herself. I don't know what she thinks there is to be unsure of. She knows I'll go with her. I'm always down to do anything with her.

"Don't you have to work?"

"It's under control."

I stand up and step closer to her. She's not as tanned as I remember from last year, but that's probably because it's so early in the summer. She's wearing another pink tank top, only this one is darker, and it makes me want to smile because I don't think I saw her in anything pink before. She used to make fun of Sadie for wearing it.

I also notice her neck is bare, not that I can blame her. Why would she want to wear the necklace I gave her when I was such a prick for six months?

"Sure. Want me to grab us something for lunch?" Just looking at her makes me a little out of breath and then that makes me feel like a douchebag.

"I'll take care of it."

Charlotte jogs off, around the back of her house and heads in the side door, staying far away from the store up front where her mom and sister work so often. It takes her less than five minutes to come back out with a backpack on and her hair tied up in a knot.

"Come on," she says, moving briskly. We head up the trail between her house and the cabins.

We walk through the field where everyone played night games a summer ago and hang a left up a path winding up the mountain. It isn't too steep, and the trail is worn from the feet of many others who have taken this same route.

"I feel like a pussy."

"Ugh! I hate that word. Why do guys use it like that?"

I shrug. "Sorry. I feel like a wuss. Like you're riding to my rescue or something."

We're walking side by side and she slows down a little. "Girls can't ride to a guy's rescue?"

"No, no. They can. It just makes us feel like pu—I mean, wusses."

"You're different. Than you were, I mean," she blurts out before speeding up again. I think she's trying to get away from me because of what she said.

Those words percolate around inside of me for a minute. I *am* different. I know it, but I don't want to seem different to her. For better or for worse, I actually liked the way she seemed to need me last summer. Like I gave her something that no one else did, but now I'm the one who needs her. The thought makes my muscles tighten.

"I don't want to be different. Not with you at least."

She stumbles a little at my words. I grab her hand to steady her. I think about what it was like to hold her last night and I'm not sure I want to let go. Still, my hand pulls back. I'm not sure I have the right to hold her for no reason like that.

"Tell me how I've changed." It's not like I don't know, but it's different hearing it from her.

"You curse more," she says. "And you're quieter." She pauses and continues onward, and I know she's working through whatever she has to say. She did that summer. I always wondered if it was because everyone just assumed everything about her instead of asking her opinion and listening to what she had to say.

Finally she continues, "Last year when we were quiet...it felt okay. Like it wasn't a big deal because words aren't always necessary. Now, when you're silent, it's feels like you have too much on your mind to talk."

This time it's me who stumbles. How does she always know the thoughts going through my head, sometimes even better than I do?

I don't want to be too sad to talk when I'm with her. "I'm okay," I tell her because I want to be and it makes me feel weak to say anything else. I don't know why I get sad sometimes. I mean, I guess I do because of what happened, but I don't know if it should still weigh down on me like it does. Then, I feel like shit for thinking that way because Chrissy has to still be dealing with it, right?

"You also didn't lie last year." She smirks and then I do the same.

"Whatever." The air around us isn't has heavy as it was. I wrap an arm around her shoulders and pull her to me playfully.

Charlotte laughs as we keep going up the mountain, but then she whispers, "You didn't fake it last year either."

I don't have to fake when I'm with you, I almost tell her, but it sounds too cheesy.

We hike for about an hour before we find a place to have lunch. I open Charlotte's bag and see it's packed with sandwiches, water bottles, and a blanket. Geez, I should have packed the food and I definitely should have carried the bag.

"You should have let me carry the pack up here." Trying not to look at her, I lay the blanket down.

"Why?" she asks and those words draw my eyes to hers. I can tell she really doesn't get why I would want to carry the bag. Little things like that are my favorite aspects of Charlotte. She doesn't rely on anyone.

"I don't know. You just should have."

"I'll remember that." A small grin tips one side of her mouth up.

"You've changed, too." We sit down and I open the lunch bag and give her a sandwich before grabbing one for myself.

"Yeah, right." Charlotte rolls her eyes. "I'll always be the same old Charlie Rae Gates. I'll spend my life in Lakeland

Village, take it over, and Alec will work with me. If you ask our parents, we'll probably even get married one day—"

"—What? You're planning on marrying Alec? Did you forget you're sixteen?" Plus, *Alec*? I don't want her to buy into all the crap that people expect to happen.

She shrugs. "Probably."

I toss my sandwich down. "I thought you said you guys were just friends."

She sighs and takes a drink of her water. "We are. You just don't get it. He'll be here. I'll be here. He loves The Village."

"But you don't have to be here, Char."

I don't realize I used the nickname until I see a quick flash of what almost looks like panic in her eyes, though I'm not sure why she could panic over that. Maybe just because it's the first time I used it.

"You don't understand, Nathaniel. Never mind. I don't want to talk about it with you."

"Whatever," I reply. And I think both of us know that's the end of our hike for today.

Almost the second we come through the clearing and up to the main part of The Village, Mr. Gates and Alec look up at us from where they're fueling the boats. One look and I can tell her dad is pissed.

"Charlie Rae Gates! You better have a good excuse why you disappeared when you knew I needed your help today. Your mom and you sister are both gone and Alec was supposed to have the day off."

My gut sinks. She bailed on work because of me. Knew she'd get in trouble, but she did it for me.

"I'm sorry. I just—"

"There is no just about it!" Mr. Gates interrupts. "You know I depend on you. It's not like you to skirt your responsibility like this. I'm extremely disappointed in you."

"It's my fault." I hope like hell a lie will come to me quickly, and it does. "I got lost up on the mountain...and I called my brother's phone, but I guess he left it and Charlot—I mean, Charlie found it. She came up and showed me the way down." It feels strange to call her Charlie, but I have a feeling it's the best thing to do around her dad.

"You got lost?" Alec tries to hide his laugh. I've never felt like punching him as much as I do right now. *He'll be here, I'll be here...*

Her dad gives me the evil eye. "I'm sorry, sir. It won't happen again. I can help you guys out, if there's anything I can do."

Charlotte looks at me. "You can help me with—"
"No. That's not necessary. We can't put you to work. You're a guest," her dad says, but it feels like there's more to it than that. I almost tell him I've helped her before, when he wasn't around, but I don't want her to get into more trouble.

"Come on, Charlie. We have work to do." Mr. Gates turns around and leaves, but not Alec, he walks right up to Charlotte, grabs her hand, and starts to walk away with her.

"Bye," she blurts out over her shoulder. Still, she lets him lead her away.

Chapter Five
July

Last year my parents made us go to some Fourth of July celebration with them, but this year, they've decided to stay at the cabin. I've held back a million times from telling them I thought this was supposed to be a *family* vacation, but it's not like I really want to spend all sorts of extra time bonding anyway.

Brandon talked our parents into letting us take the car to town for the carnival. I'm not sure why he wants to go anyway. Sadie still gives him the evil eye whenever we're around her. She's still with whoever the guy is, but it doesn't seem to bother him. I think she's surprised he hasn't come crawling back to her—I honestly am, too—but since he's suddenly playing football with Alec and his friends again, I guess he doesn't care about anything else.

"You haven't been sneaking out the past few weeks." Brandon takes a right turn to get onto the windy road that takes us to town.

"Thanks for telling me. I thought I had." I don't want to talk to him about Charlotte. He wouldn't get it. He's still always giving me shit about screwing her. It's not like I can make him see that we're just friends. It's also not like he'd understand why things are awkward with us. Hell, I'm not even sure I get it.

"What's up with you and her?"

Damn, what is this? I don't get why he wants to start talking all of a sudden. We've never talked about girls before. "What's up with you and Sadie?"

"I think it's pretty obvious that nothing is. Whatever. Be a douchebag. I was just trying to talk."

For a second I wonder if that means he needs to talk to me about something. It doesn't take a genius to see something went down. Especially when you factor in he hasn't really been seeing any girls since. Did Sadie somehow break my brother's heart? Doesn't seem likely, especially since he's the one who ignored her. Plus, he doesn't really seem to care about her, but I don't know what else it would be.

"Brandon—"

"Shut up." He turns up the music, so look out the window, hoping things don't ever get screwed up enough with Charlotte that we can't be friends.

It doesn't take us long to get there, because Lakeland Village is so damn small. I'm shocked to see how many people are here though. The biggest group I've seen in the past two years is at the bash Charlotte's family throws at the beginning of the summer and it's nothing compared to this.

We park the car and buy wristbands before going inside. Brandon pulls out his phone and texts. It's only a few seconds later he gets a reply and says, "Everyone's over by the Ferris Wheel. They're waiting."

"Why do you want to hang out with them so much since you and Sadie don't get along?"

Brandon shrugs. "Because the only alternative is only hanging out with my brother or parents all summer and that makes me feel like a loser. Plus, Alec's cool. He's a kickass running back."

"He's pretty good at being a prick too."

Brandon just shakes his head at me as though I'm being stupid.

There's a big group of people waiting right where Alec told Brandon they'd be. Sadie with her boyfriend, Alec, Charlotte, and a few more girls and guys that I've seen around a lot since last year.

"Hey," I say to everyone as we approach. Brandon fist bumps the guys and I nod at them. Charlotte is off to the side, behind Alec, and I look over at her, but her eyes are steering clear of me. What a way to put me in a shitty mood.

"We're going to play some games," Alec says.

"Yeah, Brice promised to win me a stuffed animal." Sadie grabs her boyfriend's arm, and I'm pretty sure it's obvious to everyone but Brice that she's doing it because of Brandon.

As the group begins migrating through the carnival, I notice Charlotte sort of hangs back from Alec. I step up to her because

I only have about six weeks left here and I don't want to spend them being all weird with her like we have been.

"Want me to win you a teddy bear too?" I tease.

She gets it just like I knew she would and nudges my arm with hers.

"You done ignoring me now?" I ask.

"I haven't been ignoring you."

"Yeah, you have, and we both know it."

Last year I knew she liked me. More than a friend, I mean. I told myself it didn't matter and she knew we were just friends. We couldn't really be more, but now I find myself looking for it. Wondering if that went away, but then I tell myself to chill the hell out because nothing has changed. She's here, Alec is here, and most of the time...I'm not.

Doesn't stop me from wanting to knock him out, though.

"It's hard," she whispers. I want to ask her why, but don't know if I should—want to make it easier on her because I care too much to see her hurt. I'd do anything to make it easier on her. I wish more people did, but then the thought of Alec helping her pops into my head and I'm pissed again.

"I know," come out of my mouth and I realize I get it more than I thought. It's hard for me, too. It's been like that since the beginning. She's cool and I like spending time with her. Hell, I remember the feel of her lips and wish I could do it again, but then...she's like a friend too. I can tell her anything and I want to know everything about her. Maybe I already do. "I wish we lived closer."

She doesn't reply to that. Looking up, I see we have fallen pretty far behind the rest of the group. Everyone's standing there waiting for us. Brandon's giving me this stupid ass smile that means he's thinking all the wrong things about what is going on. Alec is next to him and I don't see the anger. Not as much. It's almost like he's confused.

"You guys coming or what?" Alec shouts.

"We're coming," Charlotte calls before jogging to catch up. It's déjà vu. We never really get anywhere when we talk and she's always running to him.

We play tons of games. I beat Charlotte in a basketball shootout and she takes me at flipping coins into fish bowls. She's the only person I've ever seen really do it, so we're walking around with a betta fish in a bag. We've stopped to eat and ridden a few rides. We will have about forty-five minutes until the fireworks start at ten.

Looking up, I see a ride that looks like it was designed for ten year olds. It's not very big or anything, with one big cart where people ride in, but it has a huge shooting star on it. All the thing does is go back and forth, like a shooting star would, but still, I grab Charlotte's hand and nod toward it.

"Wanna?"

She's quiet and she gets this sad look on her face. I wonder if I said something wrong or how I screwed up, because she's still not speaking and she's just looking at me.

"We don't have to... I just thought..."

"I do. Want to, I mean," rushes out of her mouth.

"What are you guys doing? You're always the ones lagging behind. Need me to carry you so you can keep up, little bro?" Brandon teases.

"Fuck off," I call back. "We're going on this one." I point to the shooting star. Someone laughs. A few people grumble.

"Dude, that's lame," Alec sneers.

"Dude, no one asked you," I shoot right back at him.

He takes a step like he's about to come at me and I do the same. No way am I backing down to him. It's been a long time coming with us, but Brandon grabs his arm and shakes his head.

"I don't need you to fight my fights for me."

"Whatever. I'm not fighting you," Brandon says before Alec pulls free of him. "We'll catch you guys later."

I face Charlotte, not giving a shit about him, or if they're leaving or not. "What the fuck is his problem? One of these days there's not going to be someone there to stop us."

"Alec and I have always been best friends. He's been pretty much the only person I care about. He's protective of me."

I back away from her, an unexpected pain piercing through me.

"I mean, he's pretty much been the only person I really hang out with. It's been *us* and he's never really cared to be friends with people who stayed here before. It's always been a job."

I close my eyes, not able to believe she's defending him to me.

"I don't want to fight with you anymore. You know that's not how I see you. Can't we just...I don't know, just forget about everything else and have fun. Last summer..."

Without her continuing, I get what she's saying. Last year we just had fun. It wasn't always perfect, but it wasn't like this.

I want that, too. Want to wipe away the past seven months and all of our fights. I just want to *be* with her.

"Yeah...yeah, we can." I grab her hand, feeling it fit inside mine. "Come ride a shooting star with me."

She gives me another smile, and I'm already riding high.

Chapter Six

We ride the shooting star twice and Charlotte laughs more than I've ever heard her laugh. When we're done, we grab her fish from the worker before going to buy a drink. I glance at my cell phone and see it's almost time for the fireworks to start.

"Do you wanna find everyone else before the show kicks off?" I hope like hell she says no.

Charlotte shakes her head. She has her fish in one of her hands. "Nope. I have a secret place to watch them. I go up there alone every year."

Crossing my arms, I look at her. Not mad or anything, but wondering if that means she wants me to leave her alone.

"Do I get to go see this special spot?"

"You already know all my secrets anyway."

It doesn't matter if I should or not. That I'm leaving soon or that she thinks one day she'll be with Alec. We have *now*. I want some piece of Charlotte, and to let her have some of me. This time when I grab her hand it's not because I'm pulling her away from Alec or because it's easier to weave through a crowd that way. When she grabs mine back, I hope it's not because she only wants to comfort me, but because she wants the contact.

Her palm is a little sweaty, but it doesn't bother me. I think she's nervous which makes my pulse race because whatever it is that I think she's feeling; I'm feeling it, too. Or maybe I'm hoping like hell she shares the same heat bursting through my veins.

We weave our way through the crowd to the far end of the carnival and sneak through a sizeable storage building before halting in front of a fence.

"We have to go over," she says, and I smile thinking it's really fucking cool that this girl climbs fences to sneak in and out of carnivals.

"Hey." I grab her shoulder, right before she's about to begin to climb. "Thank you."

Her eyebrows come together. "For what?"

"Being you, I guess. And for this. Showing me your secrets."

She bites her lip shyly but then says, "You know, the first time I saw you, I thought you were a pretty boy. I didn't think you would do stuff like climb fences or win night games with me."

Ouch. That kind of sucks. I remember her saying something like that before. "And now?"

"Now I know who you are."

Who, I want to ask her. I always thought I knew who I was but now I'm not sure.

"Come on. We need to hurry."

"Let me go first. I'll help you on the other side." I know she doesn't need my help, but I want to give it to her. Maybe I'm just selfish and want my hands on her. It's like I don't know my own head anymore.

After taking the fish from her, I scale the fence and drop down on the other side. Charlotte comes up right behind me. When she gets to the top, she slides down a little. I reach up and grasp her waist and she slips right down into my arms. We're standing there, without any space between us, the bag still clutched in my hand. I feel her stomach and her breasts up against my chest and I'm not letting go. God, I totally don't want to let go of this girl right now.

She licks her lips and I'm leaning forward and I'm eager, like I've never kissed a girl. Like I need to know how she tastes again.

Boom!

The sky lights up in reds and blues. Charlotte pulls away and grabs my hand again. "Come on. We're going to miss the show."

Right now I don't care about anything except her, but it seems to be important to her so I follow. We run up this grassy hill right behind the building. Trees stand all around us and I wonder how we're supposed to see around them. A few more pops take off, the colors so bright we have no trouble seeing. It's not a huge hill and only takes a couple minutes to get to the top. The trees are thick behind us, but there's a perfect clearing up here. A circle, with an open sky above it. When another firework goes off, they look like they're right above us—like they could fall right on top of us, the only two people in the world.

"It's beautiful," she whispers, her eyes on the sky, but not me. I'm looking at her.

"Yeah...it is." I've never really thought of Charlotte as *beautiful* before, looking at her with that huge smile, colors reflecting in her eyes and on her face. Cute, sure, but right now I wonder how I wasn't always conscious of the fact she is so beautiful.

She glances at me. "Watch them," she says, so I do.

Holding hands, we stand in middle of the clearing and watch the show.

When it's almost over, I turn to her. My finger brushes the hollow spot at the base of her throat while I watch it. It's so crazy touching her like this. It doesn't matter that we've kissed once last year. This feels different.

"You got rid of your necklace," I say.

Her breath hitches. More fireworks go off. "You don't wear yours anymore, either."

From my pocket, I remove the black leather necklace with the star on it. "I felt like a jerk wearing it after how I treated you..."

"I wore mine every day until the day you came back... It made me feel like, I don't know, like maybe I really could have the stars."

"You can."

She's already shaking her head. I don't get it; I don't see why she doesn't think she can have more than this. If I bring it up, I know we'll fight again and I'm tired of fighting with her. I lift my hands and latch the necklace around my neck. Charlotte nods and I know that means she'll wear hers again too.

Pop after pop sounds in the distance. The colors of the finale flash the night sky alive. I cup Charlotte's cheek and she shivers.

"It's just me," I say and then feel stupid. "I mean, you know it's me and who am I really but—"

"You're Nathaniel."

I set the fish on the ground. That's all I need to hear, and then I'm leaning forward. My lips touch hers and I wonder if I should go slowly, but I can't really do it. My tongue slides into her mouth and I push a hand into her hair. I pull her closer, resting my other hand on the curve of her hip.

She moans, and I kiss her deeper. Charlotte's arms wrap around my neck. We're kissing like crazy with the fireworks going off, but then she pulls back. Steps away.

Shit. "I'm sorry. I didn't mean..."

Charlotte shakes her head. "No, it's okay. It's just..."

She's the kind of girl who needs to go slow, isn't she? Guilt rumbles through me. My mind flashes back to that night with Adam and Chrissy. I could never push myself on a girl like that.

"You didn't push," she says, reading my mind again. "I swear, it's just..." But she doesn't continue. We watch the end of the finale. For a second, I worry we're right back where we didn't want to be, but I won't let us. I reach for her hand and she's doing the same. When she laughs, I do, too.

It's a few nights later, Charlotte and I aren't meeting until one a.m. so I pass out for a little while and set the alarm on my phone to wake me up. When I get out of bed, Brandon is gone. I have no idea how he made it out without me hearing him.

I shake my head and climb out the window, hoping we don't see him and Sadie going at it in the woods again. I should have known it wouldn't be long, and I hope my brother knows what he's doing. The last thing we need is him getting into it with Sadie's boyfriend.

Charlotte has her telescope with her tonight. She doesn't bring it often, but when she does, she spends a lot of time looking through it. I wonder what she sees up there. The look on her face makes me wonder what I'm missing. It's like it's her miracle or something.

"We might want to hit our spot by the lake tonight, instead of the fort. Brandon was gone when I got out of bed..."

Charlotte doesn't need me to continue. "Oh my God! Sadie was asking about him. I can't believe that. I feel so bad for Brice."

"Sucks for him."

We head over to our spot. I lay out the blanket Charlotte brought with her and then we set up her telescope. "What are we looking for tonight?" I ask. We're close and I really want to kiss her again.

"Nothing specific. I just wanted to explore."

Sitting down on the blanket, I watch her look for whatever it is she sees up there.

"You should explore in real life one day. Away from The Village."

She groans. "I'm not an idiot. I know that."

"Sorry." I touch her back and she jumps a little. "I don't want to be a dick."

"You're not. I mean, I kind of like it when you say stuff like that. You almost make me believe it, ya know? But...there's my dad. This is my life, Nathaniel. My past is here, and it's my future, too." She's quiet and I know there's more. I lean away from her and lay down on the blanket again, giving her space.

"They're fighting a lot again...my parents. Have you ever had that feeling in your gut, that you know something's going to happen?"

"Yeah."

"She's going to leave. I know it. And then...who will he have? Dad's always been in my corner. When I was young and Mom tried to force me into dresses, he told her to leave me alone. He taught me how to build forts and didn't treat me like I couldn't do the same kind of work him and Alec did, just because I'm a girl."

He made her who she is. I'll always respect him for that. "But those things aren't all you want anymore, are they?" I start to sweat a little. Maybe I misread her. Maybe she's changed and I didn't know.

"But this is how I can repay him. I can't leave him alone."

"What if you helped in the summers? Couldn't he find someone to work for him during the rest of the year?" I ask her.

"Hiring extra help isn't always cost efficient and, that's not all it is. He wants this as our legacy, ya know? He wants it in the family."

I'm not sure what to say to that. I get it, but it's still shitty and not fair to her.

She wipes at her eyes. It turns me inside out to see her cry. I sit up and pull her to me, into my lap, and she sits there, wrapping her arms around my neck. "You really think they'll leave?" I ask.

Charlotte nods. "I think so. It wouldn't be bad here, Nathaniel. I just..."

"You want more."

She nods and we sit there like that, her on my lap as I touch the tender skin of her side.

"Want me to tell you?" she asks after a few minutes. "If I could do anything, do you want me to tell you what I'd do?"

"Yeah."

And then she talks. I hold her while she tells me she would study astronomy. "I want to learn everything there is to know about the stars. I want to see big cities and little ones. To travel and see what the night looks like from other places in the world."

"You should. You could do it."

"I've never been farther than a few hours from Lakeland Village."

She asks about New York so I tell her about places I would take her, if we ever had the chance to go.

"I've always wanted to go to the West Coast," she admits. "Los Angeles or maybe San Francisco."

"I want to go far away for school too." Then I whisper against her cheek, "I think you'll go one day."

"Yeah?" she asks.

"I do." And it's the truth.

Chapter Seven
August

"I'm bored. You wanna go outside with me and throw the football around or something?" Brandon asks.

It's evening and we spent the day hiking with our parents. Charlotte had to work with her dad, and I have no idea what time they'll be done. "Sure." I shrug. "I guess."

We go outside and around to the side of the cabin. Brandon throws the ball at me and I catch it before tossing it back to him. A laugh comes from the direction of Charlotte's house so I look over to see who it was. Sadie's sanding on the back deck with Brice. Alec's parents are there, too, his mom sitting on his dad's lap. It's his mom who laughed at something someone said. Her head is tossed back and a huge smile is on her face.

Mr. Gates is standing at the grill, cooking as he looks on. Even Mrs. Gates is out there, a glass of wine in her hand. She looks happy, too. Off to the farthest side of the deck, Charlotte sits on the ledge with Alec standing in front of her. They're in some kind of conversation and she doesn't seem to notice anything else around her.

Which means she doesn't notice me. I shake that thought out of my head. Looking at her over there, her family and his, I see it for the first time. She does fit in here. It might not be all she wants, but she could be happy. I never wanted to see that before. Her dad is here and they're good friends with Alec's parents. Alec is here and as much as I hate the guy, I know she cares about him.

This could be her life.

I think I wanted to believe she hated it here. And maybe she does, but I see that maybe she might not too.

It sends a cold blast through me. Then I feel like shit for thinking that way. I shouldn't want her to be unhappy.

"What the hell, man?" Brandon says, jogging up to me where he's able to see the deck.

He stares over there for a second too before he sighs. "One big happy family, huh?"

I look at my brother. "I'm not. I don't. It's not my business what Charlotte does." That doesn't feel right, though. The words turn the cold inside me to an angry fire.

Brandon shakes his head. "Whatever you say. And who said I was talking about you?"

Shit. He really does care about Sadie. I shouldn't be shocked that he lied before. It's not like we've ever been really close or that either of us really go around talking about how we feel. "I'm sorry," I tell him. "You can...you know, talk to me or something. Tell me what happened."

Brandon opens his mouth and I think he might say something real, but he shakes his head. "You wouldn't get it. No one would." He nods toward the other side of the house. "We'll head over that way. Go long."

I don't tell Charlotte that I saw her with Alec's family. There's really no point. It doesn't change anything and it shouldn't make me feel as shitty as it does. We sneak out that night like we always do. She could be with him, if she wanted. Maybe it makes me a dick, but it feels good to know I'm the one she spends her nights with. It's like she's choosing me over him, when I shouldn't want her in the position to choose anything.

She tells me that she has to work with her dad for a little bit in the morning and then her and all their friends taking one of the boats out, so Brandon and I should go.

When I get back to the cabin, my brother tells me he already planned to go with them and I wonder how in the hell him and Sadie are keeping this up. How he can sneak out with her at night and then watch her with Brice during the day. I've only kissed Charlotte twice in my whole life and I hate to even see her stand next to Alec.

Though I guess that's probably because I hate him.

The next morning we get up and ready. Charlotte is outside working with her dad and I hear him yell, "God damn it!"

My head whips that direction. They're over at one of the boats and I see Charlotte shake her head and bend to pick up a tool and then hand it to him. He puts it back to the boat and then drops it again. His back is to me so I can't tell if he threw it down or what, but he looks pissed. He says something to Charlotte and then takes off toward the house.

Before I know it, I'm walking over to her. I've never heard him curse at her like that, but I don't like it.

"What was that about?" I ask. Her face is a little pale when she looks at me. "Is he...he's not violent with you is he?"

That snaps her out of her daze. "What? No! I don't know what just happened. All he did was drop the wrench. He grabbed it, but dropped it again and then he got all pissed. He's not usually like that at all."

She's watching the direction he went. I step toward her. "I'm sure he's just having a bad day." I pick up the wrench and then look at what he was trying to tighten. "I'll help you."

"Okay." She smiles.

Charlotte and I are only there for about five minutes before all their friends show up. Brandon makes an appearance and we begin packing things into one of the other boats.

"I need to go change real quick." Charlotte doesn't wait for my reply before heading for the house. All of the other girls are already in bikinis, some wearing short skirts over them and some not. I wonder what Charlotte's going to wear. Last year I only saw her in her swimsuit a couple times, and it covered a whole lot of skin. It didn't surprise me that she wasn't the bikini type, but I'd be lying if I said I didn't want to see her in one.

When she comes back, she's wearing a white button up shirt, and a pair of shorts.

Damn. No answers yet.

We get out on the boat a few minutes later. Alec drives and that pisses me off, because it's totally rational that everything he does annoys the hell out of me, right? We go down the lake for a while before he pulls the boat up next to another set of docks. It's way quieter out here without all the people from the cabins swimming and hanging around.

They turn on some music and people pull out beers and we're all hanging out and having a good time. A little while later some people jump in the water. Alec, Sadie, Brandon, Mike, Danielle, and Brice are all swimming while me, Charlotte and two other people are on the boat.

"Nate! Go swimming with me!" Danielle calls from the water. "It's fun!"

Guilt slithers its way through me and then I wonder what I have to feel guilty for. "Nah. I'm good for now."

Looking over, I see that Charlotte is gone. I'm hoping like hell she's decided it's time to swim. Yeah, I seem to have a one track mind right now, but I'm sure every other guy here is glad to see all the girls in their bikinis.

I spot her sitting on the dock, wearing a white hat. Shaking my head, I walk over and sit next to her. "Why aren't you swimming?"

"Why aren't you swimming? Danielle wants to go with you."

I lean over, right next to her ear. "Danielle's not the girl I want out there with me."

Charlotte shivers and I like that I can do that to her, so I speak again, so close to her. "Go swimming with me, Star Girl."

Her eyes go wide and she looks at me, before smirking. "You don't play fair."

I know she means that she realizes I'm flirting with her. I love that she's not afraid to call me on it.

"Come swimming with me," I say again.

She looks down, the shyness coming out in her again. "I don't...I don't look like they do in my bikini, Nathaniel."

Wow. Didn't see that coming. Maybe I should have. "Who gives a shit about them."

"Boys."

That makes me wonder who's seen her in a bikini (or less) and what they said to her about it. "Come on, it's just me." I nudge her.

"Pfft." She nudges me back. "But it's not just you."

"Would it make a difference if it were just me?"

She doesn't hesitate to say, "I think so."

I smirk at her and flick the white hat off her head. "Then we'll do that later. But for now..." I grab her. She tries to fight me off, but I'm not about to let go. I manage to get her in my arms and head straight for the water.

"Nathaniel!" Charlotte screams. "We're both dressed!"

"I'm in my swimming trunks." Not like I've ever swam in my shirt, but I'll make an exception to get her in the water with me. She's still complaining, but she's not fighting me too much. It's getting hard to hold onto her so I rush with her into the water. When she slips out of my arms, I grab her hands and keep pulling her with me.

She's laughing and I'm laughing and I keep going out farther and farther with her. If I wanted to, I could let go of her. She's moving with me now, but I keep her in my arms as we get out to where neither of us can touch. "Don't go anywhere." I grin at her before ducking under the water and coming back up again. I shake my head, water droplets splashing her, and then she goes under and pops back up again.

I can't help but look down and see the way the white shirt molds to her skin. I see the yellow outline beneath.

Charlotte follows my eyes down. She knows I'm looking. We're close, just bobbing in the water, my arms around her and there's a drop of water on her lip that I really want to lick off.

"Charlotte," I whisper and—

"—Hell yeah! 'Bout time my little brother got in the water!" Brandon yells before splashing water at me.

"I'm going to kill him," I say to Charlotte. And it's not because he splashed me, either. He interrupted my time with her.

Chapter Eight

"Go swimming with me," I say again in Charlotte's ear after we finish the water fight. Most of the people are heading back to the boat, but I'm not ready to get out yet.

"We are swimming." She ducks under the water, and when she comes back up, she's facing me.

"Then follow me before they turn around." They have their backs to us right now as they head for the shore. I wouldn't put it past Alec to try to drag her out, so I head off in the opposite direction as the boat. The shore comes out a little bit so if we go on the other side of it, we'll be out of sight from the boat.

Charlotte is right behind me as we swim into the little hideaway. "What are we doing?"

"Don't know." It's an honest answer. "I just didn't feel like being around everyone else. I wanted to swim with you." She swims closer to me and again I notice how the shirt hugs her. "What happened, Star Girl? Who said something to you?"

She shakes her head and turns away, but I move to the side, so I'm in front of her again. "You don't have to tell me..."

"It's not really that big a deal."

The water is shallower here and I'm able to touch the ground. I can tell Charlotte can't so I put my arms around her waist. Hers automatically wrap around my neck.

"I went out with this guy from school last year—"

"You had a boyfriend?" When she starts to pull away, I amend, "Shit. I didn't mean it like that. You know I didn't, it's just...I didn't know."

"You would have known if we'd been talking."

I nod because I would have. If I hadn't cut her out. "I'm sorry."

"I know. But, anyway...we only went out like twice. We went to the drive-ins and we were kissing..."

My body tenses up. I try to relax because it shouldn't get to me like this, but it does. "What happened?" I make myself ask because I want her to know she can talk to me, even though I'm going to hate hearing it.

She bobs in the water a little before saying. "He put his hand up my shirt and well...obviously, I have the world's smallest boobs and—"

"They're not *that* small." Her cheeks turn pink and I realize I just admitted to checking her out. "Tell me what happened, Star Girl."

She chews her bottom lip for a second before she says, "I pulled away. I know it makes me sound like a prude, but...I just don't want some guy I hardly like feeling me up."

"You don't sound like a prude." Take that, fucker.

"Anyway, he got pissed and when we got home, he told me he didn't want to go out with my anymore. I didn't really care. It was one of those things that happened because...I don't really know. I guess it was nice to have a boyfriend. I don't really date. The next day at school, he'd spread all these rumors about feeling me up and about how small I was."

Anger bursts inside me. "Fuck him. I'd kick his ass if—"

"Alec did," she interrupts.

I try to hold back a groan, but I can't help it. Of *course* he did. Alec cares enough about her to do things like that for her and he's here to always do them. I'm suddenly shaking a little. It sucks not being able to protect her. To know Alec will and that he thinks it's his job to protect her from me too.

I don't let myself think about the words, just lean my forehead against hers and say, "If I had been here, I would have been the one to kick his ass for you."

"I know...because you're like, my best friend, right?" she asks, and I nod even though it feels off. They aren't big enough words.

"But you're weren't here... You'll never really be here."

There's a truth to her words that I hate. Instead of thinking about that, I brush my hand along her hip. "Why do you think Alec didn't care if you went out with him, anyway? I can't even talk to you without him being a prick."

Her answer is simple, easy, and she doesn't shy away from it. "Because he knew I didn't really like Thomas."

My pulse jumps. She likes me. This totally cool girl who I would do anything for. Who trusts me with her secrets and who makes me forget for the first time in months. I knew it last year, but this doesn't feel the same. It feels like more.

"I wish things could be different." I push the wet strands of her hair behind her ear. "There's nothing wrong with the way you look. You're beautiful."

She gasps. I can't stop myself from leaning forward and taking her mouth. I'm used to the feel of her by now. I know the way she moves and how she tastes. She was so tentative the first few times, but now she's opening up for me right away and pushing closer and I want her closer than anyone has ever been.

My mouth slips from her lips, trails down her neck, and I lick water from her skin. Charlotte fists her hand in my hair and her body quivers, making me pull back a little because I never want to push her.

Our foreheads come together again and we just stand there in the water, me holding her up while she has her arms wrapped around my neck. The mood darkens, sadness creeping into her features. "Don't be upset." I'm not exactly sure why she's so sad; I just know she is.

"I'm going to miss you," Charlotte whispers.

I pull her tighter against me. "We'll still be here a couple more weeks. And we'll talk this time. I won't be stupid."

That makes her laugh. "Boys seem to have a problem with that."

"Low blow."

"Do you ever talk to her?" she asks. "The girl who got hurt?"

I sigh, thinking back to when I emailed her. "After we moved, I messaged her once. I just wanted to check in, ya know? But she said she wanted to forget about it. They were moving, too, I guess. She took a lot of shit. People blamed her. Adam has this promising future and all that bullshit."

"People suck." For the first time, Charlotte leans forward and kisses me. It's quick, her lips briefly touching mine. "You did the right thing, though. Not that I'm surprised."

"Charlie!" Alec's voice shouts from the direction of the boat.

"Douchebag!" my brother yells, too.

"He's such an idiot." I shake my head.

"I guess we better go back," Charlotte says.

"Unless we want Alec over here, we do."

She rolls her eyes. "I know he's an idiot sometimes, but... He loves me."

I must frown because she continues, "Not *loves* me, loves me, but we've always been a part of each other's lives."

And they always will.

I won't.

I get it.

"Nate!" Brandon yells again.

I turn to Charlotte. "Come on, I'll race you back." But her words are a weight tied to me, holding me back, pulling me under. *We'll always be a part of each other's lives...*

Chapter Nine

The next couple weeks fly by. Charlotte and I sneak out every night. Sometimes I kiss her and sometimes I don't. I remember every time Roxi and I got together, we made out. It's not that I don't want to do the same with Charlotte. It's not like I don't want to do a whole lot more with her, but we talk a lot too. I enjoy talking to her and listening to her and I know she tells me things she doesn't share with anyone else.

I also really, really want to keep kissing her. It's in my mind way more than it probably should be.

It's our last night at The Village and Charlotte and I are meeting early. I told her we don't have to because I don't want her to get caught, but when she tells me it would be worth it, I smile. There's this sense of urgency scratching at my skin. Both of us know this could be the last time we see each other. My parents could decide to go somewhere else next year or not take a vacation at all and, hell, we're sixteen. How do you know what the future holds?

She plans to end up with Alec one day and the thought makes me feel like I'm breaking apart, so I try not to think about it.

When we meet, she has a bag with her, but it's not the one she usually carries with her telescope in it. I take her hand and she squeezes my fingers, but Charlotte stops me when I move to head toward the woods.

"Let's go somewhere different," she tells me. I nod because tonight, I would follow her anywhere.

We head the direction where we've sat by the lake a million times. The first place I talked to her our first summer. Charlotte keeps going and I keep following. We walk for at least a half hour down the lake. We turn, following the water around a corner, which makes it feel more secluded.

All the cabins are far behind us, nothing here but Charlotte and me, the water, trees, moon, and her stars.

"If you wanted to get me alone, you just had to ask," I tease, expecting some kind of smartass comment.

"I thought I did."

Her answer makes my skin feel tight. Heat bubbles inside me.

She lets her bag slide off her shoulder and moves to open it, but I reach out and grab it, telling her, "Let me."

I lay the blanket on the ground, and pull out the towels she brought, wondering what's going on. She sits and I sink down beside her. "What's on your mind, Star Girl?"

She shrugs. "Everything."

I don't want her to be sad, not on our last night together. I'd do anything to make her happy, so I ask her about the stars and she points out a few different things. I pretend to see them, because I think she needs it. The longer we talk, the more she seems to relax.

"Brandon was gone again tonight," I tell her.

One of the flashlights is facing the sky between us, but with the moon so bright, we don't really need the light.

"I'm sure he and Sadie wanted to give each other a proper goodbye." There's a smile in her voice and a blush on her cheeks.

"I guess. I tried to ask my brother about her, but he threw a pillow at my head and told me to mind my own fucking business."

Charlotte laughs. "I don't even ask Sadie. It's not like she would tell me. Last year she was pretty bummed he never called her, though. I used to hear her crying at night. It was strange. Usually Sadie doesn't let guys get to her, ya know? She's too strong for that."

I think about her sister. The way I've seen her try to get Brandon's attention and knowing they sneak out together, while she's still with Brice, and even the way she treats Charlotte. "You don't want to be that kind of strong, if 'strength' is even the right word for it."

She looks over at me, all tender like she's going to cry and it freaks me out a little. I'm not ready to deal with the tears. Don't know how, but the longer she stares the more she softens me up. Charlotte surprises me by crawling over and getting on my lap. She's straddling me; her legs wrapped around me. My body immediately starts to respond.

I know she feels it when her eyes go wide.

"Can't always control it." Damned if I'm not embarrassed. I don't get that way easily, but she probably didn't expect a boner just from crawling onto my lap.

But then she leans forward and pushes her mouth against mine. It's all the incentive I need to slide my tongue between her lips. Pulling her closer to me, I take the kiss deeper and it's urgent and needy. I kiss her neck and behind her ear and take her mouth again. My hand slips under her shirt and I move it across her skin. She feels so good and even though it about kills me, I pull my mouth away from hers.

"We should probably slow down." *Shut up! What are you doing?* A voice inside my head yells, but this is Charlotte and I'm pretty sure she's only kissed me and one other guy. There's no way I can go farther with her when I'm leaving tomorrow.

"What if I don't want to slow down?"

My head drops back and I groan. She's totally trying to kill me here.

"Oh," she tries to move away, but I hold her tightly to me.

"No. Don't do that. I want you, Charlotte. I do. This is killing me, but..." Her words from earlier about her sister pop back into my head. "You don't have to do that. I don't expect you to give me that kind of goodbye." Would I like it? Yeah, but that's beside the point.

She looks away and I hate that I hurt her, but I know I'm right about this.

"Talk to me." I tilt her head up so she's looking at me. "It's me. You can tell me anything." My hand is itching to touch her so I keep it moving under the back of her shirt.

"I ...I want something for me. For us. You're leaving and I don't know if I'll ever see you again and..."

Her words feel like a fist to my stomach. How can I never see her again?

"I want you to see me...Ugh. That sounds stupid, but I'm not like Sadie. I can't just seduce some guy and I get embarrassed and—"

"That's not a bad thing."

"But it's a hard thing. I don't even want to wear a bikini in front of guys and I'm sixteen years old. And you said I'm beautiful and I trust you more than anyone else I know. I just...I wanted you to see me and know if you still think I'm beautiful."

Holy. Shit. "You are so totally brave. I don't know anyone who would have laid that out there like you did."

"I trust you." Her hand teases the back of my hair. It's probably the most amazing thing anyone has ever said to me.

I don't give myself time to think about it. To realize it's wrong or to try talking myself out of it. I can say I'm doing it for her, and maybe a part of me is, but I'm doing it for me, too. Because who wouldn't want to see her? Who wouldn't want to give her another first? And that makes me feel selfish.

"I don't even have any condoms, but...we don't have to have sex for me to see you, Char. We don't have to...but if you want to..." I'm wondering how in the hell I got so lucky. What it is about her. Why she trusts me, but then I think maybe it just *is*. Maybe everything doesn't have to have an answer.

"I wasn't talking about sex..."

Nice. Now I feel like an idiot.

"But I still want you to see me. I want to see you too," she adds.

I nod, not able to trust my voice. I'm sure I'm supposed to be a lot smoother about this, but I'm seriously dying here. I don't know what to do, so I slowly move my hands to the buttons on her shirt. "Can, I?" I ask.

"Yes."

"You sure?" My voice breaks and I feel like an idiot.

Charlotte nods. One by one I push the buttons through the holes until her light blue shirt hangs open. She's wearing a white bra underneath.

I wish I knew what to say, but I don't, so I nod, trying to tell her to stand up. She does and I'm right behind her, before I draw the shirt off her shoulders and let it hit the blanket.

Charlotte is standing in front of me, in nothing up top, but a bra. I feel all jittery. My heart is going crazy. It's killer to pull my eyes off her, but they dart to the water and I get an idea. "Wanna go skinny dipping? I've never done that, but—"

"It'll be both our first," she says, and I know it was the right thing to say.

I pull my shirt over my head and throw it to the blanket. Reaching out, Charlotte touches the necklace around my neck that matches her own. Not sure if she wants me to undress her or not, I go to my shorts first, pushing them down and kicking out of them.

My palms are sweating and I'm as nervous as I've ever been, standing here in front of her in my boxers. "What now?" I ask.

She doesn't answer, just moves her hands to the clasp on the front of her bra and it pops open. She covers herself with her hands, but I still suck in a deep breath.

"You're perfect," I tell her.

That gets me a huge smile. "You didn't see anything yet."

"I've seen enough to know you're perfect."

Slowly, like, so slowly I think I could die, she drops her hands. Nothing could pull my eyes away from her. Charlotte. Star Girl. I can't believe she trusts me with this. "See?" my voice creaks. "Perfect."

Her eyes are watery. "Thank you."

We stand there for a few minutes and I'm sure I'm supposed to do something, but I can't. I'd seen Roxi without her shirt on but she wasn't Charlotte. This is different.

"For the rest...how about we close our eyes and then run in the water."

I laugh; glad she's getting cold feet too. I don't want to be the guy who freaks out.

"Deal."

"One," she says.

"Two," I reply and it reminds me of that time we decided to go for it in the paintball game. We weren't afraid, we trusted each other to have our backs and we just went for it. This is Last Man Standing all over again.

"Three." That voice is my head is back, telling me I'm stupid for closing my eyes, but she trusts me and I won't do anything not to deserve it. I push my boxers down my legs and then go toward the water. I hear her next to me, but I'm not sure so I ask, "How do we know when we can open our eyes?"

"Umm...we'll walk until our waist is covered. Mine is, now."

I take a couple more steps and then say, "Me too." We open our eyes and look at each other. I think she's blushing, but can't completely tell because of the light. Trying to lighten the mood, I splash her and she does the same. We play around in the water and pretty soon I forget I'm naked. Not her, I'll never be able to forget she's bare.

After a little while, we run out of the water, neither closing our eyes but not really looking either. I toss a towel at her and she wraps it around herself. Not wanting to get our clothes wet, I only put on my boxers and Charlotte her bra and panties before we sit on the blanket again. This time, I hold her between my legs with her back to my chest.

"Thank you," she whispers after a few minutes.

"It was my pleasure. Believe me. You have absolutely nothing to thank me for."

It's a little cold so I pull the blanket up around my shoulders and wrap it around her. We sit like that for hours, sometimes talking and sometimes quiet.

Before we know it, the sun is a threat in the distance, warning us that we'll soon be going our separate ways. Leaning forward, I put my mouth next to her ear, "We should probably get dressed."

She nods and leaves my arms. I instantly miss her. She slips on her shorts and her shirt and then I do the same. I can't believe it, but I'm shaking. Really shaking, and I don't understand it. I pull her toward me and kiss her, before just holding her against my chest.

Charlotte cries there as I rest my chin on the top of her head. I squeeze her tightly, knowing soon we'll have to let go. "I wasn't joking when I said you're beautiful...that you're perfect," I tell her.

"I don't want you to go," she mumbles into my chest.

"I know..." I don't tell her it'll be okay. Don't say we'll keep talking. Both are true, but neither are enough and we both know it.

"What do we do now?" That, I need to know. There's a part of me who says we'll do this. She can be my girlfriend and it will be enough because we'll talk every day. But then, there's the realist in me. The one who knows there are no promises. That we're fucking young and she's here with Alec and there's a real possibility that maybe he's better for her than I am.

"We keep living. There's nothing we can do, Nathaniel. You'll go back home and you'll meet girls and you'll play baseball and be happy and I'll be here. I'll work with my dad and hang out with Alec and life will just...keep going."

"I hate it." I kiss her forehead.

"I do, too."

We stand there for as long as we can before heading back. She wipes her eyes a couple times and I wish I was doing it for her. Or kissing her tears away. When we get close to the cabins, I grab her hand and we stop. "I think...if things were different. If we were closer... You'd be it for me, Star Girl. Is that stupid to say? That I think I could love you?"

She shakes her head and she's crying more now. I don't like seeing the tears blur her green eyes. "No, it's perfect."

Charlotte pushes up on her toes and presses her lips to mine. Then, without a word, she walks away. I stand there, watching her go.

Summer Three

He met a girl in September, only a few weeks after school started. I could see it in his face while we Skyped. He didn't have to tell me because I knew, but he did anyway. He's honest like that. When he told me he wished it could be me, I believed him. When I went to Homecoming with Lance, Nathaniel told me I looked beautiful in my dress. When Dad was diagnosed with multiple sclerosis in November, Nathaniel called to comfort me. When Mom and Sadie left us, we stayed on the phone all night. Nathaniel's girlfriend Hailey came and went, as did the next one, Monica. Lance and I went out for three months before it ended. Alec had a girlfriend for a while, too. I found our betta fish belly up one morning. The only thing that stayed the same that year was us—how I felt about Nathaniel.

Charlotte Gates
Chapter One

"Thank you!" The bald man takes a key for the cabin he rented before walking out. I turn to Alec.

"Are all the cabins clean?" I ask. "We need to make sure we double check all the empty ones and replace linens for current guests, oh, and what time does your mom have to leave today?" Maggie helps out a lot now that Mom and Sadie are gone. His dad once in a while too, but it's harder for Randy because he has a fulltime job. Plus, him and Alec aren't getting along as well as they used to. I'm not sure why.

Alec grabs my arm as I turn to pick up the piece of paper that's hung in the office where Alec's mom writes down the hours she can help.

"Charlie. Chill out. You're running around like you're on crack or something."

"I am." The words bite out of my mouth. "Did I forget to tell you I picked up the habit?"

He frowns and I immediately feel guilty. I don't know why I'm freaking out. Actually, I do know why, and it makes absolutely no sense. And even if it does, I shouldn't be taking it out on Alec. It's not his fault Nathaniel is coming today and I can't seem to get my head straight about it.

"I'm sorry," I say at the same time Alec asks, "What's wrong with you?"

Then the light bulb goes off in his head. "Oh, yeah. Lover boy comes today."

Now I have a reason to be annoyed with him. He's not my lover boy...though I do wish he was. "It has nothing to do with Nathaniel. It's the fact that we're busy."

Alec shakes his head as if to say, 'yeah right'.

"Why do you hate him so much?" I ask. "He's never done anything to you."

"I don't hate him." Crossing his arms, Alec leans against the counter.

"Sure you don't."

"I hate the way you look at him. The way you treat him like he's perfect or something." He turns to leave, but this time it's me who grabs his arm. I don't have time to reply because he's speaking again. "You're different with him, and you know it. I just don't want you to get hurt. What do you think is gonna happen? You guys live totally different lives. He uses you while he's here. When he's home, he's going out with girls and—"

"How do you know that? It's not like you talk to him. Plus, why shouldn't he? We're not together. You didn't seem to care when I went out with Lance!"

Alec sighs, a strange sort of sadness changing his facial features. "Because Lance wouldn't hurt you. He wouldn't leave you. This is it for you and me, Charlie. We both know it. Especially since..."

I hold up my hand and Alec stops talking. We both know what he was going to say. Especially since Dad was diagnosed. How could he ever do it on his own? It sends an ache deep into my bones.

I open my mouth to reply, but a bell dings and Dad comes through the door. He does good most days and today is one of them. He gives Alec and I a huge smile, which I know he doesn't really feel. Not since mom left and his body stopped working the way it used to.

"What are you guys up to?"

Alec recovers first. "Deciding on a schedule for the cabins."

Another fake smile from Dad. "I don't know what I would do without you two. You make a good team."

Dad winks at me and then walks away.

I'm nervous all day. It's so different talking to Nathaniel than it will be seeing him again. Nine months of talking, of Skyping, but that's safe, because I have no idea how to act or what to do in person. Our second summer, we held hands and he kissed me and he told me I was perfect, but nine months is a long time. There have been girls for him and, well, a boy for me, so what the heck do I expect?

Alec's out on a boat tour right now, and his mom's in the store. Dad had to run to town, so it's just me working on getting the cabins ready. I keep checking the time on my new cell phone. It's important that I have one now, Dad says. That way we can keep in touch, which means he needs to be able to contact me if he needs me.

Every few minutes that pass, my gut churns more and more. They're late. What if something happened? What if they changed their minds and don't come?

Why can't I ever stop thinking about Nathaniel?

Once the cabins are done, I go in to check on Maggie. She's fine to stay until the shop closes at five, she tells me. We close early the night of the welcome party.

Alec and I start to decorate, and soon Dad is home helping, too. I watch him to make sure he's not struggling. There are days his hands don't work right or one of his legs goes weak. You can tell he's in pain, but he tries to hide it and as horrible as it makes me feel, I try to pretend I don't notice. Drawing attention to it only upsets him. Plus, I'm not really sure how to deal with it.

"What time were they supposed to check in?" Alec stands on stepladder, hanging the lights. The back of his blond head is to me and though there isn't any sarcasm in his voice, I still don't want to talk to him about Nathaniel.

"Why do you care?"

"Awesome. Because I never care about anything that has to do with you. You're not my best friend or anything, Charlie."

Guilt hangs like a weight from my heart. "I'm sorry. You know I love you, Alec. Its just...there's a lot."

Alec climbs from the ladder, steps up to me, and grabs my hand. "I'm sorry, Charlie. You know that. About your dad and your mom...you know I'm always here for you. I'll always be here."

My eyes feel wet all of a sudden and I squeeze his hand. I know that. I do, but it makes me kind of sad. Then I feel like a bitch for even thinking it. "Thanks, Alec." And it's true. Alec is Alec and Nathaniel is Nathaniel. They each hold different places in my heart and life.

The sound of tires on gravel comes from behind Alec. We both let go of each other's hand, and turn to see who's pulling in. It's a different car than they had the last two years, but I remember Nathaniel telling me a couple months ago that his dad was having a mid-life crisis and bought a new car. I get what he's saying now when I see the bright red convertible pull in.

Alec and I stand side-by-side watching the car. I don't know what he's thinking, but I know where my eyes are. The top is down and Nathaniel's brown hair is windblown in the back. Brandon is sitting beside him, which shocks me. Nathaniel told me he wasn't coming. He's eighteen and off to college next year. With Sadie being gone, him not coming made sense.

A little pang hits me when I think about my sister and my mom, but then my eyes are drawn to Nathaniel again and seeing him sends a wave of happiness, which eclipses the pain.

Nathaniel gets out of the car and turns, his eyes meeting mine. My heart jumps, dances, and then my feet are moving. I don't let myself think about it, I just run to him. I knew I missed him, but didn't realize how much until I saw his playful grin.

He holds out his arms and I jump into them. As we hug and the first thing I think of is, whoa, his body feels firmer, and then I think he feels taller, too.

"Hey, Star Girl," he whispers against my ear, and I can't help, but think of that last night before he left. I little stab of jealousy pierces me as I wonder if he did any of that with Hailey or Monica, but I try to push it aside because he's here and that's what matters.

"Hey."

Nathaniel is holding me by my waist. My feet are off the ground and I wonder if he can feel my heart going crazy. And then I think about my breasts pressed against his chest and the fact that they've grown over the last year.

My cheeks flush, which makes me remember the fact that we're not alone. His parents are here and Brandon is looking at me over the car and I left Alec behind me. I don't even want to think about Dad seeing us. It's just a hug, but I know he doesn't get my friendship with Nathaniel.

"Sorry," I say as I slide out of Nathaniel's arms. His eyebrows crease together and my stomach flips. I've seen him over the computer all year. At least once a week, but it doesn't change that fact that I want to stare at him. Study all the ways he's changed and how much older he looks.

He's always been cute to me, but now he looks more like a man.

"Look at you! You've grown so much!" Nathaniel's mom says. She's hardly spoken a word to me in the past couple years, but maybe that's because she's never seen me attack her son before.

"Thank you, Mrs. Chase."

"You don't have to call her that," Nathaniel says as his mom offers, "Please, call me Judy."

"Oh...okay. Thank you, Judy."

Alec is the only person my age that doesn't call my dad Mr. Gates.

Everyone except Nathaniel and I start talking and moving toward the trunk, discussing bags and keys and everything else. When Alec joins us, I'm afraid to look at him and see the disappointment there. I did nothing wrong. Nathaniel's my friend.

My friend who I've been in love with for two years.

"Sorry we were late. Everything in the world went wrong." Nathaniel moves forward like he's going to reach for me, but then lets his hand fall again.

"It's okay." *Stop staring, stop staring, stop staring.*

"It's good to see you, Star Girl." And then his hand really does come forward. He pushes a piece of hair behind my ear, making me tremble. It feels so different than it would have last year, deliberately sexy, and briefly I wonder just how much practice he's had.

"You too."

"Are you planning on helping us or what, man?" Brandon says and Nathaniel drops his hand.

"I need to get back to work anyway," I tell him. "Will I see you tonight?"

Nathaniel winks at me. *Winks.* I don't remember him ever doing that before. Then he whispers. "I'm yours every night for the rest of the summer."

I know he means it playfully—that he means it as a good thing, but I can't help the sadness that sprouts from the buried roots inside me. The summer just began, and I already dread him leaving.

Chapter Two

We have a huge turnout for the summer bash. Part of me can't help but wonder if it's because the locals feel sorry for us. They all know Dad's diagnosis. They also know Mom left him soon after. It was the one thing to push her over the edge, I think. One more thing she couldn't handle.

Because it's so busy, I don't have time to do a lot of visiting. Dad needs me more than ever now and it seems like every two seconds he's calling me away for something. Alec helps too, of course, but like always he's into being around everyone else. He keeps making his way back to the group of people from school, which Brandon and Nathaniel are hanging out with.

It was a big deal when Danielle found out Nathaniel was coming back. Last year she wanted him to swim with her and the year before she was into him at the drive-ins. I kind of wanted to lie to her. Or ban her from the bash. Anything, because I know she likes him, but I have to keep reminding myself that Nathaniel isn't mine.

"I'm yours every night for the rest of the summer."

Bands of silky heat wrap around me at the memory of those words.

"Boo."

I jump, even though I immediately recognize the voice. "I was just thinking about you." I turn to look at him, but then wondered if I should have said that or not. What if he wonders what I was thinking?

"Good. Your friend won't stop hitting on me. I kept hoping you would come save me."

A burn of jealousy scalds me that she gets to flirt with him while I'm working, but I try to ignore it. There's a difference in his voice. He talks to me in a way he didn't before. This flirtatious edge that he must have practiced a lot since last year. "You're a flirt now. Oh God. Say it isn't so. Who stole my best friend?"

I turn and pretend to walk away, but Nathaniel's hands on my waist stop me. "Hey. I'm not—"

"Charlie Rae! The oil is running low on the torches." Dad's voice is firm and I wonder if he really needs me as much as he wants me to think. Or if he just doesn't want me around Nathaniel.

"I'll help you." Nathaniel lets go of me and I don't argue with him. If Dad's going to keep me busy all night, I'm going to let Nathaniel stay with me as long as he wants. I deserve that much. It's just the summer. All I really think about are my summers with him.

We fill the tiki torches, and then fix a strand of lights that fell down. After that, the trash bags need to be replaced. I feel guilty for not telling Nathaniel to go hang out with everyone else. I give so much to everyone else that I want to grab onto whatever time I can have with him. It's the one thing I get that's for me.

Only once does Alec come over and offer to help, which partially makes me mad, but also doesn't. It's nice not to feel like I'm letting him down, but it also sucks that he seems to hate Nathaniel an awful lot, but only when it suits him.

Before I know it, the party is winding down and people are leaving. Once our friends are gone, Alec and Brandon find their way over to us and Alec starts cleaning up like he would have any other time.

"What do you need me to do?" Brandon asks.

Umm, what? I don't think Brandon has offered to help me with anything or even talked to me much in all the time I've known him. He must see that knowledge on my face because he adds, "What? I help."

"Yeah fucking right." Nathaniel laughs.

"You don't have to help. It's not your job. You're on vacation." I don't do pity real well and that's the only thing I can think of for him to hang around like this. Nathaniel must have told him everything that happened and obviously he knows Sadie isn't here.

"Doesn't matter." He shrugs. "You guys are all out here so what else am I going to do?"

"Don't argue with free help," Nathaniel adds before bending to put his mouth close to my ear. "The sooner we get done, the faster we can disappear."

Disappear. With Nathaniel. How much would I really love to disappear from this place? To leave and go where I want and do what I want without having my past and my family crumble apart. Family? I can't even say that. It's only Dad.

"You kids go on and head in. You don't have to help. Charlie, Alec, and I have it." Dad places one hand on my shoulder and one on Alec's. Misplaced guilt suddenly slithers down my spine. I feel bad standing here, with link between Alec and I when Nathaniel is standing right there, and I shouldn't.

"We don't mind—"

"It's not right," Dad cuts Nathaniel off. "You guys have better things to do."

But I don't. Never me.

"The Village isn't your responsibility."

But it's mine, even though I didn't ask for it.

"Yes, sir." Brandon tells him. Nathaniel doesn't say anything to him at all, but he eyes my dad. I have no idea if Dad notices, if anyone who didn't know Nathaniel like I do could read his face. *She has things she wants to do, too. It isn't her responsibility*, his look says. If it's possible for me to fall more in love with Nathaniel Chase, this is the second I do it.

"Come on, bro. Let's go." Brandon claps a hand down on Nathaniel and in that moment, I envy their relationship. Most of the time they're picking on and fighting with each other, but right now, I see that they would do anything for one another. I wish I had that with Sadie. Turning, they start to walk away, but don't get very far before Nathaniel stops and looks back at me. "I'll see you soon, Charlotte."

Dad frowns.

And just like that, he disappears into the night.

I want nothing more than to go with him.

Nathaniel is standing outside my window when I crawl out. I almost scream, but he puts a finger to his lips as if to say "shh." He takes my hand and we walk around the side of the house to the stretch of beach by the lake before taking the path we've walked together so many times. He has a duffle bag in his hand, and I can't help but wonder what's in it.

Does he expect a repeat of our last night together?

Do I want one? Risking a quick glance at his tall frame and the rougher jaw than he used to have, I admit that I do. I want just about anything I can have with Nathaniel Chase.

We're quiet when we get to our spot. I open my backpack and lay the blanket out, still wondering what he has in his. Nathaniel opens his backpack and pulls out another bag, this one long and slim.

"I got you something, Star Girl."

I love the nickname. Love it so much. He's started saying it more since last year. Almost every email or instant message.

"You shouldn't have," I say, because I can tell by the shape of the bag, what it is. "It's too much. I could never..." I shake my head. I could never get him something like that.

"You deserve it," is all he says before handing the bag over.

My fingers shake as I open it and see the beautiful white telescope inside. "Nathaniel..."

"I wanted to. It's a good one. I did research on them before I bought it and this one is—"

"Expensive."

"Perfect," he adds. "For you. You'll love it. I want you to have it."

I need to feel my arms around him again. I set the bag down and lock my hands behind his neck. He pulls me close, holds me tight and lifts me off the ground.

"I do love it," I say into his hair. He squeezes me tighter and I wish he would never let me go. "Thank you."

I feel his lips on the side of my head before he pulls away and looks at me. "It's different with you. You know that, right? You said I flirt more now, but I'm never playing games when I'm with you."

He touches my hair. Pushes it behind my ears and I love the fact that he can hold me up with only one arm. "I know." It sucks so bad to know that. To know he does care about me, and that he does see me as a best friend, but can still be with other girls and have a life separate from me, the way I have to with him. He talks to me about everything and wants to know every piece of my world. That doesn't come around often. My parents were together since they were in high school and they didn't have that. It should be freeing and make me float, but it doesn't change anything. That's what makes it harder and that's what sucks.

It's not that I think Nathaniel loves me. I know no matter what he'll be happy and he'll live his life and do whatever it is he wants to do, but...I think he *could* love me. Actually, I know he could. I think we could be happy together. Even if we stayed just friends, there will always be this bond between us that no one can ever replace, but it doesn't count when I know I'll be so far away. That I'll never have as much of him as I have during our summers ever again. Why would he come back when he isn't with his family?

"Good," he whispers. "I really want to kiss you right now, Star Girl, but I don't know if I should...I don't want you to think I'm using you. I dated those other girls, but the second I see you, it's like there's no one else in the world, like there never has been anyone else."

I don't think I will ever in my life hear words that fill me up so much. Pump me full of happiness the way what he just said does. It doesn't make sense that I, Charlie Rae, could mean so much to someone like Nathaniel, but I trust him and know he always means what he says.

So I don't answer him. I don't wait for him to kiss me. I kiss him instead.

We move together quickly. This frenzied, messy kiss is filled with passion, bridging last summer and this summer and trying to wipe all the distance and time from between us. Our lips fight to make it disappear. Our tongues tasting and exploring to remember, so it feels like yesterday when our lips last met instead of nine months ago.

He pulls me tighter against him as his mouth leaves mine. It trails down my neck, his rough voice saying, "Put your legs around me."

So I do and it feels bad and good at the same time. No, not bad, *naughty,* but then I remember he's seen me without my shirt on and this is nothing compared to that. This is Nathaniel so it doesn't matter. I'd trust anything with him.

He walks, backing me up and I wonder where he's going or why we're not laying down, or standing still when he presses my body between a tree and him.

"I don't want to drop you." His breath on my neck. "Not that you're heavy."

And then we're laughing before he says, "I should have known you wouldn't take it that way. Not you." And then he's kissing my throat and behind my ear and it's crazy how one set of lips can feel so different than another. Lance's touches didn't affect me like this. If I was blind and deaf I would still know the difference between Nathaniel's mouth and anyone else's.

"Why didn't you just lie down on the blanket?" I drop my head back and then he's laughing against my skin again.

"Because I'm stupid and anxious and didn't think about it."

He kisses me again and it's a little slower this time. Still all passion and wonderful, but like we have a little more time. I play with the hair at the nape of his neck, and savor how he tastes and wish that I'd never kissed another guy since him and that he'd never touched any other girls.

All too soon, the kisses stop, but he doesn't pull away. "Does it make me an asshole if I say I hate Lance, even though I've never met him? Because I do."

"No, because I can't stand Monica or Hailey."

I wonder how many people have this kind of honesty. If it's normal to be able to just say what's on your mind to the person you care about. Even though I'm not sure if he loves me, I know I could tell Nathaniel that I love him. Even if he didn't feel the same, it wouldn't change things and I think that's kind of a miracle. Still, those are words I won't let myself say. Not when I know I won't leave The Village.

"Do you wanna try your telescope?" he asks.

I can't stop the grin that pulls at my lips. I really, really don't want to let go of him, but I want to look into infinity with him too.

"I take that as a yes."

I unravel my legs from around him. Before he steps away, I touch the star at his throat. "Do they know anything about me?" It's a stupid question to ask, but one I'm curious about. "I know they wouldn't know details...but just that there is a girl name Charlotte out there, who knows you too?"

I wonder if that question makes me sound weak, but I don't think being honest makes people weak. It's lies that do that.

He touches my hair again and I like that it's starting to be his thing with me. "Everyone knows about Charlotte from the lake. I wouldn't hide you."

"I'm glad you're here," I tell him. He answers with a swift kiss to my lips before leading me to the blanket, where we explore the sky together.

Chapter Three

Dad has to take more breaks than he used to. He struggles with some of the same work, but we don't talk about it. All of us pretend it's not the case.

For the next week I spend my days with Dad and Alec and my nights with Nathaniel. We don't stay out late because we both need sleep and morning comes too quickly, but we have our time and there's always kissing and there's always talking which are two of my favorite things to do with him. He asks questions and makes jokes and he feels more like the Nathaniel from our first summer than our second. Not that I don't love them both.

It sucks that so much of my time is now spent working, but then I think about Alec and how much freedom he's sacrificing and I feel guilty. All that guilt is wiped away when I remember he, at least, gets paid to do it.

My cell vibrates against my hip and without looking, I know its Nathaniel. I gave him my number and we spend a lot of our time texting. His parents seem to have realized Brandon's out of the house next year, on a football scholarship, and have been out spending family time with them every day that they've been here so far.

Pulling my cell out, I take a quick peek at it.

FYI, I'm coming to talk to your dad.

He's coming to talk to my dad? I type out a quick question mark, but my reply is their car pulling up to their cabin. All four Chases climb out and Nathaniel looks toward me, the sun shining from behind him, and smiles.

"Hey, Mr. Gates. Hey, Charlotte." Nathaniel holds out his hand and my dad grudgingly shakes it.

"How's your summer going so far, Nathaniel?" Dad's question surprises me. I've never really understood why he is so standoffish with Nathaniel, but we all know he is.

"It's going well. I go by Nate now, though."

The shovel falls out of my hand at that. I know last year his family started calling him Nate, but he didn't like it. My mind flashes back to our Skype sessions, when Brandon or one of his friends would walk in. They all called him Nate.

Bending over, I pick up the shovel, suddenly a little annoyed that he didn't tell me. That maybe he's wishing I called him something other than what I do.

Nathaniel's eyes dart toward mine, but then settle on my dad again. "I wanted to talk to you about helping Charlotte out around here sometimes. When I'm not out with my family, I'm always looking for something to do. I—"

"That's okay. I appreciate the offer, but it wouldn't be right." Dad's voice sounds different. Not the annoyance he usually shows where Nathaniel (or Nate?) is concerned, almost regret.

"With all due respect sir, I don't see how it's any different than Alec working. I've been around enough. I love it out here. A little extra money never hurts."

Dad sighs, making me turn to study him. See the beads of sweat on his forehead and the tiredness in his features. Suddenly, I want to cry. I didn't cry when he was diagnosed or when Mom and Sadie left, but my eyes beg for release right now.

"I can't pay very much."

Those words mean so much more than anything else he's said or done because last summer, he never would have said them. He never would have considered letting Nathaniel help out. He would have been too proud. What does it mean that he's not too proud anymore?

"I don't need much. It really just gives me something to do and a little spending money."

That we both know he doesn't need.

"Your parents okay with it?"

"Yes, sir."

Dad nods, and the expression on his face almost looks like it says, *thank you*. I wipe my eyes, realizing a tear broke free. I need it gone, not wanting him to know that I see what's going on. That already he worries about how much he can handle. Are things progressing faster than we thought? Is he having a harder time then he admits?

Is he going to need me even more?

"We'll fill out some papers later, okay? If you want to help Charlie out now, I'd really appreciate it."

Just like that, Dad is gone and Nathaniel starts working with us.

"Do you want me to call you Nate?" I ask Nathaniel as we sit by the old fort. I'm not sure why we came out here tonight. It's much easier to stick to the lake, but I didn't bring my scope, and I always feel like we're more alone out here.

We're lying on the blanket. I'm on my back, Nathaniel on his side, leaning on his elbow, his other hand on my stomach. I love how we just fell into this easy closeness. Both last year and the year before we had this awkward time where neither of us could get it together. It's part of being older I guess.

"Why do you ask that? Because of what I told your dad today?"

"Yeah."

"I want you to call me whatever you want to. Whatever comes naturally. It really doesn't matter either way." Leaning forward, he kisses my forehead. "Nate and Nathaniel are the same person."

"I wish Charlotte and Charlie were," I blurt out and then immediately want the words back.

"They are. Charlie wants the same things Charlotte does."

"I know. And I do. I don't think I did two years ago."

"It's wild that I've been coming here for three years. You had that deer in the headlights look the first time I saw you.

Then you looked a little sick and I was scared you were going to puke on me."

"Shut up!" I push him, but he laughs and grabs me. Rolls with me until I'm on top of him.

"I still thought you were hot."

Hmm, I think I could get used to hearing that. "You did not."

"I thought you were cute and I was intrigued by you. One look at you, Charlotte, and I knew there was something different about you. You weren't like any other girls I knew. You were like this mixture of badass and..."

"Lost," I fill in for him.

"Nope. You know your way. You just need to take it."

At the thought of what he's suggesting, I groan and roll off him, missing the feel of his body. "He's worse, Nathaniel. Something's going on he's not telling me about, or he's scared or something. He wouldn't have let you help if that wasn't the case."

Nathaniel moves and sits up next to me. "I hate that, Star Girl. It fucking sucks, but...it's not your fault. You shouldn't sacrifice your whole life because of it."

Now I push to my feet, walking over to stand next to the creek. Words rattle around in my head, but I can't make sense of them so I don't say anything. Instead I look up to the sky.

"What is it about stars that you love so much?" he asks.

That answer comes quickly. "Because they're infinite. They're miracles, and anything is possible when you look out into the massive space that goes on and on." Because I want that. I want to explore and see what's out there and feel as free as those stars in the sky.

"You can have that. You deserve it. Alec loves it here. He's a bastard, but he's like family to you. He can stay."

"Don't," I shake my head.

"Char—"

"I can't do this with you. Not right now, okay? I just...I just want to be with you right now."

His arms wrap around me and pull me close. "I don't mean to push. And I definitely want to be with you, too."

When he kisses me, I forget everything else. It's like my stars times a million. He makes me forget how things are. Forget what I've lost, and how I'm scared that, without him, I'll always feel as alone as I do when he's not here.

Chapter Four
July

Nate works with us at least a couple days a week. It's not all day, but it's enough that we get to see each other a lot more which, according to him, was the whole reason he brought it up to Dad.

It's hard being with him in the daytime and not having the same kind of relationship that we have during our nights. No kisses, no touches. We talk about things that don't matter, and even though he doesn't flirt back, I have to see girls hit on him. And I have to remember that I'm the one who wanted it this way. That when he started working with us, I didn't want to deal with Dad or Alec or anyone else so I pushed to keep anything that's more than friendly to our nights.

Easier said than done.

The other day I sprayed a girl from my school with a hose and then had to pretend it was an accident. I've never been so mortified in my life, and all Nate did was pull me behind a building and whisper in my ear. "I want everyone to know you're mine, too. Just so you know."

He put the ball in my court, but I've been afraid to do anything with it. Admitting it makes it more real. And Dad will freak out and Alec will be worse. It's stupid, but I can't help how I feel.

Around six, one evening in early July, a truck pulls up, packed with people from school. They're all people Nate and Brandon have met before. Guys from Alec's football team and girls I pretend to know how to relate to.

Matt, stands up in the back of the truck and yells, "Where's Alec? We wanna a plaaaaaay baaaaaall!"

"Douchebag. That's baseball," Nate mumbles to me. I practically hear Alec perk up from where he's standing about fifty feet away from us. His football sensor is going off.

"We're in! Let me hit up Brandon!" Alec jerks out his phone and starts sending a text.

"God forbid two football obsessed guys play a game without each other."

Nate doesn't reply, so I look over at him to see he's staring at me. One of his eyebrows goes up and he has a mischievous look on his face.

"What?" I ask.

"We're playing."

"Yes, sir?" I tease and he rolls his eyes.

"Don't act like that. I know you wanna play. Plus, it gives me an excuse to be able to tackle you."

My neck heats. I still can't make myself stop blushing with him. "We play flag football."

"That's good, because I might freak out a little if someone else tackled you, but on the other hand, oops. My bad. I didn't mean for you to end up under me like this, Star Girl."

More heat. And excitement.

"What if we're on the same team?" I ask, trying to be flirty with him and not sure if I'm pulling it off or not.

Nate shrugs. "We will be. Did I ever tell you I have a problem with accidentally tackling my own team?"

I smirk, thinking there might not be anything in the world a good as being on the same football team with Nate.

I'm not a violent person, but I really, really want to kill Danielle. Logic doesn't matter. Who cares that she doesn't know I'm with Nate. Am I really with Nate? He leaves in August and he has a life several states away. I try to have one here. It's not like I expect a seventeen-year-old guy to try to have a long distance relationship, but for now, yes, we're together. And if she doesn't stop trying to stand by him in every huddle and talk to him every two seconds, I'm likely to lose it for the first time in my life.

I'm not jealous. I'm not jealous. I'm not jealous.

"Nate, over here! I'm open!" Danielle calls. Never mind that she really is open, I hate that he throws her the football.

I'm totally jealous.

Danielle drops the ball and I almost cheer. What is wrong with me? She's on my team. I shouldn't be cheering when she misses the ball.

"What's wrong?" Nate asks a few minutes later when we take our places, ready for the other team to come at us.

"Nothing."

When I try to keep walking, he grabs my waist. Nerves push at my jealousy and I step back, not wanting to have to deal with Alec finding out Nate and I are whatever we are.

"Whatever," Nate replies. I can't blame him for not pushing. For turning and walking away because not only has he done nothing wrong, but I'm the one who stepped away from him. Who lied to him. That doesn't stop it from hurting.

The game keeps going. I'm dirty and sweaty. The game is tied and Nate hasn't tried to talk to me anymore.

I can't stop thinking that he tried to touch me and I stepped away. My head isn't in the game and even though we manage to stop them, I'm not sure how.

Our ball.

We get into our huddle, like we ever really do what we say we're going to do anyway. I run up the field, dodging Alec. He's strong, and fast, but I'm hoping to keep myself ahead of him.

"Charlie!" someone yells and when they do, I turn to see the ball flying in the air at me. It's over thrown a little so I'm still running, trying to grab it, and before I even have the chance to reach for the ball, I hit the ground.

Hard.

"Shit! I'm sorry, Charlie. I couldn't stop." Matt's tangled in me and even though there's a little bit of pain in my back from hitting the ground, I'm okay.

Slowly, I try to stand as Matt does the same. "It's cool. No—"

'*Worries*' doesn't have time to come out of my mouth before Nate's yelling, "What the fuck, man!"

And then Matt stumbles back as Nate pushes him.

"Dude, it was an accident!" Matt yells back.

By then I'm to my feet. Brandon gets to Nate before me and grabs his arm. "Chill out, bro."

"Did you see how hard he hit her?" Looking back at Matt, he shouts, "You need to watch what the hell you're doing."

Nate turns to me, right as I step up to him. "It's cool. I'm good." Maybe this makes me sound like a bitch, but it feels good to have him stick up for me. That he cares that much, but I also don't want him and Matt fighting.

I wonder why I won't risk Dad or Alec's wrath so everyone would know that, for now, he's with me.

"I'm good." Then I push up on my toes and press my lips to his. It's a quick kiss, but that's all we need. Danielle gasps, Brandon laughs and...nothing at all comes from Alec. It doesn't matter. None of it. Nothing but Nate and me.

"Oh, I got you." Matt says with a laugh.

Nate shrugs. "Sorry, man." We all start moving again.

"Our ball," I say to everyone else, and then to Nate, "Let's do that play again. This time, you and me. I won't get hit again."

The look he gives me makes my heart stutter. It's something like...awe. But then, what reason would he have to look at me like that?

"Let's do it."

When I look over, Brandon's hand is on the back of Alec's neck and as they walk back to their side of the field, he kind of shakes him, like boys do trying to pump each other up or whatever. If they're talking about Nate and me, I don't care. If they're making a plan to defend me, they're not going to have a chance.

A few minutes later, I'm running down the field again. Nate's arm goes back and he throws the ball at me, and it's perfect. It falls right into my arms as I pass everyone to make a touchdown. And, somehow, Nate is right behind me. He grabs me and lifts me up. We don't kiss again, but we don't have to. We don't win the game either, but it doesn't matter. Right now, I feel like I've won the world.

"I can't believe you didn't tell me!" Danielle says. "I mean...I wondered for a little while last year, but then nothing happened and you never said anything. Why the hell didn't you stake your claim on that boy? He's hot. Oh, wait...didn't you date Lance last year?"

I glance at Danielle. I don't even know how to reply to all of that. "This is...new." Though it's not really. We've been dancing around it since the first summer. Nate feels as much a part of my life as breathing. "Kind of new this year. He's only here for the summers though."

"Awww! So have you guys have, like, this secret love affair every summer? Only one more year left until you finish school, though. Then you can go to college together and live happily ever after!"

Her enthusiasm is freaking me out a little bit, not to mention the pain that her "happily ever after" vision conjures up inside me.

"Poor Alec... I've always thought he was secretly in love with you."

I throw a glance over my shoulder to see all the guys are still standing in the middle of the field.

"Alec's not in love with me." I don't think. Could he be? Could Alec really be in love with me instead of it being about The Village and our friendship? No, it's been too much time. He would have told me.

"Heads up!" Nate yells. The football that Brandon brings every year comes flying at me and I catch it before tossing it into the truck. I think I hear Danielle say, "swoon" before walking back to everyone.

"I'm totally going to kiss you right now. Watching you play football gets me hot." Nate says into my neck and I can't help but laugh. He feels good. No, incredible, like he always does.

Chapter Five

It's 8:30 when we get back to The Village. Alec's mom had been the one to tell Dad they could handle things for a while if we went to play football and now she's sitting on the back deck with him and Alec's dad.

"I should probably go over there," I tell Nate, who gives me a nod.

"I should probably check in with my parents and see what's going on."

We nod like we both aren't sure how to act. It's one thing to show affection in front of our friends, but Dad is a whole different story. Nate works for him. They're renting a cabin from him. I don't think Dad would make them leave, but what if he did?

"See you tonight, Star Girl." Nate winks before jogging over and playfully shoving his brother. They screw around back and forth while they're walking to their cabin. I can't stop myself from watching them until the door closes.

"Can we talk?" Alec asks and I jump, unable to believe I forget he was standing so close.

"Sure." I shrug.

"We're going to go for a walk!" he calls to our parents, who just nod and smile without a second thought.

"I don't want you to get hurt," is the first thing out of Alec's mouth when we hit the beach. He automatically walks the opposite direction as I go with Nathaniel and as ridiculous as it is, I'm glad.

"Nothing's changed. You can't tell me you didn't know something was going on. Seeing it doesn't—"

"Seeing it does make it more real and you know it, Charlie Rae. If you didn't really care about him, we either would have been seeing it all along, or we never would have at all. Don't pretend like I don't know you."

My eyes close for a second before, resigned, I force them to open again. "Of course you know me. We've been friends our whole lives. So...maybe you should trust me."

Alec stops walking. "What is that supposed to mean? You know I trust you."

"Do you?"

"Yeah. I don't trust *him* not to hurt you. I mean...what do you think will happen? Or what are you planning on happening? Do you not want The Village anymore?"

I never did! Not like you. Not like Dad. Not that I have a choice. Those sentences scream in my brain but I don't let any of them out. I trap them there because all they will do is cause pain.

"Nothing's changed, Alec. I know that. I would never leave Dad. You know me better than that. Nate and I both know whatever is going on will be over with the summer."

Understanding, which I didn't expect, sparks in his eyes. "I know... I hear ya. You know I love you, right? I would do anything for you. I just...don't want you to get hurt."

"I know." There has never been a doubt in my mind about that. Alec has always tried to take care of me. We've looked after and been there for each other. Even when we fight, I know it won't last long, because we just don't work that way.

Alec was the first person I ever told how I felt about my sister. The first person to get it, and tell me that I mattered. He beat up boys who called me names, and taught me how to climb trees and play ball. We will always be a part of each other's lives.

"I'll be okay, Alec. Just trust me. I can't get hurt when I know what I'm getting into."

But really, I have no idea.

"Have you made any plans for college?" I ask Nate as we lay on the blanket, the water not far from us. Rolling over to look at him, I wince, a little pain stabbing into my back.

"Your back still hurt?"

"Yeah, it wasn't that bad after Matt's hit, but then I think I lifted wrong today."

He frowns, but then his demeanor changes when he says, "Take off your shirt."

"Excuse me?" That totally came out of nowhere. Yes, I went skinny dipping with him last year and we've had some pretty heavy make out sessions this summer, but I still didn't expect that.

"I'll massage your back," he tells me.

"You don't have to do that."

"Believe me. I'm doing it for totally selfish reasons. I'll take mine off, too, if you want."

I roll my eyes. "You have your shirt off half the time anyway." He goes shirtless a whole lot more this year than he did last. I like it. But before he has the chance to do anything, I hold my breath and pull my shirt over my head. Nate's eyes go wide and I try to remind myself that I have a bra on this time.

"They're bigger," I blurt out and then almost die. Covering my face with my hands I say, "Oh my God! I can't believe I just said that."

"I can't believe you think I didn't notice." Nate laughs before pulling my hands away. "We're going to be in some serious trouble here if you don't lay on your stomach."

"Boys." Playfully, I roll my eyes before lying down. Nate straddles my butt and I'm really hoping it doesn't feel too cushiony.

"Can I undo this?" His fingers touch my back, under the strap.

The first time I try to speak, nothing comes out. The second time I manage to squeak out a, "Yes."

He does, and then his hands start kneading the tender muscles in my shoulders...down, down to my lower back before he goes up again.

"So...college. Do we really want to talk about that?"

Is it just me or does his voice sound a little rougher than it did a minute ago?

"Why not? It's an important part of your life."

"Yours, too. Don't make it sound like that. Just because you might go to community college locally doesn't mean you're not going to school."

I nod because he's right.

Nate continues, "I haven't made specific plans. I still have my whole senior year. But there are a couple places I'm considering. You know I wanna study architecture, right?" His hands keep moving, keep massaging as he talks.

"Of course I know. You told me that your first summer here. I'm not surprised you didn't change your mind—"

"—You remember that?" he cuts me off.

I wonder if it makes me sound pathetic to be honest, but I do it anyway. "I remember everything."

"Shit..." Nate curses, making me wonder what's wrong. "Will you roll over?" he asks, pushing up onto his knees so there is more room. There's only about two seconds of hesitation before I do as asked.

My bra still covers me, but it's looser being unstrapped. I expect his eyes to drift down to my boobs, but they don't. "UCLA. It's my top choice."

California. The place he knows I want to go. My heart starts going crazy because I don't know what that means. If it means anything. Maybe he's always wanted to go to California. Hell, maybe he has family there. But maybe...maybe he's saying he wants to go because I do.

"Nate—" His finger against my lips quiets me.

"Shh...Just wanted you to know." Then the look in his eyes switches and he does what I thought he would do a few minutes ago. His gaze lands on my chest. When our eyes meet again, I see the silent question there. I nod my head and with slow hands, he slides my bra off each arm before tossing it aside.

"Still perfect."

My heart does all sorts of somersaults and back handsprings that he remembers exactly what he told me last year. And then he starts kissing me. His mouth exploring more than just my lips. I arch toward him and fist my hand in his hair.

I love you, I want to tell him, but something deep inside me thinks he might already know.

Chapter Six

"Do you think I've changed?" I ask Nate one day as we're going on a hike. It's not often that guests ask us to take them, but we have a family of five who wanted to go Indian Rock. Dad named it that himself and took pictures of it before I was even born, hanging them up all over the store. It's become somewhat of an attraction now, the locals and visitors all wanting to see the tall rock up on that mountain that looks like a Native American, headdress and all.

Dad usually took any tours we had up to Indian Rock, but, well, that's one of the things that has changed. He wanted Alec to go with me, but he had something else to do, so Nate was his only choice.

Both of us were a little shocked.

"Changed like how?" he asks. The family is about ten feet behind us, but not paying much attention to what we're doing. It's then I realized we talked about how we were different on our hike last year as well.

"I don't know. Changed. Like in any way. Every year you come back you're different in one way or another. Last year you were sadder. This year you're more like you were the first summer, just..."

"Hotter? Sexier? Impossible to resist?" He grins.

"Conceited?"

He feigns shock, but then reaches for my hand. Two of our fingers link like a chain as we keep walking.

"I was going to just say more grown-up, but I'm rethinking that."

"Oh, so I'm more manly? Basically the same thing as sexier." He laughs before pulling me to him, wrapping an arm around my shoulders. "I mean, yeah you've changed in some ways. You wouldn't be normal if you didn't, but there are some things about you that are always the same."

"Like what?" I ask him.

"Your honesty. The way you say whatever's on your mind."

"Only to you."

"That's all that matters." I pinch his side and he pushes my hand away. "I'm kidding. No pinching, woman. You're adventurous in a different way than any girl I've ever met. You're comfortable playing football or looking through a telescope and telling me about the stars." He leans closer to me. "You trust me in a way no one in my life has ever done... Even when I didn't trust myself to make decisions because of Chrissy. You trusted me. Those things are the same about you, but...I guess it's like you said about me, you're more grown-up. Sometimes, I don't really know how to say what I'm trying to, but it's like you're this old soul trapped in a seventeen year old's body. I think you see the world different than anyone I know, Charlotte Rae Gates."

I look over at him. "I don't want to see it differently."

"Why?" he asks. "It's one of my favorite things about you. You wanna see and do so much, but you have this kind of nobility or something about you that makes you put all your dreams aside for other people. I couldn't do that. Not many people could."

I think that might be the best compliment I've ever received. "No one makes me feel like you do," I tell him.

He looks down at me as we keep walking up the mountain. "You do the same thing to me, Star Girl."

"I..." Before I can continue, my foot comes down the wrong way on a rock. I fall forward, but Nate catches me. I wonder if one day, I'll ever be able to catch myself.

"My brother wants to go camping, Charlotte. He told me to ask you if you can hook it up. I think he's feeling lonely because he's stuck in his room every night alone."

Brandon flips Nate off. "Screw you. That has nothing to do with it. I just thought it would be fun, you asshole."

Nate laughs, but then he turns to me, looking panicky. "I didn't mean...not because we're out or every night or...shit." Something else seems to hit him. He leans down so his mouth is by my ear and whispers. "I'm an asshole. I shouldn't have said it that way because of your sister."

Because of Sadie leaving. I get it, reaching over, my hand grabs his shirt by his stomach. "No worries. I know what you meant."

I turn my head, "Brandon, I'm not inviting girls on a camping trip because you're lonely."

"That's not what I meant." He crosses his arms, looking every bit of the jock-ish, football player he is. "I just thought it would be fun to get out, but I know my brother doesn't go anywhere without you, so..."

"Would you?" Nate asks, while I say, "You guys can go camping. I don't have to tag along."

Now Nate's attention is on me. "Who said I want to go without you? I'm with him all the time."

"See!" Brandon adds.

"I used to love camping. Me, Dad, Alec and his dad went a lot when we were younger."

Nate stiffens at that. "Of course."

"I don't like him like that. I never will." It doesn't matter to me that Brandon is sitting right there when I say it. All that matters is Nate hearing it and believing it.

"Yeah, she doesn't like him like that. My baby brother is jealous of Alec."

"Screw you," Nate tells him before turning to me. "Camping could be fun."

Camping could be a blast. But... "The only way I'm going to be able to go is if I go with Alec. And Alec's probably going to have to talk him into it." Suddenly all sorts of plans are forming in my mind. Spending the night, the whole night and part of the day up in the mountains with the stars and Nate. I can't imagine anything more perfect, but...who would help Dad here?

"Your Dad would really let you go camping with Alec? Does he know guys?" Nate asks.

"He trusts him. He's known Alec his whole life."

"And he can get your dad to let you go with all of us? We'll get caught otherwise. There's no way someone's not going to realize that Brandon and I are gone, too." Nate still looks a little tense, but like he's trying to hide it.

"Dad trusts him," I say again. "And there's no promises...I can probably make it look like Danielle and some of the others are going too..." I'm suddenly really glad that I never let Dad see that there was anything more going on with Nate and me.

"We doing this?" Brandon jumps in.

Nate shrugs and I say, "Let's do it."

"You're sure you're not going to be the only girl there, Charlie Rae?" Dad asks for the millionth time. My camping supplies are all sitting by the door, waiting for us to head out.

"Yeah, Dad. We're meeting up with Danielle and some other friends." Liar, liar pants on fire. "We just want to do some fishing and sleeping out. Brandon leaves for college soon and he wants to do some different stuff before he goes."

"You can fish here."

Yes, yes we can. "But it's not the same to camp here. I live here! How many times did we used to go? It's fun to get out like that."

Dad sighs before sitting on the back of the couch. "I know, kiddo. I get it. And you deserve to have some fun. With..." he closes his eyes and I wonder if he's trying not to cry. "With your mom and sister leaving, I know that puts a lot more pressure on you."

He doesn't mention his MS and I wonder if it's on purpose. He doesn't talk to Mom when they call, only Sadie. I don't really talk to my sister, only Mom. None of us ever discus his MS. I think we all want to pretend it's not true.

"You know how much I need you, Charlie, but I want you to have fun too. That's why I'm letting you go. You work so hard, kiddo."

You know how much I need you.

I know more than I wish I did. "I know, Dad. I want to be here for you."

He nods and then I hear Alec's voice outside.

"I better go. You'll have help here, right?"

Alec's parents are helping while we're gone. I know that, but have to ask anyway.

"I'll be okay. You just have fun."

Dad follows me outside and walks almost to the truck with me, but stops at Alec.

"Take care of her, son." He touches Alec's shoulder. "I'm trusting you."

My eyes lock with Nate's. His face says everything I need to know. He heard. And it hurt him.

"Absolutely. You know I'd do anything for Charlie," Alec tells him, as Nate climbs in the back of the truck with his brother.

Alec drives up to the area we used to go to when we were kids, which is about forty-five minutes away. The back of the truck is packed with tons of fishing stuff, a football (of course), along with the rest of our supplies, which includes four tents; one for me and then one for each boy, because they're guys and apparently that means they can't sleep next to each other.

We park in this little turn out and then walk a trail to look for our spot. All our hands are full and packs on our backs until we find the perfect spot nestled between a large group of trees. It's perfect because it's secluded, hidden away, but not too far from the water.

Somehow all my stuff gets tangled together as I'm trying to get my backpack off. I'm about to scream when Nate walks up to me and says, "I got it."

They're the first words he's spoken to me since before we left. He screws around with the fishing pole before getting it untangled and leaning it against a tree.

"You're free now," he says at the exact moment I'm blurting, "I'm sorry about my dad."

Nate hooks his finger in one the belt loops on my jeans. "It's not your fault, and I'm being a prick about it. It just…it fucking sucks, honestly. Remember when we talked about Monica and Hailey? It's like..."

He steps closer to me, wrapping his arms around my neck and resting his chin on my head. "Imagine seeing one of them with me every day. My parents raving about her. I know I'm going to leave and you'll still be here with him and that your lives are tied together in this way I'll never be able to have with you. That if some asshole hurts you, he'll get to be the one to protect you. And then I feel like shit for thinking all of that because he's your best friend. You've known him a whole hell of a lot longer than me."

He pauses and I slide my arms around him. Fist my hands in his shirt and wish everything he said wasn't true. That he wouldn't have to leave or that I could go. That we could have more than just our summers. I try to tell him with the way I'm holding him that I feel like that, too.

"So, yeah...that's where my head's at, and like I said, it just really fucking sucks."

"I want it to be you. I'll always want it to be you."

Nate pulls back, and for the first time there's insecurity in his face. Doubt, which is something I never expected to see from him.

"Yeah?"

"Yeah...I—"

"Come on, you guys!" Brandon steps up to us. "Do that shit later. Let's get camp set up."

The moment is broken. Nate and I pull away from each other, and get to work.

Chapter Seven

We set up the tents and pack the food away so it won't lure the bears. Brandon and Alec decide they want to go fishing so we get all the gear ready. I slip into my tent to change, putting on the new yellow bikini that I'm determined to wear today. Without a shirt over it. I don't want to be one of those girls who hides who she is. I want to be proud, because I'm me and I don't want to think there's anything wrong with that.

Still...I put on a pair of cut off shorts, because walking around in a bikini, especially if we're going to be fishing, just isn't my style.

Nate is standing by his brother and Alec when I climb out. The guys are already in their shorts and of course none of them are wearing shirts. I might be the luckiest girl on the planet right now, because all three of them are gorgeous. Nate and Brandon with their dark hair and strong builds. Alec sunny and blond, but just as muscular as the other two.

"Hey." The corner of Nate's mouth pulls up in a grin when he sees me. He walks over and in that second, I decide not to hold anything back on this camping trip. I lean up and kiss his lips.

"Perfect," he says into my hair, before we pull away.

Alec shakes his head, but then Brandon says, "Dude, cut them some slack." Obviously pissed, Alec heads toward the water. Brandon follows behind him and then Nate and I take up the rear.

It's even prettier up here than it is at The Village. Mountains surround us with the water sparkling in the middle of it. I set up the chairs while Brandon and Alec screw around with their poles, laughing over something in a way that only boys do.

"Do you want to fish or go swimming with me?" Nate asks. There's no question about what my answer will be. After unbuttoning and unzipping my shorts, I step out of them. Turning to walk toward the water, I'm suddenly swooped off the ground and Nate is running with me in his arms.

"You're going to piss off the fish!" Brandon yells.

"Go somewhere else then!" Nate isn't even looking at him as he wades into the water with me in his arms.

We spend what feels like forever and also two seconds at the same time, splashing around in the water. Nate dunks my head and I wrap arms around his neck and realize that's kind of our thing.

When we are tired of holding ourselves up, Nate runs to the shore and grabs an inner tube. Brandon and Alec have moved out of sight, giving us the space I want and keeping their precious fish calm.

When Nate gets back to me, we lie down together in the tube and float along the water.

"You and Brandon are closer than you used to be, aren't you?"

"Yeah...kind of. I'm mean, we've never really been that close. Even now. Why?" His hand splays out across my stomach.

"Because he told Alec to chill out earlier and they're not on top of us right now."

Nate shrugs. "I guess I've talked to him more about you this summer. He knows I like you, and I guess he gets it."

Rolling over, I lie with my stomach on his. My cheek on his chest, while his hands do the same thing to my back that they just did on my belly. "Are you still playing baseball your senior year?" I ask. He'd mentioned before that he wasn't sure if he would.

"That came out of the blue."

"I want to make sure I know everything about you."

So we talk. He tells me that he is playing ball because he figures he might as well continue what he started. We talk about classes and he asks when was the last time I talked to Mom and Sadie. "A couple days ago," I tell him. "They call about once a week."

We talk about stupid things like our favorite drinks and he tells me about the time he did two keg-stands at a house party and how it's the only time he's ever thrown up while drinking.

We talk about my dad, and Nate's parents and how he never would have thought he'd miss Brandon, but he's kind of bummed his brother is leaving for school. It's like any other conversation we've had. It's everything and nothing out of the ordinary too.

Suddenly, water comes splashing at us. I don't know how we didn't hear Alec and Brandon approaching. Nate rolls with me and we're off the inner tube sending water right back at them. It's the first time the four of us have really hung out like this.

Soon, the water fight is over and we're heading back to shore.

Nate and I decide we want to fish, but Brandon says he's tired and wants to go back to camp for a nap. Alec looks unsure at what to do.

"It's cool. You can chill with us if you wanna," Nate tells him, which I know isn't easy for him to say.

Brandon shakes his head. "How in the hell am I supposed to find my way back then? I didn't grow up out here like you guys."

"Idiot," Nate laughs and even Alec joins in.

"I'll help you," Alec says.

When the two of them are gone, Nate and I each sit in the chairs, side-by-side, with our poles in the water.

He's looking out at the lake, as am I. Then, out of the corner of my eye, I see him turn and stare at me...forever.

"I wanna be with you," Nate blurts out. His voice sounds a little huskier than usual, but still strong. Firm.

"What?" I thought we were already pretty much together.

"I want to be with you. I know it's stupid, but I think we should do it. We should give it a try, Star Girl. We'll talk every day and I know it'll suck and it'll be hard as hell, but how will we know if we don't try?"

My heart is beating a million miles per hour. My eyes sting, but at the same time a smile stretches across my face. "Really? How...I mean."

"We talked all year, and we *weren't* together. We'll do it when we are."

Little blips of our conversation from earlier filters in. "Is this because of Alec? I don't want—"

I actually see Nate's defenses go up.

"I don't give a shit about Alec. This has to do with you and me. What do we have to lose? We're both pretty friggin' miserable when we're not together."

I don't want to talk him out of it, but he needs to know the magnitude of what he's saying. "We'll never see each other. It's not fair... It's your senior year. You'll want to date and go to prom and..."

He shrugs. "Who cares? I want you, Charlotte. *You.* I'll be eighteen in October. I have money saved and can get plane tickets. I'll come see you. Fuck, I don't know if it'll work. I just know I wanna be with you. I don't want to say goodbye like we do every year, ya know? Maybe I'm not supposed to admit stuff like that—"

"You are," I tell him. "You so totally are."

This makes him laugh and I love it. It's impossible not to join in with the deep, throaty sound. Him being happy makes me happy and I know I'm one of the lucky ones because I feel it in the way he treats me. I know I make him feel the same way.

"I want to be with you, too. But what about college?"

He rolls his eyes at me as though I'm being crazy. "It's a year away. Stop trying to fast forward to the future. We can apply to some of the same schools, just in case. You never know what can happen. Hell, even if it's just pretend, let's do it.

I don't let myself think. Don't want to think about all the ways this can go wrong or how it will kill me if we somehow make this work for a whole year and then I lose him. But he's right. Or maybe I just want to pretend he is. If we don't give it a shot I'll always wonder—and always regret not having tried. The only thing I know is I'm opening my mouth and letting the word, "yes," jump free.

I smile and look over at him, little water droplets on his skin and his dark hair wet. Nate leans toward me. "Yeah?"

"Yes."

Then he kisses me, his tongue stroking me slowly, and it's the best, most amazing kiss he's ever given me. Maybe better than any kiss in the world.

When he pulls back he touches my hair and I know it's all messy and stringy from being wet, but I don't care.

"Holy shit, we're sappy. Maybe I should throw you over my shoulder or something to show you how manly I really am."

I push at him. "Oh my God! That doesn't make you manly, and why do boys care so much if they sound sappy once in a while? Ugh." I get up, pretending to walk away, but he hooks his arms around my waist and pulls me to his lap.

"I'll be sappy with you, Star Girl. No one knows me like you do."

Later, I'll realize I should have told him I love him. That moment would have been the perfect chance, but unlike the first time I saw him, I didn't realize this was one of my *moments*.

Instead I sit here while we finish fishing. Once we're done we go back to camp and hang out with Brandon and Alec. We cook dinner on the fire and roast marshmallows, doing all those things you're supposed to do while camping.

When it's time for bed, I don't bother with going into my tent. I climb right into Nate's with him and we spend half the night kissing, touching and exploring before we fall asleep in each other's arms.

And for once, everything feels perfect. I can forget Dad has MS, and Mom and Sadie are gone. That Dad needs me and Alec wants me to stay here with him and that in less than a month, Nate will be leaving.

We're together. We're going to stay together. For now, I'm focusing on that.

Chapter Eight
August

Each day seems to go by faster and faster. It's always in the back of my mind, and it makes my stomach ache, but not with the same ferocity it could have. It's different knowing we both want to make a go at this. Even though we're young and everyone would tell us it's stupid, we care about each other enough to try.

I think Dad knows something is going on with us, but I don't even let that bother me. Nate works with us almost every day and even though you can tell it about kills Dad sometimes, he appreciates it.

Even Alec is being okay. I don't know if it was because they got along well on the camping trip or what. It's not like they'll ever be super good friends or anything. That much is obvious, but they don't look like they want to murder each other half the time.

For once, everything feels okay. Like maybe if you want something enough or you earn it enough, maybe you can get the things you want.

Not that I think I'll be with Nate forever. We've talked about schools to apply to and wondered what it would be like, but I don't know if I really believe that will ever happen. Dad is still sick. Sadie and Mom are still gone. And I'm still needed here.

It's a slow day around The Village. It gets like that toward the end of the summer sometimes. People leave early or they stay in and relax more. Dad gave Alec the day off, and him, Nate, and I are working on the back deck of one of the empty cabins. Some of the boards are rotting out so we have to replace half of it and then stain it. Luckily it's not too big.

"Can I get your hand over here for a minute, Nate?" Dad asks him and I can't help but look up from where I'm working to watch them. They're working together the same way he would have with Alec and it makes fizzy hope bubble over inside me.

What if things could really work out? What if they aren't as hopeless as I always thought they were?

"Shit. Be careful. You almost got my thumb." Dad laughs and shakes his head playfully at Nate. "You haven't let Charlie teach you how to use a hammer, have you? She's made me lose a nail and lost one herself, getting a little over anxious."

Nate glances at me, his face full of mischief. "No, but those definitely sound like stories I'd like to hear."

"Dad! Don't," I yell which of course makes him launch into the story. Even though I pretend it bothers me, it doesn't. It's cool seeing them converse and hear Dad talking about the past. We have so many memories together and I'm lucky, so lucky, that he's taught me all the things he has. I know I wouldn't be the person I am without him.

After teasing from Nate, we get back to work again. It's not long later when Dad says, "I'll be right back. I need to stand up for a few minutes."

My eyes immediately dart to him as I watch him struggle slightly to stand. It might not be obvious to everyone, but it is to me. I flinch as Dad pushes up and the second he's to his feet, I want to die. I know it's nothing, nothing compared to how he must feel.

My eyes fill with tears as the wet spot in the font of his pants grows.

Nate turns away, picks up a tool and I know he's pretending not to notice that my dad lost control of his bladder. They said things like this could happen, but hearing it and seeing it are two different things.

Without a word, Dad drops his tool belt to the deck and walks away.

Nate is to me before right as the first tears rolls off my face and hits the deck. "Shh. Come here. It's okay. I got you."

Climbing onto his lap, I wrap my arms around his him, bury my face into his neck and give into my cries. Nate just holds me, rubs my back and tells me it will be okay. That he's sorry, but all I can think is that my dad, the big, strong man who's run The Village since he was twenty years old, the one who built a fort with me and taught me to fish and play football and drive a boat, just peed his pants when he stood up.

My legs shake as I walk into the house a little while later. Seeing Dad right now is the last thing I want to do. Maybe that's not what I should be thinking, but I am and it's not just because of me. It's for him. After what just happened, I know he wishes he'd never have to see Nate or me again.

But I also can't walk away. It's not right and no matter how hard it is, I have to try and show him that it's okay. That nothing has changed.

Yeah right.

"Hey," Dad says, changed into a fresh pair of clothes. "You might want to get changed. We're leaving soon."

Confusion pushes words out of my mouth, "Where are we going?"

"Randy and Maggie."

Huh? I have no idea why we'd be going to Alec's all of a sudden. "Okay...when will we be back?"

"Who knows, Charlie? Do you have plans I don't know about?"

Every night. "No. Let me go take a shower. I'll be out in a few minutes."

After grabbing my clothes, I lock myself in the bathroom and text Nate.

Don't know if I'll be able to make it out 2night. Dad suddenly wants to go to Alec's.

Everything cool? He asks almost immediately.

Think so. We used to go there a lot. Maybe he just misses old times?

This time it takes a minute for him to reply. **K. See ya 2morrow. Let me know if u need anything.**

Thx

Nate doesn't reply after that. I wonder if he's mad, but I don't know what he would expect me to do. I have to go with Dad.

My shower is over quickly and before I know it we're in the truck heading over to Alec's. I don't ask him about The Village—who he has working it or if he just closed it down early for tonight. None of those things really matter.

Alec and his family live in a small house about two miles from us. The short drive doesn't give us time to talk, and honestly, I'm not sure if I want to.

Dad knocks, but doesn't wait for an answer before pushing their front door open.

"We're out back!" Maggie yells, so we weave our way through their house to the deck where Randy stands in front of the grill while Alec and his mom sit at their picnic table. It's like déjà vu to so many other evenings of my life that for a second, I actually feel like I've been transported back in time.

Sadie and Mom's empty seats jerk me right back to the present.

"Charlie Rae! It's been much too long since you came to visit." Maggie hugs me. Yes, we see each other at least a few times a week because she helps at The Village, but she's right. I haven't been to Alec's house all summer.

"Hey, kiddo," Randy says.

"Hi." My reply was means for them both.

"What's up?" Alec asks when I sit down by him. Our parents are all on the other side of the deck by the grill now.

"Hey."

"Surprised you could make it away from your extension tonight." It's the first smart aleck comment he's made about Nate since the campout.

"First of all, screw you. I hate it when you're a jerk for no reason. Second," and now I lower my voice, "Dad peed his pants in front of me today, so excuse me if I'm not in the mood to fight with you."

Alec's facial expression goes hard. Not angry, but...upset? "Shit. I'm sorry, Charlie."

I shrug. "It is what it is."

Reaching over, he gives me a hug. For a few seconds, I let myself be comforted from my oldest friend.

Soon we're all eating dinner together outside. Dad is laughing with Alec's parents like nothing happened. From dinner we go into card games and it isn't long before I'm laughing, too. It's so easy, the time we spend together. Like second nature. I know his family as well as my own. His dad has always been a little more standoffish. Not rude, but he's just one of those silent, manly types who make people nervous, but still, I know he's a good guy. I know he cares about my family. For a second, I think about how much easier it would be if I loved Alec the way I do Nate.

Holy shit.

I have Dad in my sights now. Is that why we're here? Is he trying to manipulate me?

"Wanna go inside for a while?" Alec asks as though I'm not having an internal breakdown here. Without a reply I push to my feet, knowing if I stay out here, I'm not going to be able to keep my mouth shut. As much as the words want to come out, I don't want to do that in front of Alec and his family.

As soon as we get into Alec's room, I fall into the chair by his desk and he sits on the bed.

"Can't believe summer's almost over," he says.

"Yep."

"We're seniors next year."

"Uh huh." The short answers are about all I can manage right now.

"Wanna run away with me and have all my babies?"

"Sure." As soon as I reply, I realize my mistake. "Alec!"

"It's your fault. What? You can't talk to me anymore?"

My instinct is to yell at him, but there's a genuine sadness to his words. That little bit of vulnerability that Alec doesn't often show. "I just have a lot going on right now. It's not you, and you know it."

He nods, because no matter what, he really does.

"It's crazy how much things can change sometimes, isn't it? I mean...everything. It's like you expect your life to go a certain way and then you get thrown this huge curveball—"

"Baseball metaphors? You're inner football player must be pissed."

"I'm serious, Charlie. I never would have expected someone to come between us. I just...always thought no matter what, there would always be certain things I'd know. You are one of those things. I never expected that to change..."

In that moment, I see someone different in Alec than I've ever seen before. It's hard for me to even say what it is; I just know it's not the Alec I thought I knew my whole life. For the first time, it's out in the open, that the future we both thought we would fall into won't come to pass.

"You are and will always be my best friend, Alec. Please tell me you know that." Getting up, I walk over and sit next to him.

"Yeah?" he asks.

"Absolutely. Nate or no one else will ever change that. I'd do anything for you."

Alec pulls me into a hug. "I've got...there are some things going on with me too."

I cock my head and look at him. "What is it? Your dad?"

"Yes and no. Never mind. I don't want to talk about it right now."

"I'm here when you're ready."

He sighs. "I know. I love you, Charlie. You're a good friend."

Bruises cover my heart, as everything seems to drain out of me. "I love you too."

I knew nothing could stay perfect for long.

The truck is silent except for the rumble of the engine as Dad and I bump down the road.

"I'm sorry about today," he says, after what feels like an eternity.

Which part? I wonder. The thing on the deck or trying to manipulate me. "Why did we go to Maggie and Randy's tonight, Dad?"

"They're our friends—"

"Who we haven't visited forever. Why tonight?"

Dad sighs. "Look, Charlie. I'm tired and I've had a long day. If you have something to say to me, you need to just say it."

"Fine!" I cross my arms. "Did you bring me to Alec's to pressure me into wanting to stay? To remind me what I have here and..." To make me feel guilty for wanting to leave him. Or maybe not that. He has no reason to know I want to leave, but he doesn't like how things are between Nate and me. Maybe that scares him.

To my surprise, Dad whips the car over to the side of the road and turns on the interior light.

"No matter what, I'm still your father and I don't appreciate you accusing me of something like that. We went to see them because I needed it. Jesus Christ, Charlie! I pissed my pants in front of you and that kid tonight! Did you ever think how that made me feel? Maybe I just wanted a distraction. I've lost my wife, my daughter, and the ability to work all in the past year, and now I can't even control my God damned bladder!"

Dad's open hands slam down on the steering wheel. Tears are running down my face. I've never seen him get angry like this. Never heard so much pain in his voice. I feel guilty for assuming this night was about me.

"I wanted to forget and try to make myself believe things were like they used to be. Christ, I miss her. I miss them both so much, kid. I should have known. She never wanted a life here, but I thought I could make her happy. I assumed that after she left and came back to me—"

"What?" I cut him off. "When did Mom leave?"

He looks at me, his eyes as red as they were when Mom told him she and Sadie were leaving. "She was young...nineteen. I knew I loved her, even then. She left with some kid she met one summer. Two months she was gone before he broke her heart by being with another woman, and I healed it for her. There's nothing I wouldn't have done for her. I loved her in a way he never could have. So yes, maybe I did subconsciously bring you to Alec's tonight partially for that reason. You look at Nate the way your mom used to look at him. I'll be damned before I let him hurt you the same why she was hurt."

Light off.

Truck started.

Dad pulls back onto the road and starts to drive away.

My heart is too heavy and my mind too full to say anything. But there's one thing I do know: I'm not my mom, and Nate would never hurt me like that.

Chapter Nine

All the lights are off in Nate's cabin when we get home. Dad and I don't talk further and I go straight to my room.

Hey.

Hey he replies.

Just got home. What ya doing?

Lying in bed. Have fun?

No.

What happened?

Nothing...fight with Dad. See you 2morrow?

Always, Star Girl. 'Night.

Goodnight

Dad and I stand in front of the deck on the empty cabin. The completely finished deck that wasn't done when we left it yesterday.

"Wow..." Dad runs a hand over his head.

Yeah. Wow.

The parking spot in front of cabin 3B is empty. Nate texted me to let me know his parents wanted them to all hang out together today, since they'd be leaving soon. Leaving. That word pries my chest wide open.

"Did you know?" Dad asks.

"No."

There's remorse in his voice, but not enough. I know it doesn't change anything. Neither will my words. "He's a good person. He'd never hurt me like that guy hurt Mom. I'm taking the day off."

Dad doesn't reply and I don't wait. It doesn't matter that Nate won't be here until this evening. I can't spend my day with Dad. I go swimming, something I haven't done by myself in a long time. Afterward I change clothes and go for a hike, hoping my head will clear in all the open space.

Nate leaves in a week. I thought the fact that we're going to stay together would change the empty feeling inside me. It's crazy how you can feel empty and full at the same time. It's exactly what has taken me over. The emptiness fills me.

When I get back down to the house, I pack a bag with my telescope, blanket, and all the other things I bring on our nights out. Nate texts when they get back and we pick the time to meet. Dad and I have dinner together, making small talk, but he knows I'm mad and I'm not ready to be over it. Mom left. Sadie left. But I'm still stuck here. And it sucks and it's not fair and I wish he would see that.

"Hey you," Nate says after I climb out the window.

"Hey." We lock hands before I say, "Let's go to the fort tonight."

We take the same path we've taken so many times together over the past three years. The path that I wonder if we'll ever take together again. If I leave—though I don't know how I will—we might not take this walk again.

If I stay, we might not either. Next summer he'll be getting ready to go wherever he decides to go to school, ready to live his life. I'll be helping here and going to school locally, which isn't horrible, but not my dream either.

I stomp those thoughts down, not wanting anything to cloud this last time we have together.

When we get to the fort, we sit in our chairs behind it like we always do. I look through the telescope a little bit, but I'm not really feeling.

"You finished the deck," I finally say while sitting on his lap.

"It was nothing. Dragged Brandon out there to help me, then went back out to stain it after you got home."

"Hey!" I tease. "You lied! You said you were in bed."

Nate only shrugs. "Wanted to do it for you guys."

He looks down and picks at the peeling paint on the chair. A tense prickle covers my body, making me worried about what's going on. "What is it?" I finally ask.

He stalls before answering. "I get it... What's going on with your dad? Seeing that yesterday? I get it. I know why you feel like you can't leave him. I don't think I realized it before, but...I guess I'm selfish because it doesn't stop me from wanting to keep on doing what we had planned, ya know?"

"I know." Because I feel the same way. I lay my head on his shoulder.

"I was stressing out on saying anything or not, but I knew I had to. I want you, Charlotte. I still want to be with you and see what happens. We can apply for schools still together or not. I just want you to know...I want you to have your stars and that has nothing to do with me...but I get it, okay? I know you're scared, but don't be. If you decide you can't go, I'll understand."

Love over takes that empty feeling, kicking and shoving it out of my system. There's no room for it when I'm with him. "You have the biggest heart of anyone in the whole wide world," I say before kissing him.

Nate kisses me back, urgently, taking the kiss deeper like he's afraid I'll disappear. He twists me so I'm facing him, straddling him, and his hands go under the back of my shirt.

And I know I don't want him to stop. Nathaniel Chase gave me my very first moment. He gave me my first kiss. He was the first boy to see me naked. To take me skinny-dipping. The first boy I loved, and I want him to have every one of my firsts. Not that I think I'll ever be with anyone else, but if there's one thing I've learned it's that nothing in life is a guarantee.

"Do you..." *Breathe, Charlotte. It's Nate. I can say anything to Nate.* "I want to really be with you. Do you have any condoms?"

Nate's eyes go wide and his hands tighten slightly on my waist. He gives me a small nod, but then says, "You don't have to."

"I want to... Do you want to?"

"Are you kidding me? Of course I do."

I can't help but chuckle at that.

Nate trails one of his fingers down the side of my face, torturously slow. "You are so incredible."

Nate grabs my hand and I let him help me stand. He's right behind me, picking up my bag. "I wish I could take you somewhere better," he whispers, before leading me into the fort. It's clean inside. I keep it that way because it's important to me.

He lets go of my hand, grabs the blanket and lays it out, then sets the flashlights so we can see. He kicks out of his shoes and I do the same. Taking the edge of my shirt, he pulls it over my head and drops it to the floor, then takes his off.

"Okay?" he asks, his fingers on the button of my shorts.

The only reply I can manage is a nod. My heart is beating so hard. My pulse a loud bang in my ears. He pushes the button through the hole. Slides the zipper down. I hold my breath as he pushes my shorts and panties down my legs. His come off and I gasp a little, really seeing instead of catching a quick glimpse like the time we went skinny-dipping.

"I probably should have waited to do that until we were lying down."

I love that he's as nervous as I am. I don't know if he's done this before, and right now I don't care. "It's okay."

"You're beautiful." His eyes trace my body.

And then we lay down and he kisses me, touches me. I touch him, too. Nate grabs the condom and his hands shake as he rips it open. I watch in fascination as he puts it on.

"It'll hurt," he says. "But I'll be careful."

"I know."

And it does hurt, but he's careful. His kisses help to dull the pain. And the whole time I know, this is another of our moments. And it's what I always hoped it would be. What I hope we'll be able to do a million times in our future. This is *Nate* and we're doing something together I've never done with another person.

When it's over we lay next to each other. Nate pulls one side of the blanket up and over us. His hand is in my hair like it so often is.

"You okay, Star Girl?"

"Yeah."

"Was...was it okay?"

I lean up onto my arms so I'm looking down at him. "Was that your first time, too?"

Nate nods and I close my eyes, wishing to stay in this moment. I guess it's something neither of us has ever done with someone else. It surprises me. I know Nate it popular and he's gone out with a lot of girls, but I'm glad. "It was perfect," I finally tell him.

"What are we going to do?"

My answer is automatic. "I don't want to lose you. Like you said, we can talk every day." It'll be hard, but if anyone can do it, it's Nate and I.

He rolls me over, kisses my lips, then the star at the base of my throat. "I love you."

My eyes are wet when I say, "I love you, too."

Chapter Ten

We've been out to the fort every night. He leaves tomorrow and I want to stall as though keeping busy will somehow make the night take longer to get here, but at the same time, I want it to hurry. Want to be alone with him so we can talk and he can hold me and make me forget we have to say goodbye.

It's not goodbye, I tell myself. I'll see him soon. He said in October.

I lie in bed, staring at the ceiling. I'm not supposed to meet him for a while yet, but I can't stand being in this room. It's driving me crazy. I push off my bed, grab my backpack, and crawl out. I see Nate sneaking off to the side of their cabin. He must have had the same idea as me, wanting to come out early.

Not wanting to wake anyone, I don't shine the flashlight his way, but quietly try to catch up with him. I have a little ways to make up because I don't want be too loud and his cabin is a whole lost closer to the woods.

Once I hit the trees, I hope I'm going the right way. Where the heck is he going? "Nate." I whisper loudly, as though he can hear me.

I get this strange feeling in my stomach, but I try to ignore it as I keep going. There's no reason to freak out. I know these woods like the back of my hand and Nate is out here somewhere, but he's not going to any of our usual locations.

I stumble into one of the trees and lean against it and that's when I see him. Them.

Only it's not Nate. It's Brandon.

And he's not with some girl.

It's Alec.

What the heck are they doing out here? Brandon's back is to me and I see Alec give him a huge smile. One that I've never, ever seen him give me, or any other girl for that matter.

"What about your brother?" Alec asks.

"He thinks its Danielle."

Everything in my world turns upside down in that moment as I see Brandon lean forward and kiss Alec. Kiss him the way Nate kisses me. The way I've never seen two boys kiss before. My brain keeps telling my eyes to look away because this is their private business and I have no right to intrude on it, but I just can't do it.

Betrayal shoots through me. Alec is gay. How could he never have told me he's gay? Did he think I would look at him any differently?

But suddenly, a whole lot of things make sense—why Brandon is even here this year, how Alec seemed to know things about Nate I didn't expect. I think of the football Brandon has every time he's here and realize it has a big "X" on it and remember the time Alec was screwing around and drew it on there, saying X marked the spot because he liked football so much. He did that before we even knew them, and now I know Alec must have given the ball to Brandon. His favorite football.

Brandon's hand goes under Alec's shirt as his mouth leaves Alec's lips to slide down his neck, and that's when Alec's eyes find mine. I'm frozen. Scared, guilty, confused, hurt, every feeling I could possibly have is battling inside me.

"Shit. Charlie. It's...it's not...." As Alec is jerking away from Brandon, I run. I'm not quite sure why I'm running, but my feet won't stop.

"Charlie! Wait!" Alec's voice comes again, closer. A few seconds later he grabs me and pulls me to a stop. Everything about him looks frantic, his eyes, his facial expressions.

"I don't understand." It's a pretty stupid thing to say because what's to understand? Alec is obviously gay and never told me.

"I didn't mean for it to happen. I didn't want—I thought—I was confused."

"How long?"

He shakes his head. "Charlie..."

"If you don't want me to walk away right now, Alec, I need you to be honest." My whole body is shaking though I don't know why.

"Officially? It started last summer."

Oh God. The whole time we thought Brandon was sneaking out with Sadie last year, it was Alec.

"Wait. What do you mean officially?"

He looks guilty and I want to tell him not to. Despite everything, guilt for his feelings about Brandon doesn't belong here.

"We've talked all year...every year. Even after the first summer."

I'm not sure what to say, or how to react. Brandon blew off Sadie for Alec. It's crazy.

He's frantic now. "Swear to me. Swear you won't ever tell anyone, Charlie. You say I'm your best friend, and you know I would do anything for you. Swear you won't tell anyone."

"But...don't you want to be with him?" It's not right that he has to be so scared to be with the person he wants. It's not right that he felt like he had to hide it from me.

"Swear it."

"Of course. I swear. How long have you known you're gay, Alec?" My voice softens, still trying to wrap my mind around this.

"I'm not gay. Seriously."

"You've been seeing a guy for a year. I'm pretty sure that makes you gay." Reaching out, I touch his arm. "It's okay. You don't have to hide it from me. You can tell me anything."

"No," he shakes his head, looking slightly frantic.

The next thing I know, Alec's lips are on mine. I'm so shocked that it takes me a second to register what's happening. A second to try to push him away, but that one little stall ruined it. A moment can change everything.

"What the fuck?" Nate yells. I'm jerking away from Alec and then Nate's fist flies through the air, landing a hard hit to Alec's jaw. Alec staggers backward, but catches his footing and then he's charging at Nate.

"No! Stop it!" I scream.

Alec shoves Nate to the ground and punches him in the stomach. Nate groans, but rolls them quickly so he's on top. Nate punches him again. Before I can get to them to try and separate them, Brandon is there, pulling his brother off Alec.

All I can think is *thank God*. We can get this sorted out and everything will be okay.

"What the hell? Charlotte?" Nate is trying to pull away from Brandon who has a tight grip on his arms.

"It's not what it looks like. I swear. I don't know why he kissed me. He—"

"Charlie, please." Pure fear shines in Alec's eyes, making a bone deep sadness spread throughout me. The first thought in my mind is, is how sad. How horrible to be so afraid to be able to admit who you are. I can't imagine that feeling.

"*Please.*" He stresses again. When I make eye contact with Brandon, the same fear reflects back from his eyes.

And my heart breaks for them. It's not my secret to tell.

"Tell him," I say to Alec. "Tell Nate it's not what it looks like."

Alec is silent.

Brandon is silent.

"Get the fuck off me!" Nate jerks free from his brother's grasp.

"He kissed *me*. I was pulling away."

"And he's here!" Nate screams. "He'll always be here to keep trying to do it again."

"So? You'll be back home, with other girls too! You go out with a whole lot more people than I ever have!"

"Not girls I planned to end up with one day." His voice cracks, pain shining through, but it's not the kind of shine you want. It's dull, aching.

"I don't love him. I love you. You know that." I don't know what else to say. How to explain without telling him what I saw—something I'm still trying to work out. My brain isn't working right with so much overloading it at once. "He kissed me, and I was shocked. I swear it's not what it looks like. I love you." I say again.

"Why are you even out here with him?" I've never heard Nate's voice sound like it does right now. Broken.

I look at Brandon, silently pleading for help. His eyes go wide. Alec scrambles to his feet and I'm afraid to look at him, but I do and I see exactly what I knew I would. More fear mixed with a reminder of what I just promised him.

"Charlie, you *promised*." Alec's words light a fire in Nate's eyes, no doubt wondering what kind of promise I made. My body is weak, but primed and on edge too. I can't find the right words to say to fix this for all of us.

"I can't say, but it's not because I don't want to. It's a misunderstanding, though. You know me, Nate."

As long as I live, I will never forget the anger on his face when he looks at me. The dark red, edged sadness.

"I thought I did, but I obviously don't. Or I didn't want to believe it. You'll always pick him over me."

"What? No." I reach for him, but he steps out of my grasp. "That's not what this is. You know that! I'm not picking him over you. I've always picked you."

"Are you kidding me right now?" Nate shouts. "We've had to hide because of him. You didn't even want him to know about us in the beginning. We've said it before a million times. He's always here. You've known him your whole life and you're always going to pick him over me."

"Alec. Tell him." I look at him. "Tell Nate the truth. *Please.*"

Alec is pale in the moonlight. Terrified. No one says a word. I'm shocked. Can't believe what happened or that Nate doesn't believe me.

"You know what? I'm done. You wanted easy, I'll give you easy. You can have your life with him. Then you'll make everyone happy: your dad, Alec, his family. I sure as hell hope you're happy too." Nate's hand goes to his neck and he rips the star necklace off and drops it to the ground before walking away.

"Nate! Don't go. Please!" I call after him, tears streaming down my face, but he just keeps going.

"I'm...I'm sorry," Brandon says before running after his brother. Nate has walked away from me every summer for the past three years and none of them hurt like this one. Because this time, there is no doubt in my mind I've lost him forever. Logically I know all it would take is for me to tell him, but I can't. Not this. *Why didn't he believe me?*

I fall to the ground and cry.

"Charlie?" Alec steps up beside me.

"Get the fuck away from me! I hate you! You ruined everything!"

I push to my feet and run away from him.

Chapter Eleven

I go to the fort and lie on the ground and cry. Cry so much my eyes hurt. I'm crying for Nate and losing him and how much I love him. Even though I hate them, I'm crying for Brandon and Alec, too. That they'd be able to hurt people they care about because they're so scared for anyone to know who they're attracted to. I don't understand that and I never will. And as much as I want to tell Nate the truth, tell him why, I know I can't. How can I be the one to out them on something as deeply personal as that? I swore to Alec, and I won't break my promise, but I'm so upset he'd let me lose Nate to keep his own secret.

Soon I'm also crying for me and for Dad and what's happening to him. For the fact that Mom and my sister left us, and they're living their lives in Atlanta while I'm left alone to deal with this.

At some point I stop crying, and fall asleep. The sun peeking through the cracks in the wood wakes me up. And I run. All I can think about is Nate. Maybe I can make him understand. Maybe I can get Alec or Brandon to be honest with him. Maybe, maybe, maybe, maybe. I deserve that, right? After everything we've been through.

My chest hurts from running so hard and fast.

When I break through the woods and to the ground of The Village, their car is gone, and Alec sits on the porch of their lonely-looking cabin.

"I told your dad you were with me last night. That I have some stuff going on and you were helping me deal with it. You're good to go for today."

"Fuck you, Alec."

"I'm sorry, Charlotte." I freeze at his use of my real name. "I'm so sorry that you got hurt, but I can't say anything. Don't you understand that?"

Without realizing I started walking, I'm standing at the porch with him. "No, I don't. I know it's hard, but I don't get letting us get hurt because of it. At least you guys should be able to tell Nate. He's Brandon's brother. He would understand." I sigh, still unable to believe what I'm about to say to him. To Alec. "There's nothing wrong with being gay."

"Pfft. That's easy for you to say when you haven't lived it. Some people don't come out till they're forty fucking years old because of how people react. It's...it's *hard* and you can never understand that unless it's you."

"Alec—"

"Brandon has a football scholarship. How many active professional football players can you name that are gay? You think they won't give him shit in college? Not want to share a locker room with him; afraid he's going to, what? Attack them or something? Rub off on them? You don't know what it's like for him, Charlie." For the first time since we were kids, there are tears in Alec's eyes. "He can't do it. He's scared to tell anyone, even his brother."

"You love him," I whisper, sadness bleeding through for him. For Alec and Brandon.

"It doesn't matter if I do." He shrugs.

"Yes, it does. What about you? You had a whole list of reasons why his is hard for Brandon, what about you?"

"Come on, Charlie. You've heard my dad talk. How many times does he talk about "those faggots"? How disgusting they are? I might not be as good as Brand and I might not have the same future as him, either, but I don't want people giving me shit when we're playing ball."

"Does your Dad know, Alec? Is that why you guys aren't getting along as well?"

He blanches at that, real fear on his face. "Of course he doesn't know! It's just...I hate when he says shit like that and it's hard not to pull away from him. We got into an argument one day because he said something about this guy at the store and I just...I lost it. After that, things have been different."

I try to find the right words to say to him, but nothing comes. Soon Alec continues. "I just wanna be me. Alec. I'm gonna find a way to be the Alec everyone wants me to be."

There's a part of me who hates him so much for what he's done, for how things turned out, but my heart is crushed for him too. "You need to be the Alec you are. You're one of the best people I know. There's nothing wrong with who you are."

Stepping forward, I pull him into a hug. We stand there for so long my legs ache, but I keep holding him. Keep being there for the boy who has always been my best friend. The only person I've known as long as my family, while he cries.

The world is so screwed up sometimes. How we make people hate who they are, hide who they are. It's one of those things I hear about on TV or read about, but I never thought it would affect me until Alec.

"We could be happy, you know, Charlie," he says after forever.

"What?" I pull away from him. "What are you talking about?"

"You know I love you. You're my best friend and I'm yours. We could be happy. We'd never have to worry about getting hurt. About being left…"

Because I'm not the only one who got left behind today—or the last two summers before, either. This whole time I thought I was alone in my pain, but I wasn't. Alec suffered silently.

"We'd always be there for each other and I love your family and you love mine. No one would ever know. We'd be happy," he says again. "We always figured we'd run The Village one day anyway, and—"

My hand flies up and I slap him. "You asshole." Suddenly everything makes sense. Why he hated me with Nate so much, but didn't mind the other boys. Why he didn't date much and let people assume we'd be together one day. Why he always, always kept me in the wings, because if he tried to help me with Nate last night, or didn't care if I was with Nate, I couldn't be here for him.

He's always wanted me as his cover. To use me to pretend he's straight. To live a lie. Nate threatened that. I feel used and cheated by the one person I never thought would hurt me.

"Charlie...I love you," he says again. "I want to make you happy. I'd forget all about Brand and we could...ya know..."

No tears are left to cry. Nothing I can do to change anything. There isn't doubt in my mind that Alec loves me. I don't believe he tried to hurt me, but that doesn't matter because he did nonetheless. "I know you do, Alec. But it's not enough. Stay away from me. I never want to talk to you again."

It's not just Alec and Brandon I'm upset with either. Nate didn't trust me. If we really knew each other the way we thought, he would have.

This summer took away from me the only boy I've ever loved, and my best friend. I've always depended on having Alec there...then Nate came and I wanted to always be with him. It's time I leave that in that past, and only count on myself. I walk away knowing nothing will ever be the same.

Summer Four

The next few months are hard. Alec and I aren't talking. I miss my friend. Nate is never far from my mind and my heart aches for him...but I keep busy. I apply for schools I'll probably never go to because it helps to pretend and feels good to do something because I want it. Dad asks about Alec, and I won't say more than we had a fight. No matter how hurt I am, I'll never tell his secrets. Danielle and I get close and I date a couple boys and try not to compare them to Nate. In December, Dad meets Nancy. In February I ask Alec to the Valentines dance, because I can't stop talking to him forever. We have too much of a past for that. He knows I'll never play his game, but no matter what, we'll always be best friends. I can't imagine how it feels to be willing to do anything to keep a secret. Alec has enough on his mind, and I can't abandon him. Some days I'm happy, some I'm sad, but I'm always wishing and hoping for my future—for my stars. Everything changes on a rainy afternoon when Dad tells me we need to talk...

- Nathaniel Chase -

Chapter One

"You and Marisol broke up, huh?" Brandon asks me as we head toward Columbia University. Brandon's back early from Ohio. We took the train to the city and we're on our way to meet Dad for lunch.

"Yeah... What's the point? It's not like the long distance thing would work." I didn't want to try and make it work. Neither did she, so it wasn't a big deal.

"That's a shame. She's hot. Especially when she speaks Spanish," my brother teases.

"How are you ending your freshman year in college and you're still a douchebag? You never even met her."

Brandon nudges me. "I didn't need to meet her. Pictures and her voice were enough." He winks.

"Fucker," I call him. "You talk about girls enough, but I never see you with one anymore. We're going to have to work on your game, man."

"There's more important shit than girls."

When I look at Brandon, I see he's staring in the opposite direction. "Yeah, football. How could we forget? Nothing can ever be as important as football."

A woman walks right between us like we aren't even there. Brandon drops the conversation and says, "I can't believe you're staying even closer to home than I did."

"Columbia's awesome for architecture," is what comes out of my mouth, when really I just want tell him, *me too*. My mind tries to wander back to plans I had with Charlotte that we both should have known would never happen. It's easier to slam the door now.

We're quite for a few seconds as we make our way down the street. Brandon's the one who speaks first, "It's kind of crazy isn't it?"

"Not a magic eight ball. Can't read your mind."

"That doesn't even make sense," he tells me, but then adds, "Being in New York for the summer. I mean, it's not that I care, because there's a whole hell of a lot more to do here, but it's just..."

"Crazy," I finish for him. It sucks that he brought it up, but it's true. Not that I really would have expected Brandon to say it. Yeah, he had fun at The Village, but that second year, he was pissed he had to go. The third, it was just for something to do. He never looked forward to it the way I did. Probably because he wasn't a dumbass kid who thought he was in love with some summer girl.

Brandon's quiet again and I wonder what the hell is going on. It's usually hard to shut him up. You can always tell when he's freaked out about something because he's not blabbing about stuff.

I'm about to ask him what's up when he asks, "Do you ever...you know, talk to her or anything? I ask because I know how you guys were so I didn't know if you made up or whatever."

My skin suddenly feels too tight. My mind flashes back to seeing her kissing Alec that night. Fuck, I thought I was over all this. It's been nine months. "Nope. We don't talk."

"Oh... That sucks." His voice sounds weird. Soft or something. "I'm sorry, man."

Brandon stops walking, so I do, too. "What are you sorry for? It's not your fault I was an idiot and thought she wasn't really into Alec. They have their history or whatever. Nothing we can do about that."

It probably makes me even more pathetic because that doesn't really feel right. I know her and get her and can't imagine her really wanting to be with him. But then she had her chance and no matter what the reason, she chose him when she kissed him that night. Chose to keep quiet about whatever Alec wanted her to and that says a whole hell of a lot. How could I trust her after that?

"Nate...do you love her?"

Brandon's question socks me in the gut. Do I love Charlotte? I thought I did. Or is it I think I do? How the hell do you really know the answer that question? I know there has never been anyone like her. She made me see things and feel things no one else ever did. Something ripped me open when I saw her kissing Alec. Like she yanked out all my insides and I still feel the aftershocks from it. If he would've asked me that last summer, I never would have hesitated. I actually fucking talked to my dad about her and all I got was *you're young and at that age,* blah, blah.

But I felt her in my bones, saw her when I closed my eyes, and would have done anything to be with her. If that's not love, what is?

I don't say any of that to my brother though. Brandon's always busting my balls about something and even though I bust his right back I don't want to go there when it comes to Charlotte.

"Because if you did...well..."

"It's over man. I'm starting college in a few months. Charlotte's in the past."

I feel like the world's biggest liar. And when I look at Brandon, for the first time I wonder if he sees more than he lets on, because he looks all expectant. Apparently I'm not only a liar, but also a shitty one at that.

Later that night, I'm in my room at home, lying on my bed when my phone beeps with an email. I pick it up, hit the blue square and see her name pop up. Charlotte Gates. I want to rush to open it and delete it at the same time.

It's the first time she's contacted me since everything went down last year and she happens to do it on the same day my brother started asking questions about her, digging everything up and making her fight her way to the front of my thoughts again.

I click it to open because there's no way I can't. After all this time, I'm curious what she has to say to me.

Nate,

Hey...Hope you're well. I won't keep you long because, well, you know, but I just wanted to tell you I'm in New York for two weeks. I thought you'd be proud. Or maybe not, but I want to think you would be. It's crazy being here and knowing you're in the same state. I'm in your territory now, not that we ever saw it that way. But yeah, I wanted you to know...and wanted to tell you again that I'm sorry everything went down the way it did...but I stand by what I said that night, it wasn't what you thought. I didn't do anything wrong.

I miss you. Hope it's okay that I said that.

Charlotte

The rest of the day, all I can think about is Charlotte. It pisses me off and I want her out of my mind, but she's there and I can't stop running a million questions through my head. Why is she here? How are things at The Village? Is her dad okay? Is she reaching for her stars? Is she with Alec?

That's when I get even more pissed and tell myself it doesn't matter if she's here. An hour away from me.

About ten PM, our parents go to bed and Brandon and I head downstairs to the game room. I beat him in a couple games of pool, the whole time wondering if I should tell him about Charlotte. It's ridiculous that I get so tied up like this. What I should do is call Marisol. Hit a party with my brother. There are a million different girls out there; too many to let only one of them take up so much space inside me.

I don't do any of that.

Around three a.m. I pick up my cell and start a new text, with one simple word.

Meet?

Her answer is just easy.

Yes.

Too bad things have never been that simple for us.

It's time to get some answers.

Chapter Two

Mom is sitting on the couch when I come down the next day. She's still in her pajamas and eating from a bag of chips. She gives me a guilty smile when I see her. "They're only chips, Mom. You don't have to look like it's the end of the world."

"I thought you were your father," she says, like he would have thought it was a big deal either.

"How ya feeling?" I ask her. Some parents have a mid-life crisis when their kids are both at college and decide to move to Hawaii or something like that. First mine started working to get close to Brandon and I—which is cool. Then they decided to have another baby. It's not like I know much about being pregnant, but apparently it's harder on you in your forties than when you're younger. She's already on light bed rest, which is part of the reason they didn't try to get us to go back to Lakeland Village this year.

"I'm doing great. What about you? Where are you headed off to so early?"

"I'm going downtown. I'm not sure what time I'll be back." I'm definitely not in the mood to answer questions about Charlotte so there's no way I'm saying who I'm meeting.

"Okay. Be careful. Have a good day. I think I'll finish my chips and then take a nap."

It's a little wild seeing Mom like this. She's always been one of those girls who thinks she has to look perfect all the time. Even if she's in the garden or at The Village she always looks perfect. I think that's part of what intrigued me about Charlotte. She was so different than what I was used to.

"See ya later," I say before walking out.

It's a long ass ride to the city, but I've done it a million times. I pull out my iPod and listen to music, wondering what the hell I'm doing.

It's a couple block walk once I get off the train. As soon as I round the corner on 52nd Street, I see her. She's already standing in front of the coffee shop that Mom goes to. I didn't know where else to tell her to meet me and now I don't know why I'm thinking about stupid things that don't matter like why I picked the coffee shop.

Her hair is shorter. It's up to her shoulders and I wonder when she cut it. She's wearing jeans and I realize that as long as I've known her, I've never seen her wear pants. What does she look like in the winter? It's crazy just seeing her not surrounded by her lake.

When I look at her from this far away, all our summers slam into me and it's almost like from this distance, just looking at her, I can almost forget all the bad shit that happened.

For the first time, I think I want to, but then that last night body slams its way in and I remember how many more of her moments that Alec has than me and I wonder *what's the point?*

We were young, stupid kids and we tried to make something work that never would have.

I'm about to turn around and walk away, but of course that's the second Charlotte turns around. The crowd doesn't matter. There aren't hundreds of other people around us like there always are in New York. Her eyes land right on me.

This would be way, way easier if she wasn't so beautiful. I almost forgot how she goes right to my head with just one look. It's always been like that, even from the first glance in front of the cabin when I didn't understand what it was.

Charlotte lifts her hand and gives me a small, nervous wave. There have been so many people who've come and gone in my life. We've never seen each other for long periods of time or really known each other beyond our summers, but every time I see her, even when we were confused or I was depressed or whatever, things always feel a little better when I look at her. No matter the time that's passed or how one of us might have changed we always still knew each other. I could look at her and see through her to the bits and pieces of her I knew so well, but standing here now, for the first time, I feel like I don't know Charlotte anymore.

And it really fucking sucks. Which then makes me pissed at myself because she kissed Alec. She let me walk away and she never even told me why.

I've never been a pussy before, and I refuse to let myself be one now. I shove my hands in the pockets of my shorts and walk toward her. "Hey." I nod my head at her and then feel like a douchebag.

"Hey...thanks for meeting me."

"No problem. Let's go get a drink." I open the door for her and she walks in. It's crazy and stupid, but I could swear she smells like The Village; all open air and trees and water.

I try to buy her drink, but she doesn't let me. It probably shouldn't bother me, but it does. If it were Alec, would he be buying one for her?

Charlotte and I head back outside and we're lucky a table opens up. It's close to the building and toward the end, which means we'll get about as much privacy as possible out here. Which isn't much.

"You're taller," she blurts out and then her cheeks go a little pink. "I mean, I think you are. Maybe you're not, but you look like it."

"Your hair's shorter."

She touches it, making me remember when I used to do that. How she'd shiver and I wondered if she could feel it deep inside her the way I could.

"Yeah. I cut it a couple months ago."

I think maybe I should tell her it looks good, but I don't let myself. Just like I don't tell her it's good to see her outside The Village. Or ask her how she likes it. Or tell her I'm proud of her. All I ask is, "What are you doing here, Charlotte?"

Disappointment creases her brow, before she says, "It's kind of a long story. So much has happened, Nate. I want to tell you all about it, but I don't know if you want to hear and—"

"—Is your dad okay?" I cut her off. Yeah I'm pissed, but I would feel like a prick if something happened to her dad and I never knew. Wasn't there for her.

"Yeah. He's fine. As fine as he can be. He's hanging in there. The MS seems to have slowed down a little which is good. He met someone."

"Wow." I never expected him to. He seemed like not much mattered except his family and The Village.

"He says it isn't serious, but of course it is. She's at The Village all the time. She helps out there, too. She's a nurse and works three days a week. If she's not a work she's at The Village."

I can't help but wonder if that's why she's here. If her dad has help now and she's coming for school or vacation or what. But then...I know she wanted California, so if she's going to school, I'm sure it isn't out here.

"That's cool."

We're both quiet and it's the kind of silence I hate. It's not like I'm real chatty. Marisol could get like that sometimes and it drove me crazy. This silence is strangling and awkward. "What are you doing here?" I ask again.

She seems distracted, watching people as they walk by.

"Is there somewhere else we can go to talk?"

I almost say yes, but I feel like she's stalling. "Here's as good as any place."

Charlotte flinches, making me hate myself a little. I don't want to be the guy to make her feel that way.

"School...I'm going to Vassar in Poughkeepsie this fall. Alec and I are out here for two weeks getting to know the city a little bit."

Aaaand, now I'm pissed. She's here with Alec, but she called me. That's not even the worst of the thoughts injecting anger into my veins. A familiar ache in my chest develops that I haven't felt since last year. She left The Village for him. She's going away to college with him. Maybe it makes me a selfish bastard to think that way. Her dad needed her and I always understood that, but I still wanted her with me too.

But now she's here, in my city, with him.

"Bet your dad loves that. I'm sure he's cool with you leaving for school since you're with his golden boy, right? Have a good visit." I push to my feet, but she grabs my wrist before I can get too far.

"I'm not with Alec. I swear. I never have been. He's my best friend and that's all, Nate."

"Then why can't you tell me what happened that night? If you're not with him tell me why, Charlotte. I deserve that much." She flinches again, but doesn't reply. "That's what I thought."

Her grip loosens and I start working my way through the tables and people. I don't know how I know it, but she's behind me. She always gave in when it came to her future, but that's about the only thing.

"Nate," she calls, but I keep going. "Nate!"

I turn a corner and I'm slowing down. Damn, I'm an idiot, because even though I'm pissed I can't make myself just walk away from her.

"I'm sorry for hurting you," she says. Her eyes are red and her face is wet.

"Damn it." My hand pushes through my hair and I duck into the alley next to us, Charlotte right behind me. "It's been since August, Charlie! You could have explained a million times. I'm not stupid. I knew when I said we should try to be together that the odds were against us. Who the hell can make it last in a normal relationship, but we had distance, too. But I was willing to try. If you didn't want to, all you had to do was tell me. It would have sucked, but I would have been okay. I've never lied to you. Even when we weren't together and I went out with other girls I always told you—"

"—I didn't lie to you, either! I've never lied to you! Alec kissed me, but it wasn't him I wanted. I was caught off guard and then you showed up and all hell broke loose."

"And if that was all there was to it, you would have told me then."

I lean against the wall. I don't want to fight with her. I've never wanted to fight with her.

"I would tell you in a second if I could, Nate, and you know that. It's not my story to tell. This whole year I've spent trying to figure out my life. How to be who I am without you and without Alec or my dad."

"And you lump me in with them? I'm the only one who ever pushed you to go for what *you* wanted."

She groans. "That's not what I meant. You're trying to fight with me, Nate. That's not why I messaged. I just want...I just..."

"You just what, Charlie?" It's the second time I've called her that today. It feels strange. She's always been Charlotte to me.

"I want out friendship back. I miss you. And I know it's crazy and doesn't make sense because you're probably going off somewhere to school. I know you didn't want to stay close to home and I'm going to be here, but it doesn't change the fact that after everything, I at least want my friend back."

My defenses are weakening, softening up with each of her words and I try to turn, but she steps in front of me the way I've done with her.

"I want to tell you about my year and explain how I ended up in New York and hear you talk about baseball and I want to look at the stars here with you. I want my friend..."

Her words echo through me. I study her face I know so well. The curves of her body, her hands that I've held and that anger is still filling me, but there's something there pushing it aside.

I miss her.

I want our friendship back, too.

I've always wanted her.

I grab her hand and it's a little awkward, but she doesn't pull away. She's breathing hard and all I can think is she's still wild and crazy as always.

With my other hand I touch her hair and push it behind her ear. "I hate it. No one wrecks me the way you do, but I can't help it. I miss you, too..."

Chapter Three

The whole way home I'm still not sure I did the right thing. I wasn't lying when I said she wrecked me because she did, but she's also here and I never really expected her to be. I've given her so many of her firsts and she's had so many of mine that I want this. I want to be the one to show her New York and pretend it's the world.

I want to be with her when she looks at the stars in the city and see if she thinks they look any different than they do at home.

And I really, really need to stop dwelling over this.

I get home after six. Dad is there like he is most of the time now. Usually the only time off he takes is when we went to The Village every summer, so it's crazy to see him at home so much and the way he takes care of Mom.

"I ordered pizza," he tells me as I walk into the living room.

"Nah, I'm good. I already ate. Is Brandon here?" When Brandon's in town he's never usually home. He's off doing whatever with whomever.

"Yeah, he's upstairs in his room," Mom answers.

"Thanks." Turning, I run upstairs, my tennis shoes slapping on the tiled floors.

About three seconds after I knock on Brandon's door, he tells me to come in. The first thing I do is blurt out, "Charlotte and Alec are here." Wow...way to freak out.

"What? Here?" Brandon pushes to his feet, looking even more tripped out than I feel. What the hell is up with that?

"Not at our house, dumbass. In New York. Why do you look like you're going to puke? Your football buddy is here. And, you know, the guy who kissed Charlotte when I was with her."

"You weren't really with her," Brandon tosses back.

"How do you know? It's not like I ever told you anything. We were though." In a way I feel like I've always been with her. It doesn't make sense because she's gone out with other guys and me with other girls, but even back then, I knew she was the one for me.

Brandon rolls his eyes. "Yeah, until you got home and realized your girlfriend lived a thousand miles away."

My brother's words light a fuse under my barely controlled anger. "Fuck you, bro. It was different with her. Just because you've never had anything serious with anyone—"

"Fuck you, too. You don't know anything about what I have and haven't had." Brandon falls back into the chair at his computer desk, still looking a little sick. "And what does that even mean? Just yesterday I asked you if you loved her and you made it sound like she didn't really matter that much." His leg is bouncing up and down like it's on crack.

"Why are we even fighting about this?"

"I don't know, man. You started it." Brandon shakes his head. "So...what are they doing here? Did she say anything? I mean, about what happened with her and Alec."

Opening my mouth, I almost tell him nothing, but then figure it can't be that bad to talk to him about something. "Kind of. She said she's not with him and that she never was. She says he just kissed her, which is all stuff she said before. I know there's more to it than that. Otherwise, things wouldn't have gone down the way they did."

Brandon looks at me, really looks like he wants to figure me out. We're cool, but we've never been all that close so I wonder what he sees. Wonder why we don't really know each other better.

"I believe her," he says.

I shake my head. "You don't know her." Not that there isn't this part of me who doesn't know he's right. I think that's why I gave in today. Why I told her I want to take her to The Met tomorrow. It's impossible to really tell her no to anything. "Regardless, I hate Alec and always will. If I see him, I can pretty much promise you I'm taking him out again."

"But... What if...what if it wasn't his fault?" Brandon asks. He has his cell in his hand and he's screwing with it and not looking at me.

"How can it not be his fault? He kissed her, man."

At that Brandon pushes to his feet. "You have a lot of growing up to do. Things aren't always as simple as you think they are."

"I have a lot of growing up to do? Says the guy who doesn't care about anything but football and getting laid."

Jerking Brandon's door open, I slam it before going into my room and falling onto the bed. His words keep playing in my head. He believes her. That things aren't always cut and dry as I think they should be. Just like that night with Chrissy, I didn't think of the consequences of telling. Yeah, it was the right thing and I wouldn't change that, but I never really thought about how it would affect anyone.

This is Charlotte. I know her. I do. And it's never really fit. If Alec kissed her and she didn't want to be kissed back, then what was the big secret behind it? That whole night has always been this strange clusterfuck that I can't piece together to make sense of it.

But I know her.

My brother might be right in at least some ways. Charlotte wouldn't lie to me. I feel that in every part of me.

Still don't get why though.

And I can't help but think my brother got a hell of a lot smarter all of a sudden. I wonder what else there is about him that I don't know.

We stand at the bottom of the stairs, Charlotte's eyes practically as big as the building in front of us. People are all around like they always are, sitting on the steps, walking on the street, and taking pictures. I try to see it through her eyes, for the first time with the oversized pillars and the intricate artwork on the upper ledge of the building, but I can't really do it. Instead I just want to watch her soak it all in. Watch her and wonder what's happened since I saw her last and then I get a little annoyed at myself for caring.

"It's so...big." Charlotte smiles and I can't help but laugh.

"Yeah, you can say that." Then we're quiet and she's still soaking it in. "It's one of my favorite buildings in the city," I tell her.

Charlotte turns to face me. "It is?"

"Yep."

"I didn't know that. Though why would I? It's not like I know everything about you."

She knows more than anyone else. "I don't know everything about you, either."

"Yes, you do." Her answer is quick. "As much as someone can know about someone else." Her words spark all kinds of questions, confusion and a little bit of anger. As if she can sense it, Charlotte changes the subject. "What's your favorite part about it?"

"The small details." I point to the top. "It's simple in a way, not over done like a lot of buildings are, but it has those little pieces to it, those little extras that make it special."

"Buildings are like your stars. I knew, but I've never seen it before." There's awe in her voice and in her green eyes that I don't see or hear from anyone else.

"Yeah... I guess you can say that."

"Can we go in?" she asks and I suddenly can't wait to show it to her.

"Come on." Reflex makes me reach for her hand, but I jerk back before I touch her. If she notices, she doesn't say anything.

We go inside and Charlotte looks even more amazed than she did standing at the bottom of the stairs. Pictures are on the walls and pieces displayed everywhere. Charlotte leads the way; excited in a way I don't remember seeing when we were at The Village. It's a different part of her here, one who is more unsure than she was at home, but eager and anxious to figure it all out.

You wouldn't think so, but it's kind of hot. It surprises me that as many times as I've seen her and everything we've experienced together that there is so much more out there to do.

"Don't they do lectures and stuff like that too?" she asks.

"For sure. Wanna go to one?"

"Oh my God! Yes!" She moves like she's going to hug me, but just like I did with her hand earlier, she pulls back.

I just want to put it out there. Ask what the fuck happened to us and how we can get it back.

"Are we going or what?" She smirks, breaking the ice.

To hell with it. Putting my arm around her shoulders, I say, "I don't remember you being this pushy... Oh, wait. That's a lie. I do."

"Nate!" Charlotte tries to pull away, pretending she's mad, but I hold onto her and keep her close.

"It's a good thing to always tell the truth, right?" I tease again.

Charlotte crosses her arms. "I don't remember you being so mean. Oh, wait. Yeah I do."

We laugh as we keep walking and then we're not laughing and her head's on my shoulder and all I can think is it feels like it did at the beginning of every summer. Like it always has. Fuck, I missed this girl.

"So...how 'bout that Eros, huh?"

Charlotte rolls her eyes.

"You have to admit it's kind of crazy. I definitely didn't expect a lecture on Eros, God of Love." Though maybe I should have.

The sun burns my eyes when we step outside again.

"Why not? What's wrong with it?"

"I didn't say there was anything wrong with it. Did you like it?"

Charlotte stops and looks at me, into me. "I loved it."

What is it about her that turns me so inside out? My hands itch to grab her, to pull her to me and kiss her and talk the way I only do with her. "I'm glad."

"Nate—"

"—Come on. I'll get you back to your hotel."

Charlotte nods.

"Subways are so cool," she says as we sit inside.

That makes me laugh. "If you say so. I'm sure most of us could think of a few other words for them."

Charlotte watches everyone, her eyes never staying still for very long. I have to remind her to get off when it's our stop. Her hotel isn't a long walk from the subway, and when we get there, I pause her before she goes inside.

"If Alec is here, it's probably not a good idea if I go up there." It's not a good idea regardless.

Sadness dims her eyes. "Nate... I need to know you believe me. Alec doesn't like me like that and even if he did...it's never been him for me. It never will be."

I'm not sure if it's smart, but my reply is automatic and honest. "I do. I believe you. It doesn't mean I'm not pissed, because I am. I wish you could trust me with the truth."

"I do. You know I trust you with everything. It's just not my truth to tell."

"That doesn't change the fact that I deserve some answers." She opens her mouth to reply, but I continue. "I'm not trying to fight with you. I'm here, Charlotte. That means something. Today was..."

"Perfect," she fills in the blank.

It wasn't. I know that and she knows that, but I can't deny her reply either. It's like that with us. Imperfections are still perfect. Just being with her is.

"I'll pick you up tomorrow morning, okay? We'll do Times Square."

Charlotte replies with a nod.

I wonder why I haven't told her I'm going to Columbia. That we'll only be an hour and a half train ride from each other.

Reaching out, I touch her hair. "I'm glad you're here, Star Girl."

Pulling my hand back, I turn and walk away.

Chapter Four

I'm exhausted from taking the train into the city again. I don't know how Dad does it, but it's worth it because I still can't believe Charlotte is here.

She's waiting outside her hotel when I get there. I have to do a double take because, standing there, she looks more like the Charlotte I remember than she did yesterday. For the first time, I see her legs again, all smooth and tanned in the jean shorts she's wearing.

And a tank top. I love her tank tops. It's yellow just like the swimming suit from the first summer and the bikinis from our second and third. It's a stupid thing to remember. I'd probably be embarrassed if it was anyone but her.

"Hey."

She's smiling so big that it takes everything inside me not to kiss her.

"Hi."

"You ready?" I ask.

"Yep."

We take another subway ride and walk to Times Square.

I almost never come here. If people think the city is busy, they've never visited Times Square. Tourists everywhere and so many people it's almost impossible to breathe.

"Holy crap, it's crazy here." Her voice is a little unsure, so I grab her hand.

"I got you. You have to learn to shove your way through."

I make way for both of us as we work through the throng of people. It's loud and there are lights everywhere even though it's daytime. I should have taken her at night, so she could see even better how it lit up. I don't know why I didn't think about that.

We watch the screens and go into shops and stores. Charlotte asks questions, reminding me how she likes to know so much about everything. And still, we've hardly seen half of it.

"How far is Central Park?" she asks.

"You wanna go? We can. That's why I came early today. There's still stuff to see here, too." It's only noon right now so we have some time.

"I've always wanted to see Central Park," she says.

I didn't know that about her. "Yeah. Let's do it. We won't be able to see the whole thing, but we have some time."

We head toward Central Park. The whole time I'm wondering if she thinks some parts of it will remind her of home. If that's why she wants to see it so badly.

When we get there, we grab some food at a little stand before walking into one of the huge grassy areas. We sit on the ground and she crosses her legs, taking a bite of her sandwich. "I think I could live here," she finally says.

"You're going to in a couple months, right?" It's still crazy for me to think about.

"Yeah, but I mean *here*. In the park. It's amazing, Nate."

"Eh. Probably not a good idea to live here, but you're going to freak out when you see the rest of it."

Charlotte watches a bike go by before saying. "Dad's been paying me a little and I've done some odd jobs. I've been saving up since last summer for this trip. Well, I guess I didn't know what it was for at the time, but I was putting money away for something. I can't believe I'm really here."

"I can't believe you are, either. How'd it all come about? Going to school here and stuff?"

She sets her sandwich down and lies down on her back. "I wish it was nighttime. Most of our talks are under the stars."

I don't know what makes me do it, but I lay down next to her, leaning on my elbow. "Close your eyes and pretend." Lightly I set my hand over her eyes. Her lashes brush my palm, so I pull away. It's such a little thing, but I love how she trusts me, even in something as simple as this.

"I'm scared to mention it because everything came about after that night," her voice whispers.

A fist tightens around my chest, but I ignore it. "You can tell me anything, Star Girl. You know that. That's why I don't understand—"

Her eyes jerk open. "It's not me. I would tell you if it was."

"So tell me the rest."

She closes her eyes again. "I missed you so much, Nate. It was different than when you left all the other years. Even though I never really knew if you'd come back, I had hope. I was so scared you hated me."

"I wanted to," I can't help but say. "I wanted to hate you, but I couldn't. Then I was even more pissed at you because you still had this grip on me."

"You had me too."

The fist loosens slightly. "So what happened?"

"I started applying places. I was so mad at the world. I felt like I was being rebellious or something. I didn't tell Dad or Alec or anyone. I wasn't talking to Alec at all so it was just me and my secrets. It felt like it used to, when no one really knew how I felt. After I met you I always had someone I could tell anything to, but I was on my own again. I applied to LA and a few other places. I don't know what made my try Vassar... Because it's close, I guess? Not too far from home, but still somewhere new."

"You knew you'd go?"

She opens her eyes and looks up at me. "Nope. I thought I'd never get out. I just needed to feel like I was doing something. Maybe I just wanted to pretend. It was after Dad met Nancy that I really started to think about it more, but I still didn't see how it was possible."

"You deserve your dreams, Star Girl." I touch her hair and I know I need to stay away. We have too much history and now it's bogged down with the last night we spent together, but I can't stop myself from wanting her.

"I missed that name."

"What happened next?" I ask, trying to find out everything about her year, but also putting some distance there.

"Dad happened... He just talked to me one day. He told me Alec's parents were interested in becoming partners of The Village. They love it as much as we do and they've spent their lives there. At first I kind of freaked out because it's ours. It's our life."

"And you felt guilty."

Charlotte nods. "It was so hard, because then he started telling me how all he ever wanted was The Village and how it was his dream...but then he said he knew it wasn't mine. He didn't want to force it on me. If he deserved his dream, I deserved mine, right?"

That surprises the hell out of me. I never expected her dad to go there, but I don't want to sound like an ass by saying it.

"Didn't expect that one, did you?"

"You said it, not me." I wink at her.

"He'd already talked to Alec's parents and Nancy and they all had this plan worked out. He said it was happening regardless and that I deserve to live my life. They're only doing summer and fall now. Nancy loves it there and loves to help, plus she helps take care of him. Add in Alec's parents and...here I am. I'm still close enough to home that I can go back and help, but I'm free too."

"You love The Village." We both know she does. Getting out never meant she didn't love it. "And Alec?" I don't mean for my voice to be so tight when I ask about him.

A sad look takes over her face. "I want him to get out of there... I don't know if he will yet. He needs it. All these years I thought I really knew him, Nate, but I didn't. Not really. He—"

I groan and rub my hand over my face. "You're killin' me here." It's not something I like to admit, but I've always been jealous of him, their relationship and the times they had together.

"Not like that!" She sits up. "Shit, I didn't mean for it to sound like that."

"I have no right to care if it does." I don't like the words, but they need to be said.

"Maybe you don't want to, but you do."

"Char—"

She counters with, "Nathaniel."

"You haven't called me that in a while."

"Maybe that will be what I call you when you piss me off."

"What? What did I do?" I don't know how the mood suddenly got so much lighter, but it did.

"You're being a guy. I understand things like that so much better since I started hanging out with Danielle."

That's the first time I realize she really must not have talked to Alec for a while. That maybe she'd been almost as pissed at him as me.

"Let's pretend we're at The Village right now, okay?" Charlotte lies back down. "It's like every other summer. Let's just...talk."

So we do. I tell her about Mom and the baby and she asks a lot of questions about Brandon. I manage to dodge the college question, but we catch up on everything else.

Its already almost evening time before I get her back to her hotel.

"You do realize I didn't get to show you any of Central Park today, right?" I ask.

"It doesn't matter." She shakes her head.

An expression that says she still had a great day plays across her face, but I'm not ready to hear it. "I better go. I'll pick you up tomorrow, okay?"

"Okay."

As soon as I round the corner, my cell phone beeps. Pulling it out of my pocket I see a text from Charlotte.

What we did was better

Maybe I am ready to hear it. Not sure what I plan to say when I get there, I turn around back around, take the corner and see that she's gone.

I don't go after her. Don't reply. Just head back to the train and go home.

Chapter Five

"Nate! Wake up!" Brandon grabs me, jerking me out of sleep.

My room is pitch black, but then the lamp from my bedside table flips on, the light stinging my eyes. "What the hell, man?"

"It's Mom. She's bleeding. A lot. We're taking her to the hospital."

I'm already out of bed before the last word leaves his mouth. I pull on the same jeans I wore today, which were on the floor, get a t-shirt from my drawer and then I'm right behind my brother, snagging my cell as I head out of my room. My shoes are already by the door so I shove my socked feet into them.

"Where are they?" I ask. My voice shakes. My hands are shaking.

"They just left. Dad caught me when I was getting up to go to the bathroom and told me. I saw her nightgown, Nate. It's..."

Brandon doesn't continue and he doesn't have to. It's bad. I can see it with one look at him. "Just drive. Let's go."

We climb into Brandon's truck and he backs out.

"We got into an argument tonight," Brandon rushes out.

"Why?"

"I guess it wasn't really a fight, but she was upset... I told her I'm not sure I want to play football anymore."

That catches my attention. "You love football."

"I never said I didn't. But it's a lot of pressure. You don't get it. You loved baseball, but it was never the same. You're also a brainiac and everyone has always known you're more than just sports."

"What are you talking about, Brandon? Mom and Dad have never been like that. Hell, Dad couldn't care less about sports."

"Who said I was talking about them?" he says quietly.

Every time I talk to Brandon lately, it's like he has another surprise for me. Another secret I don't know about him. Does he really think he's not more than football?

"If you don't wanna play ball, don't. You have to live your own life."

Brandon sighs. "Easier said than done, bro. And I don't know for sure. I just...never mind. Mom is what matters right now."

"It's not your fault." I'm not sure why I say that. "The fight. If..."

I feel Brandon's eyes on me. "Thanks, man."

We don't talk after that. I hold my phone in my hand the whole way to the hospital. While Brandon is parking I stop fighting the urge to text Charlotte.

Might not be there 2morrow. At the hospital with Mom. Bleeding.

It doesn't matter that it's two in the morning, Charlotte replies quickly.

What hospital? I'll be right there.

A deep breath pushes out of my lungs. I should have known she'd give me exactly what I didn't know I needed.

They're in the room for an hour before Dad comes out. His face is pale as he sits down next to Brandon and I. "They've slowed the bleeding down, which is good. They also did an ultrasound to check on the baby; he's doing okay for now. Still has a heartbeat and everything."

"He?" Brandon asks. They'd decided they weren't going to find out what they were having, but I guess this changed things.

At that, Dad smiles. "Three boys. How lucky are we?"

I lean back in the chair, studying Dad. It's not like I never knew he loved us or I ever felt mistreated or anything. He has just always been...busy. Even when he would take summers off and we'd go to The Village, we have never been one of those families who eat together at night and plays games or whatever. We've all had our own lives, but looking at him now, I see how much we mean to him and how proud he is of us. It's funny that I would feel closer to him now than I did when I was a kid, but maybe that's how life worked sometimes.

"He'll be okay, Dad. How could he not be? I mean, he's cool enough to have me for a brother."

Brandon punches me, but Dad laughs. "You guys are good kids. Your mother and I love you. Let's keep Mom and your brother in your prayers, okay?"

The seriousness of the situation weighs heavily on us again. "She's at twenty-four weeks now and that technically means the baby is viable."

Viable? I don't know why that word makes me nauseous. He says it like it's a good thing, but, but it sounds so...cold.

"So they'd be okay if he comes early?" I ask.

Dad awkwardly adjusts his weight from one side to the other. "There are no promises, Nate. Obviously every day we can keep him in there safely is a good thing. He needs all the time he can to get strong. The odds of survival get better and better, but it's still a tough road."

Odds of survival. That's hard to hear. I was freaked out when they told me they were having another baby, but now, I just want my little brother.

"Come here." Dad gives us each a hug before saying, "We'll be in the ER a little while longer, then they're going to admit her to the labor and delivery department. They're just waiting on a room. You guys can head home and we'll call you—"

"—No. Not yet."

Brandon nods his head in agreement.

He squeezes each of our shoulders again, before he disappears into the emergency room with Mom.

Another hour passes and then I hear another sliding door, this one coming from the entrance. My head shoots up and I see Charlotte standing there. I push to my feet to go to her, but then I see she didn't come alone. Alec is standing right behind her.

My jaw tightens. My hands fist. I need her. I need her and she came here with him.

Alec's eyes meet mine. They don't linger on me long before they dart toward Brandon.

Charlotte moves to me. "Nate, is everything okay? How's your mom?"

I know I should answer her. It shouldn't matter that Alec's here because Mom is in there bleeding, and her and my brother's lives are in danger. But it still sucks. Still feels like someone pushing a knife into my gut.

Charlotte walks up toward me, steps so close. "He wanted to come for Brandon," she whispers. "They're...friends. Brandon means a lot to him, too."

I lean against the wall, knowing she's right. "I hate it, Charlotte," I say softly. "Hate seeing him and knowing you're still close to him, even though I shouldn't. Things have changed and even if they hadn't, now sure as hell isn't the time for me to let it bother me. It's just...I need you. I'm scared out of my mind here and even after all this time, you make things feel better, but he's always there."

She gets closer to me again. She steps between my slightly spread legs. Doesn't hesitate. Just wraps her arms around my neck.

"I'm here. I'll do whatever you need. I'll always be here for you."

As if they have a mind of their own, my hands rest on her waist. Like I've done so many times, I slip them under the bottom of her shirt, seeking skin. She buries her face in my neck. I don't know where Brandon or Alec are. And I don't care.

"I'm scared, Star Girl. She wants this baby. What if something happens to my mom?"

"It won't."

We just stand there and hold each other. Her supporting me the way she's always done. The way only she can. "Thanks for coming," I finally tell her.

"You would have done the same thing for me. You have. You were the first one who told me I could get out of The Village, Nate. Even my mom who wanted out herself never told me I could leave. And when they did go, you helped me through it. You're always there for me."

"It's a trade." As soon as the words leave my mouth, I realize how true they are. "You helped make me realize everything was okay after the Chrissy thing...and you're here now."

"So we're two for two?" She laughs. "You were my answer that first summer, then me for you the second one."

"I had the third summer and now you the fourth," I finish. It's amazing, I realize. Having that with someone. Having it with her.

She licks her lips, something she does when she wants me to kiss her. It's another of those things I know about her that I hope no one else ever does. I lean forward, needing to feel my mouth on hers. Charlotte's breath catches. I want to swallow each and every sound she makes. "I'm so freaked out right now. I just need something familiar. Can I kiss you?"

"Déjà vu." She smirks, reminding me how I asked her the same question in the past. "Yes."

Only I don't get the chance. The doors leading back through the ER open and Dad comes out again.

Brandon jerks out from around a corner and I pull from Charlotte to step toward him. "Is everything okay?"

"Oh! Wow. Surprised to see you kids here. I didn't even know you were in New York." Dad says to Charlotte and Alec.

"They're here for two weeks," I say.

"Thanks for coming. I'm sure Nathaniel and Brandon appreciate the support." Dad tells them.

Brandon steps closer to Dad. "How's Mom?"

"Better. The bleeding has almost completely stopped. That doesn't mean we're out of the woods yet, but it's a good sign. They're bringing her upstairs in about five minutes. The doctor said you boys could go in and see her for a minute, and then why don't you head home? There's nothing you can do here right now. If anything changes, I'll call."

Brandon and I look at each other. My brother nods. "Yeah...okay."

"It's the third room on the right," Dad tells us. Brandon and I go in to see Mom. She's all covered up in white hospital blankets, her hair a mess, but with a small smile on her face.

"Hey, guys." Her voice is raspy.

"Hey..." I grab her hand and Brandon steps to the other side, doing the same. She has IVs in and there are machines all around.

"How are you?" I ask.

"Okay. Tired."

"Mom?" Brandon's voice cracks and his eyes pool. Shit. I don't think I've ever seen my brother cry. Not since we were kids, at least.

"Shh. Your brother and I will both be fine. You understand that? I promise you guys. The Chase boys are fighters. This little guy is going to take after both of you. My strong, brave, wonderful boys. He'll be okay and we'll all get to meet him and you two will be able to show him just how wonderful you both are, okay?"

My eyes are wet, too. I squeeze her hand, but not too tight, afraid I'll hurt her. "You're strong, too," I tell her.

Mom smiles. "I love you guys. Go home and get some rest. Your dad and I have this under control. We'll call you later."

I nod before leaning down to kiss her, and then Brandon does the same.

Dad gives us another hug when we walk back out to the waiting room. "I told Charlotte and Alec that they're welcome back at the house with you guys." He eyes me. "But be good. I'm trusting you." But he really means me since I'm the one bringing a girl home to an empty house for who knows how long.

"I will."

Brandon's quiet as Dad goes back into the waiting room. Charlotte and Alec walk up to us and I say to Charlotte, "Do you have to go back?"

She shakes her head. "No and I can't believe how long you've traveled every day, Nate. I didn't know."

"It's not a big deal."

And even though I can't stand Alec, I'm glad he took the train ride with her to keep her safe. When the four of us walk out of the hospital, I can't help but think it feels good. It feels like so many of our summers from the past.

Chapter Six

"I can't believe I'm in your house." Charlotte stands in the entryway looking around. "It's huge, Nate. How many bedrooms are in this thing?"

"Six. Wanna come up to mine?"

Her eyes go wide and it makes me crack a smile. "Just to sleep. I'm tired as hell."

"Yeah... I do. But I just have to talk to Alec for a second."

Of course he picks that moment to walk up. They don't say anything. He pushes a hand through his blond hair. Maybe it makes me a prick, but I'm not walking away and leaving him alone with her.

"I'm good," Alec tells her and I wonder why he wouldn't be.

"Brandon can show him to one of the guest rooms," I say.

Charlotte nods and then follows me upstairs to my room. When we get inside, l close the door and step out of my shoes as she walks around, looking at everything.

"Oh my God! You still have your old hat! You never wore this after the first summer." She grabs the Yankees hat off my dresser.

"It got too small."

She examines the bookshelf, my desk, the corkboard where there's a picture of us from the second summer. "You still have this?"

We'd taken it on our hike. "Yeah." I can't really manage much more than short answers. I'm tired, worried about Mom, and a little annoyed that Alec is in my house. "I'm dead on my feet. You have to be tired too." I nod my head toward the bed. "Lay down with me." And then I realize it probably won't be comfortable for her to sleep in jeans so I go to my dresser and pull out a pair of shorts and a t-shirt for her. "They'll be big, but it should work."

Charlotte nods.

"The bathroom is across the hall."

Another nod before she walks out. I step out of my jeans, pull on another pair of shorts, and toss my shirt to the floor. By the time she comes back in, I'm already laying down.

I pull up the blanket. Charlotte hesitates for a second before switching off the light and climbing in. She curls right up to me and I wrap my arm around her. "They'll be okay." The words come out for me, more than they do anything else.

"I know."

"I'm glad you're here."

"Me too," she replies and just that quickly, I'm out.

At about noon, I wake up. Charlotte is asleep beside me, this half-smile on her face. I wonder if she's dreaming and what it's about. She stirs slightly, but doesn't wake up. Grabbing my cell phone, I send a text to Dad to check on Mom. He replies back and tells me she's resting, they're monitoring the baby, but the bleeding has stopped.

A huge weight lifts from my chest.

"Hey," Charlotte says from beside me.

"Sorry. Did I wake you up?"

She shakes her head. "Nope."

"I don't know how I would be dealing with this if it wasn't for you," I tell her. She smiles up at me.

"I have something for you," Charlotte says. Getting out of bed, she grabs her shorts and pulls something out of the pocket. Once she's back next to me, she opens her hand, showing me the two leather necklaces inside.

"I wasn't sure if I should give it to you or not, but...I have to. I don't know if you'll want it—"

"I want it," I tell her, taking mine from her hand. Guilt pulls at my seams, threatening to pull me apart. "I shouldn't have ripped it off. I was so...yeah, it killed me seeing him with you and I didn't know what to do. I wanted it back, though. Even right after I did it."

"I hate what happened to us. We wasted so much time."

Charlotte has fixed the latch on the broken cord. It's the second time it's been broken, but the leather stays strong. Hopefully we can do the same. I sit up and put it on my neck. "Let me do yours," I say, and she sits up before handing me her necklace.

"I still wore it, but I took it off before we had coffee. Other than these couple days, I've always worn it."

Looking at her, I don't think I'll ever love another girl like I love Charlotte. Despite everything with Alec or the time we've spent away from each other or the fact that we're young, I still know I love her. Leaning forward, I press my lips to hers.

Charlotte gives a shocked noise, but then she's opening her mouth and I'm slipping my tongue inside. She leans back and I go down with her. Her hands trace paths up and down my back and I slip my hand under her shirt. My body is screaming, *finally*! But I'm trying to slow down because I don't want to rush her.

It feels different than the other times I've kissed her, and I wonder if it's because we're older now and if it means we're more ready. Or, hell, maybe I'm getting ahead of myself, something I only do with her.

I roll onto my back, pulling her on top of me and I kiss her deeper, wanting more and then—*bang, bang, bang.*

"Nate! My phone is dead! Have you talked to Dad?" Brandon's voice comes through the door. Charlotte jumps up and runs her hands down her clothes like she's trying to unwrinkle them. It's a lot easier for her to hide what we were doing.

I grab a pillow and put it in my lap before sitting up.

"Open the door."

Brandon sticks his head in. "Bad time?"

I pick up another pillow and throw it at him. "Screw you. Charge your phone. I just texted Dad and she's doing better today. No bleeding, but they're keeping her for now."

"Good. Okay. Alec's downstairs. Neither of us knows how to cook. Wanna go get a pizza?"

"Breakfast of champions. Go for it."

"Cool." He closes the door, leaving charlotte and I alone again.

"You okay?" I ask. "I don't want to seem like I'm pushing you..."

"You're not. You never could."

"Good." I stand up and walk over to her. "The past nine months sucked. The beginning especially, but when you're here, it's like none of it happened. Like we can just pick up where we left off."

"I feel like that, too."

Wrapping my arms around her, I pull her toward me. "What are your plans for the next week? I wanted to show you around, but I don't want to go too far from here."

"We don't really have much set. I want to take a trip to Poughkeepsie. I haven't been, but I have all week to do it. I could come back and forth. If you guys need any help while your parents are in the hospital or anything."

"That's a lot of back and forth."

"You did it."

"Why don't you guys stay here? I mean, if you want to. I don't want to ruin your trip, but I'm sure Brandon and Alec will be happy that they can do whatever the hell it is they do again.

It's not quite as exciting as being in the city, but...it's cheaper. You can stay here for free."

Of course my dad may have an aneurism but I'll cross that bridge when I come to it. He let them stay one night, so what's a few?

"That depends," Charlotte says. "What are the stars like out here at night?"

"They're perfect."

Alec and Charlotte went back to the hotel to check out early and get their stuff. Brandon called Dad and told him told him they needed a place to say. Yeah, he's stretching the truth a little, but who cares.

"What do you like so much about Alec?" I ask Brandon as we watch TV.

He whips his head toward me. "What do you mean, what do I like about him?"

"I mean, why do you think he's so cool? You know, your obsessive football friend?"

Brandon turns of the TV and tosses the remote to the coffee table. "We get along, I guess. He likes ball, but it's not like that's the only thing we have in common. I don't know. Why does anyone like anyone?"

"But anyone is Alec."

"You never gave him a chance. You always hated him because he's close to Charlie."

"Because he's in love with Charlotte."

"He's not in love with her, you douchebag. Open your eyes a little, yeah?" Brandon stands up.

I suddenly get the feeling I've been letting my brother down a lot lately, though I'm not sure why. "Hey," I call to him before he walks away. "We should like...hangout or something. Pretty soon we're gonna have another brother in the mix."

"Yeah. That'd be cool. Want to go see Mom before Alec and Charlie get back?"

"Sure." I push to my feet. "But I get to drive this time."

Chapter Seven

Charlotte and Alec have been here a couple days. We haven't really talked about anything important. I'm still being a douche and not telling her about Columbia, and I can't even say why. We're cool, I appreciate her being here, and most of the time I'm over last summer, but I feel like there's still so much I don't know.

I hate that I don't have all the answers. Charlotte and Alec exchange looks I don't understand. No matter how much I try to forget it, part of it is always there. He's always there, too. We all played pool downstairs and watched a movie and him and my brother are pretty much best friends.

I feel like shit that Alec knows Brandon better than I do, so basically the guy just pisses me off all the way around. Not a real cool thing to admit.

Mom is still hanging in there and the baby is still doing well, so I try to focus on that stuff instead.

And Charlotte.

"Hey." We just finished a game of pool and she's putting her cue up. "Sneak out with me tonight?" I wink at her. Dad comes back and forth a little, but he's spending most of his time at the hospital, but pretending we have to sneak out sounds fun.

Her face lights up. *Tell her you still love her. That you're going to Columbia and that you want to be with her.*

"Same time?"

"Nah. I can't wait that long. We'll be rebels and sneak out early tonight."

"I didn't know you were such a troublemaker. What time were you thinking?" She crosses her arms.

I look at my cell. "How about...right...now."

"I'll grab my telescope!" Charlotte runs to the stairs. I'm right behind her. We grab her telescope and I get a blanket out of the closest. Unlike at her place we have neighbors close, but the backyard is private and it's quiet.

I lay the blanket out and even though we're in New York, it feels the same as it has the hundreds of other times we've done it. Charlotte sets up the telescope and I sit and watch her as she looks through it. Of course the stars aren't bright, but she makes them seem that way.

"So?" I ask, when she doesn't say anything.

"They're incredible."

"They're the same as they are in Virginia."

"Not to me." Charlotte shakes her head. "The stars here and the ones there are each special for their own reason. You grew up looking at these, while I looked at mine. Now we've both looked at each of them together."

Not for the first time, I'm in awe of her. "No one I know looks at things the way you do. I've never known anyone like you."

Charlotte crawls over to me and straddles my lap. "You said that to me the first summer too."

"You remember that." I brush her hair from her face.

"I remember everything."

"Me, too." And then I kiss her. She tugs on my hair and kisses me back. I pull back far enough to say, "I still love you, Star Girl."

"I love you, too."

"Come up stairs with me?" I ask.

"Yes," she replies. I take her hand, and hope this time, I never have to let her go.

Alec and Charlotte are gone for the day. She's going to Poughkeepsie, and Brandon and I decided to hang out. We went to the park and played basketball. He had a friend of his buy us some beer and now we're back at the house, downstairs, drinking together.

"I owned you today," I tell him. We played two games of one-on-one and I beat him at both. Brandon can take me any time where football is concerned, but we're pretty evenly matched in other sports. Today was my day.

"Everyone gets lucky once in a while," he teases.

"Yeah. I just get luckier more often than you."

We both laugh. It's the first time in a long time that I remember us hanging out all day without fighting.

After we settle down, Brandon downs the rest of his beer before saying, "So you really are in love with her, huh?" He opens a beer and downs another big swallow.

"Yeah." I sit on the couch while Brandon leans against the pool table. "I think I've always loved her. She's...I don't know, she's just always in my head, ya know? Everything about her." Then those times come that make me wonder what I'm doing. There's still something going on that I don't know about and it sucks that she doesn't trust me with it. *The way I didn't trust her that night?*

Brandon nods. "Yeah. I know."

But really I don't get how he does. As far as I know, Brandon has never been serious about any girl.

He's fidgeting with the bottle in his hand, peeling the paper. When he sets it down, I could swear his hands are shaking. An anchor suddenly weighs down my stomach. "What is it?"

"I'm just going to say this even though I'm scared shitless to do it. I'm mean, I've never even said the words out loud before, but you're my brother and who can a guy talk to if he can't talk to his brother? Mom talking about how strong the Chase boys are and everything...I want to be strong. At least by telling you." He shakes his hands like they fell asleep and he's trying to wake them up or something.

My heart is going crazy, trying to figure out what could have Brandon this stressed out. Fear fills me.

"Don't freak out on me, okay, Nate? I really need you to not fucking freak out on me."

"Dude, I'm your brother. You can tell my anything—" All sorts of thoughts are running through my head, making me wonder what could be wrong with my brother that I missed.

"I'm gay."

I stop breathing. Totally not what I was expecting.

The bottle in my hand slips through and falls to the floor, beer foaming out. I don't even pick it up. "Excuse me?" It's not that I'm homophobic or anything. Hell, what other people do is none of my business. To each their own, but hearing my brother tell me he's gay isn't something I ever thought I'd hear. I never suspected.

"I'm gay, man."

"Since when?"

"What do you mean since when? Since forever. It's not just something someone wakes up and decides." He starts pacing the room.

"Shit." I run a hand through my hair. "I didn't mean to ask that. I just...you go out with girls. You talk about sleeping with them all the time. Hell, I saw you having sex with Sadie once."

"That's because I didn't want to be gay!" he yells. "Who wants to deal with that? People judging you and looking down on you. I'm a fucking football player, Nate. You play sports. You know how that is. You hear the shit people say. I just..." He stops moving and looks at me. I've never seen my brother look so lost and scared in my life.

"I thought maybe I could fake it...or change it. Didn't you notice I wasn't really with anyone after her? It was wrong. I had sex with her and then I went home and ignored all her calls because she wasn't what I wanted. I felt sick, but then even worse for feeling that way because I *should* want her, right? That's what everyone says. That would make me fucking normal, right?"

Wow.

Brandon falls onto the couch, his elbows on his knees and his face in his hands. And I just sit there. I don't know what to do or what to say.

"Tell me I'm normal, Nate?" Then, my brother starts to cry. It's not just tears in his eyes, but full out crying. "*Tell me, tell me, tell me,*" he says over and over.

I've never seen strength like I see from my brother right now. Because even though he's breaking down, he's manning up, too. He's admitting who he is and I hate the fucking world for making him feel like he should be ashamed about it. "Hey. There is nothing wrong with who you are. You hear me? Fuck anyone who tells you anything differently."

Brandon looks over at me with red eyes. "Yeah?"

"Yeah."

He breaks down crying again and this time and I hug him. It's awkward at first. I don't think I've hugged my own brother since I was five years old, but soon it feels more natural. He's still crying and I'm still trying to process what he said. It's hard to work through it, but I don't want him to see me struggle. I just want to be here for him.

My brother is gay.

He's been lying to us, to everyone his whole life.

But he told me now.

It feels like forever until he stops crying. I scoot back and Brandon wipes his face with his shirt.

"Shit. I can't believe I just broke down like that. That makes me feel more like a pussy than being gay."

He laughs and even though I don't feel like doing it, I laugh, too. Neither of us feels it, but we need to try to do something to lighten the mood.

"You could have told me," I tell him. "All these years...you could have said something." He's been carrying that alone and it has to be killer.

"Yeah?" he sounds like he's not sure if he believes me.

"It doesn't matter to me. You're still my brother and...I don't think I've given you the credit you deserve all these years. I just didn't know, man. I didn't know you were holding all of that in and I'm sorry for that. I'm sorry you felt like you had to keep quiet about it and...I want you to know, I've never been more proud to be your bother than I am right now."

I've obviously just said the wrong thing because Brandon looks like he's about to be sick. "I'm sorry," he whispers.

"What is it?" I scoot back, waiting for him to tell me something huge. Nothing prepares me for what he says.

"That second summer...Alec and I..."

"What?" I jerk off the couch and push to my feet. My world tilts, then things start to align. "Alec?"

"I mean, I kind of knew that first summer, but I didn't want to believe it. I tried to fight it, but we talked all that year. I thought maybe if I didn't go back, I could try and forget everything. Then the second summer...we just got closer then, ya know? I know you hate him, but you don't know him like I do, Nate. Not a whole lot happened that year, but yeah, we started..." Brandon trails off before picking up the conversation elsewhere. "We kept talking again all year after that, and then last summer..."

I shake my head. Not wanting to hear more. Somehow knowing exactly what he's going to say. "Don't."

"I have to. I need you to understand. We were scared. No one could know. His dad...and college...football..." He's throwing out all sorts of words, but not finishing a sentence.

"What are you even talking about? Alec's been all over Charlotte her whole life. He hated me. Kicked any guy's ass who messed with her. He wanted to run The Village with her one day."

One look at him tells me it was a lie; Alec was lying, just like Brandon did. That Alec wanted to use Charlotte the same way my brother did with Sadie. "Tell me," I grit out, backing away.

"Charlie caught us that night. Alec went after her. He was freaked out, Nate. He thought she would tell and he was scared."

"So he kissed her to make up for it? And you knew. You knew I was gutted all year and you never said anything!"

"Fuck you, Nate! That's easy for you to say. You don't get it! You'll never get it unless you've experienced it."

"What I don't get is letting your brother be miserable for nine months. I loved her, man and you let me think she wanted him!"

"Gutted? What about Marisol? You moved on."

"The way you did? You just admitted to me that you were with people you didn't want, so fuck you, Brandon. I love her! We had all these plans and...and you all knew. Everyone knew, but me." Now it's me who's pacing the room. "I was the only one in the dark. I was wrecked and all three of you could have said something to ease it, but no one did!" Another thought hits me and it takes everything inside me not to tackle my brother and kick his ass. "I lost her so you could what? Keep Alec? So you guys could have your secret?"

"No. That's not it! We didn't talk last year. It didn't feel right. You don't fucking get it, Nate!"

The downstairs door opens, and Alec and Charlotte walk in.

"You didn't tell me," is the first thing I say when she walks in.

Charlotte looks at Brandon, then at me and back to Brandon again, putting all the pieces together. Alec is right next to her. I can't read the guarded expression on his face and I don't want to.

"How could I, Nate? I wanted to, so bad, but it was their secret to tell. It...it wouldn't have been right."

I've always felt like I fit with Charlotte. Like we belonged, matched even though there are things about us that are so different. We made sense and I felt like I would always fit with her.

But I was wrong. Just like last summer, they're on one side, and I'm on the other.

"No matter what, I would always do anything to make sure you weren't hurt. Do you know what it felt like to see you with him? It was like you punched through my chest and ripped my heart out. You could have found a way. Someway to tell me something at least so I wouldn't spend all that time wondering what I did wrong or if everything was a lie."

"I spent months the same way!" Charlotte steps closer to me. "After the first summer you just dropped off the face of the Earth and left me hanging. Don't you think that whole time I wondered what I did wrong?"

"No." I shake my head. "That was different. We hadn't spent the summer saying we loved each other."

"So? Saying it doesn't make it truer! I always knew I loved you. I did everything I could to tell you I didn't want to kiss Alec, without telling something that wasn't mine to share. You're the one who chose not to trust me."

At that, the room goes silent. I'm breathing heavy. Alec has walked over to Brandon. Charlotte and I are standing about five feet apart, staring at each other. She's right. I've probably always known it. I've thought about it lately, how I didn't trust her, when I should have.

Words are lost. I don't know what to say. Brandon's cell ringing makes it so I don't have to.

"Dad? What's wrong?" I hear my brother say. He pauses. "We'll be right there!"

Brandon pushes around me and heads for the door. "We have to go! Mom's having the baby and they can't stop the delivery."

Chapter Eight

Alec drives Brandon's truck because we've both been drinking. How screwed up are we? Our mom is in the hospital, trying not to go into preterm labor, and we're getting drunk. Not that I feel any kind of buzz now, but still.

No one says a word, except for Brandon reminding Alec how to get to the hospital. We go to Labor and Delivery.

One of the nurses we've seen before is at the desk when we get in. She gives us a sad look.

"You guys are going to have to wait here. They're delivering right now. I should have some news for you soon, okay?"

My hands are shaking as I nod. We take a seat in the waiting room. My right leg bounces up and down, but I can't make it stop. I feel like I'm going to shake out of my skin.

I don't know what to feel right now. I'm scared to death for Mom and the baby. For Dad. Scared of losing the baby. Hurt from Charlotte and Brandon. Confused. Guilty for not believing her or not realizing my brother held such an important part of himself from me.

I lean my elbows on my knees, head down, and try to take a couple deep breaths. Without letting myself think, I reach over and grab Charlotte's hand. None of our problems matter right now. She locks our fingers together and leans into me. Kisses my shoulder and whispers, "I'm here. Whatever you need, I'm here."

Just knowing there's someone there to share some of the pain, helps.

My eyes find Brandon. Tears stain his face. He's shaking just like I am. I see the fear in his eyes. Alec sitting beside him...yet he can't comfort Brandon the way Charlotte does me.

Or I guess he can, but they're scared. I cock my head, trying to figure out what that would feel like. To be so lost and freaked out of your own mind, but the fear of letting someone else see who you are is stronger.

It's not only my pain that Brandon's fear won the battle with, but his own. Yeah, he wasn't honest with me, but it wasn't to hurt me. And seeing him hear and knowing he'd probably like to have someone share some of his burden the way Charlotte does with me, shows me he's suffered too. Longer than I ever have. Alec is within his reach, but he can't go to him. Someone to support him, but he'd suffer alone. I hate it.

"Go somewhere," tumbles out of my mouth.

"What?" Brandon asks.

"We'll stay here. Find a room or whatever you guys need. Just stay close. The second Dad comes out, I'll text you. You shouldn't be alone in this."

Brandon rushes to his feet, grabs me and pulls me into the tightest hug. "Thank you. I'm sorry. Thank you." Something tells me he's thanking me for more than just this. Maybe this whole time, he's been afraid we wouldn't accept him.

"There's nothing to thank me for," I tell him.

When we pull away, Alec looks at me. The guy I've hated for four years. The one who's hated me and maybe loves my brother, holds my stare and says, "Thanks, man. You're all right, you know?"

I nod. As they're walking away, I sit down again. I pull Charlotte to my lap, wrap my arms around her waist and bury my head in her neck. "I want my brother to be okay. Both of them."

"They will be. I think the Chase boys can do just about anything."

That one sentence gives me hope. It's not the exact same, but close enough to the same thing I said before.

There are so many words that could be said right now; I'm sorry, forgive me, I trust you, I love you, but I'm not now is the time. Eventually? Yeah, but I think deep down, we all already know them, regardless.

Only twenty-five minutes after we get there, Joshua is born. He weighs 1.5 pounds. His lungs are weak. He has to have tubes all over him, but he's here. And I know he'll be okay. He's a Chase.

Charlotte and Alec stay all night with us. Charlotte doesn't let go of me the whole time. I don't want her to. Alec is never more than a foot away from Brandon either.

In the morning, she and Alec make plans to leave. Their plane leaves to take them home in two days and they have things to take care of before they go.

Alec and Brandon have disappeared again. They've done that a lot over the summers, I realize, and it makes me feel even worse for them. So many times I could have tried to get to know my brother better. Maybe if I would have, he would have realized he could trust me. That I would always love him no matter what.

Charlotte and I walk outside. They're taking Brandon's truck back to our house for their things, and then a cab to the train station. It sucks not to be able to take them ourselves, but we need to stay here with our family.

When Charlotte looks at me, tears fill her eyes. "You'd think I'd get used to saying goodbye to you."

I cup her cheek; brush her tears away with my thumb.

"I'm sorry," I say.

"No, I'm sorry. You're right. I could have found a way."

"Maybe you could have, maybe you couldn't. I was selfish and jealous. I'm pretty sure I made it too hard for you to be honest, anyway. I don't think it matters. None of us are perfect, Star Girl. I forget that sometimes. I think we all do, but that's life, right? You make mistakes and you learn from them and you grow up." That's what we've done together—grown up. The first time I saw her, she was this skinny tomboy, who stumbled over her words in front of me and I kind of liked that I made her react that way. That I gave her something that no one else did.

And then the next year, she was giving that to me.

We've grown and changed, screwed up, but at the beginning of each summer, we found each other again. Or maybe we never really lost each other.

"Over the past four years, nothing important has ever happened in my life that I haven't shared with you. Even if it was months later, or through the computer, or in the middle of a lake, or under the stars. I should have trusted you."

The tears keep coming and I keep wiping them.

"I'm going to Columbia in the fall," I finally tell her.

Her eyes go wide, and she kind of shakes her head a little. "What? Why didn't you say anything?"

"I don't know, but I'm saying it now." I think back to last year, what I told her while we sat in those chairs by the lake when she wore her yellow bikini. "I want to be with you. I've always wanted to be with you. For three years we said goodbye at the end of each summer. We made plans to keep in contact, but that didn't always happen. We made plans to stay together and that never happened. This time we're saying goodbye after only two weeks, but at the end of the summer, you'll be back."

"We'll talk every day," she uses my same words from last year.

"And when you get back, I'll take the train to see you every weekend." It's not perfect, but it's doable. An hour and a half is nothing compared to everything we've been through.

"I love you, Nathaniel Chase. I've loved you since I stepped out of that cabin and I dropped the keys in front of you. Every first I've ever had is with you and I want to keep having them."

"I love you too, Star Girl. You're it for me." I drop my forehead to hers. Slide my hand around to the back of her neck. And then I kiss her, knowing this time, we're ready. All those other summers and those other kisses and everything else we shared, my dad choosing some random lake in some random town to stay in one year, the fights and the screw ups that helped us learn and gave us experiences with other people. They were all meant to happen, and our paths were supposed to cross over and over again. Until we found that point, the bright star in the summer sky that would be ours forever.

Out of all the years, this is the one she changed and grew the most, the one we both did.

"I'll see you soon," I tell her.

It's not goodbye anymore.

"See you soon."

As if on cue, Brandon and Alec walk up. My brother hugs her goodbye. I look at Alec and hold out my fist. He bumps it with his.

"What are you going to do?" I ask Brandon, after they disappear.

"I don't know. It's hard."

"You know Mom and Dad won't care. They'll support you no matter what."

"I know."

"And me."

"I know that too," he tells me.

"I feel like shit that you didn't think you could tell me who you are. Whatever I did, I'm sorry."

"It's not your fault. It's not always feeling like you can't trust someone...I think it's also about being honest with myself. If it was a secret, I could pretend it wasn't true. Shitty, right? That I'm not man enough to be proud of who I am."

"What?" I grab his arm. "You're a hell of a lot stronger than you give yourself credit for."

Brandon nods. "It's not just my secret. It's Alec's too."

"You have shitty taste in guys," I tease him.

Brandon punches me. "Dickhead."

"I'm kidding. He's not too bad."

He opens his mouth as if he's going to say something about Alec, but I can tell he's not ready. Brandon takes a deep breath. "Come on. Let's go see Joshua."

"I'm here, man. Know I'm always here."

Brandon nods.

I walk inside with my brother, my best friend and hope he's able to be himself one day. Hope he sees there is nothing wrong with who he is.

My phone vibrates in my pocket and I pull it out.

I'll see you soon

I smile at Charlotte's text. Maybe everything isn't perfect. I don't know if it ever is. But if you ask me, it's pretty close.

Charlotte

For the first time, everything went as planned. Alec and I went back to The Village. We worked all summer, helping Dad. His parents were always there too, even though things are still strained with Alec and his dad. Nate and I talked every day. He told me about his trips to the hospital to see Joshua, who was getting stronger all the time. Josh was a Chase boy, after all. We talked about Brandon and Alec, who kept in touch, but still didn't now what they were going to do. Brandon had to go back to Ohio for school soon. It wasn't like it was the moon, I'd told Alec. He looked at me one day and said he finally got it. He understood why I wanted out. Not that there was anything wrong with The Village, but there was a whole other world out there, too. He always thought if he stayed here, stayed with me, he could deny who he really was. I told him to be proud of who he is, I hoped he'd explore the world one day. That there would always be a place for him, for my best friend, with me.

A week before I left for Vassar, Dad told me Nancy was moving in. For the first time in maybe forever, I think my dad was really happy.

Every day, I still think about the first time I saw Nate. About walking out of cabin 3B, and having my first moment. Just like I knew I wouldn't, I haven't forgotten it. I relive it every time I see him.

The End

$\mathcal{A}$cknowledgements

My first thanks always has to go to my family. My husband and two beautiful little girls deal with my obsessiveness when it comes to my writing. To my delayed responses and those days that I just can't pull my brain away from my characters. I am so lucky they deal with me.

Wendy Higgins for always, always being there. Jolene for the quick read and those two really awesome things you caught that I totally missed! Also thanks to Heather for reading and for your enthusiasm over one of my favorite parts of this story.

To my readers. I can do this because of YOU. Your support, excitement, reviews, tweets and messages never cease to brighten my day. Every day I am thankful for all that you do for me.

About the Author

From a very young age, Nyrae Dawn dreamed of growing up and writing stories. It always felt as if publication were out of her grasp—one of those things that could never happen, so she put her dream on hold.

Nyrae worked in a hospital emergency room, fell in love, and married one of her best friends from high school. In 2004 Nyrae, her husband, and their new baby girl made a move from Oregon to Southern California and that's when everything changed. As a stay-at-home mom for the first time, her passion for writing flared to life again.

She hasn't stopped writing ever since.

Nyrae has a love of character-driven stories and emotional journeys. She feels honored to be able to explore those things on a daily basis and get to call it work.

With two incredible daughters, an awesome husband and her days spent writing what she loves, Nyrae considers herself the luckiest girl in the world. She still resides in sunny Southern California, where she loves spending time with her family and sneaking away to the bookstore with her laptop.

Connect with me online via

My site http://www.nyraedawn.com

Facebook https://www.facebook.com/nyraedawnwrites?ref=hl

Twitter https://twitter.com/NyraeDawn

Goodreads
http://www.goodreads.com/author/show/5784345.Nyrae_Dawn

CPSIA information can be obtained at www.ICGtesting.com
Printed in the USA
LVOW07s1513011013

354946LV00015B/860/P